Carly's SOUND

What Reviewers Say About Bold Strokes Authors

KIM BALDWIN

"'A riveting novel of suspense' seems to be a very overworked phrase. However, it is extremely apt when discussing Kim Baldwin's [*Hunter's Pursuit*]. An exciting page turner [features] Katarzyna Demetrious, a bounty hunter...with a million dollar price on her head. Look for this excellent novel of suspense..." – **R. Lynne Watson**, *MegaScene*

RONICA BLACK

"Black juggles the assorted elements of her first book with assured pacing and estimable panache...[including]...the relative depth—for genre fiction—of the central characters: Erin, the married-but-separated detective who comes to her lesbian senses; loner Patricia, the policewoman-mentor who finds herself falling for Erin; and sultry club owner Elizabeth, the sexually predatory suspect who discards women like Kleenex...until she meets Erin."– **Richard Labonte**, *Book Marks, Q Syndicate, 2005*

ROSE BEECHAM

"...her characters seem fully capable of walking away from the particulars of whodunit and engaging the reader in other aspects of their lives." – *Lambda Book Report*

GUN BROOKE

"*Course of Action* is a romance...populated with a host of captivating and amiable characters. The glimpses into the lifestyles of the rich and beautiful people are rather like guilty pleasures....[A] most satisfying and entertaining reading experience." – **Arlene Germain**, reviewer for the *Lambda Book Report* and the *Midwest Book Review*

JANE FLETCHER

"*The Walls of Westernfort* is not only a highly engaging and fast-paced adventure novel, it provides the reader with an interesting framework for examining the same questions of loyalty, faith, family and love that [the characters] must face." – **M. J. Lowe**, *Midwest Book Review*

RADCLY*f*FE

"...well-honed storytelling skills...solid prose and sure-handedness of the narrative..." – **Elizabeth Flynn**, *Lambda Book Report*
"...well-plotted...lovely romance...I couldn't turn the pages fast enough!" – **Ann Bannon**, author of *The Beebo Brinker Chronicles*

Carly's
SOUND

by
Ali Vali

2006

CARLY'S SOUND

ISBN 1-933110-45-7
THIS TRADE PAPERBACK IS PUBLISHED BY
BOLD STROKES BOOKS, INC.,
NEW YORK, USA

FIRST EDITION, JUNE 2006

CREDITS
EDITORS: JENNIFER KNIGHT AND SHELLEY THRASHER
PRODUCTION DESIGN: J. BARRE GREYSTONE
COVER GRAPHIC: SHERI (graphicartist2020@hotmail.com)

By the Author

The Devil Inside

Acknowledgments

Thank you to Radclyffe for believing in my writing and for the opportunity to tell this story. *Carly's Sound* is a labor of love that I've been working on for a few years now. It's my pleasure to share it with you all.

Cancer is a life-changing experience no matter your social standing, race, or religious background. It knows no boundaries and cares not about the life you lead or the family that loves you. That's not its purpose. It exists only to destroy and to win, so it takes a heroic effort to send it packing.

Years ago I faced it when my partner was diagnosed and just last year again with my mother. When this book came to me, it was a way for me to finally put to rest the pain of watching C suffer through a year of treatment. Her first comment after reading the first draft was that I had killed her. In reality the pages that follow celebrate the woman I knew before cancer and the woman who emerged afterward. Both were full of life and beautiful, but now we find that each day is a gift not to be squandered.

Having shared just how important this story is to me, I want to give special thanks to my editor Jennifer Knight. As a teacher, lead encourager, kind critic and mentor you have made something special so much more—it was an honor to work with you. Thank you so much Jennifer for your input, advice and guidance, and also for caring about these characters as much as I do. I want to thank Shelley Thrasher as well for her part in bringing this story to life. It was a pleasure to work with you again.

Thanks also to my partner for providing the inspiration I need to keep the words flowing. You have been and continue to be the muse that sparks my imagination.

DEDICATION

For C and Mami
You both beat the beast that is cancer with the
dignity and grace that make you the women I love

CHAPTER ONE

Nine hundred and seventeen days.

Raquel Poppy Valente ticked off another in her tally as she rolled over and faced the sun shining outside her bedroom window in New Orleans. It had become a habit now to wake up with a number in her head, followed closely by a curse. That she had woken up at all to face another lonely day with Carly gone pissed her off. It pissed her off because the loss swamped her hope so badly she wanted to roll right over and close her eyes.

Today was different, though. Today she stared at the innocuous yellow envelope on her dresser until her skin prickled. She'd had the damn thing for all of those nine hundred and seventeen days, but the idea of opening it had only started to germinate the night before. Now the envelope was almost screaming at her from across the quiet room.

With a deep breath she swung her legs over the bed and walked slowly to the dresser. She carried the envelope down to the den and sat in her boxers and T-shirt to rip it open. The videotape she pulled out had the words "For Poppy" written neatly across the front. For a long while, Poppy just held it before putting it into the machine.

The scene it opened with was sunset on Carly's Sound, a small, privately owned island near Aruba. Poppy leaned forward as Carly came into view, bald and wearing a large terry cloth robe. She sat on a porch that overlooked a beach with crystal blue water. Next to her was a cup, and when the camera panned back, Poppy could see that her legs were folded under her.

"Hi, sweetheart." Carly looked directly into the lens and smiled for what she knew would be a very attentive audience of one. "I finally got you to take a nap. You're so stubborn about leaving me alone. If you're watching, I hope it means you're ready for the next phase of your life, and I can't tell you how happy that makes me."

"I'll never be ready for that." Poppy clenched her fists, fighting the urge to just sit still and listen.

Carly rubbed her chest in an attempt to ease the pain that had racked her body constantly at the end. Poppy knew the gesture well, and seeing it once more made her angry over the familiar helplessness.

"It's a strange concept to wrap your brain around," Carly said in a surreal but accepting tone, "the fact you'll be dead in a matter of weeks. But I'm not that overly concerned. Don't get me wrong. If I could, I'd change my fate, but we both know that can't happen. My life has been short, but it's been good, in large part because I've lived the last eleven years with you, baby.

"Poppy, above all else I want you to know that you've been the piece that's made my life complete. I know that sounds corny, but it's true. Now that I can see the end of my road, I'm the most proud of two things—being a mother and your wife."

Carly stopped talking for a minute and took a sip of her tea. She pulled her robe tighter around her body as if she was trying to ward off a chill. For a brief moment a slight smile graced her face as she looked toward the surf.

"With you I never felt trapped or insignificant. Do you realize how lucky I felt every time you told me I was too beautiful to do anything else but spread my wings and fly? Besides the birth of my children it was the one gift that ever meant anything to me, because it meant you'd listened to me and had taken me seriously. You made me feel like I was worth more to you than all the things you accomplished and all the places you built. That's not something everyone experiences in a lifetime."

Carly stopped and pulled a tissue out of her pocket and wiped her eyes. "You loved all of me, Poppy, and that was a gift. It made choosing between quality of life, and quantity, easy. I chose quality. I wanted to be in my right mind for all the time I had left with you. Living every moment of the time you're given is what helps you accept the fact there are only a few grains of sand left in your hourglass. It's a lesson you've taught me well."

The toll of having to film this message was starting to show on Carly's face, and seeing her tire so quickly broke Poppy's heart again. Being active and productive at both work and play had been such a fundamental part of Carly's personality, it had been hard for her to accept when the cancer started to defeat her strong determination.

"We've returned here to the place we began a lifetime ago, and we'll add one more memory on this beach. Ooh la la, the stories I could tell, huh, sweetheart?" Carly's lips curved into a beautiful smile.

"I want you to do a few things for me, and the first has to do with Lizzie." Elizabeth "Lizzie" Stevens was Carly's daughter, who now worked for Poppy. "If you want, you can show her this part of the tape, but please remind her how special she was to me—my little bookworm who morphed into an extraordinary young woman. Aside from you, she's the person I'm going to miss the most. Tell her that I love her, and that I'm proud of her. Tell her to take care of herself and remember all the things we talked about. I'm going to miss those long conversations we shared."

Carly's soft green eyes watered at the admission, and she stopped for a moment as if willing herself not to cry. She tilted her head back into the wind, and Poppy could tell she was trying to find the strength to finish. She had gotten so frail at the end, but her sense of humor had remained.

When the camera lens focused on the green eyes again, Poppy felt like Carly was looking right into her heart. The parting words were just for her.

"So all there's left to say is dry your eyes, my love, and shed your sadness. I love you, and don't you forget it. Thank you for listening. You always were a soft touch when it came to me, and I love you for it. I'll be seeing you in your dreams, honey."

"I wish for so much more," whispered Poppy.

"Get yourself dressed and get going. It's time to stop your moping."

❖

As soon as she emerged from the revolving doors at the side entrance to the upscale Piquant hotel in downtown New Orleans, Poppy heard the wailing. She stared across from the closed hotel shops to the source of the noise, a red-faced, crying infant being bounced gently by a young blond woman who looked equally miserable. The two were standing in line in the hotel coffee shop, being ignored by not-so-amused customers.

"Come on, Tallulah girl, it's going to be okay. Mommy just needs some coffee before we fly out this morning," the young woman said, as she tried to juggle a diaper bag, flight bag, and her baby. "God, I should've known better and just ordered room service."

Unable to stand their helplessness, Poppy quickly crossed the gleaming marble floor to stand next to them and asked, "May I give you a hand?"

Knowing that most people mistrusted strangers, she fully expected the young woman to decline, but Julia Johnson expelled a breath of relief when she heard the soft velvety voice offering help. Without hesitation, she handed the flight bag and diaper bag off to the tall, dark-haired stranger, thanking her sincerely.

Once her savior was loaded down with her possessions, Julia distracted Tallulah with a soft toy. This ploy reduced the decibels enough that Julia could order. "A decaf café au lait, please, and a blueberry muffin."

The clerk nodded, then turned her attention to the pack mule standing next to Julia. "And what do you desire, good-looking?" The clerk's arched eyebrow looked even more pronounced because of the spike piercing it.

"A venti latte, please." The stranger glanced toward Julia, who was trying to extract her wallet from her purse, and said, "It's on me."

Moving a superbly tailored jacket aside, she slid a hand into the front pocket of immaculate black pleated pants and extracted a gold money clip engraved with a flower instead of a name or initials. She peeled off a twenty and pressed it into the teenage clerk's hand. "Here you go, kid, and keep the change. You're good for my ego."

Julia couldn't help but join the clerk in really taking in her benefactor. The tall stranger was laughing softly, and something in her bearing lifted Julia out of the frustrated mood she had been in and replaced her aggravation with a slight panicky feeling. She realized that, in her distracted state, she had not only handed over the bulk of her money, which was in the flight bag, but she'd also allowed the woman to pay for her order.

"I can't let you buy my breakfast," Julia protested as the woman started walking.

Tallulah was restless again and emitted a couple of sharp howls. Bouncing her, Julia followed her luggage, which was still attached to the woman who was also carrying the tray holding their coffees and Julia's muffin.

"Why not?" The woman paused at the coffee station and set down the tray.

"Why not what?" asked Julia.

"Why can't I buy you breakfast? Is there some law or religious reason why I wouldn't be able to?" The stranger uncapped their cups and started adding the appropriate ingredients to hers.

"No, it's just that I don't know you, and I don't want to impose," said Julia above the wailing going on near her right shoulder. Tallulah was trying to crawl over her body, and the cries sounded as if she was in pain. "Why can't they talk from the beginning?"

"How do you take your coffee?" The voice was close to Julia's ear, making her shiver.

"What? I'm sorry," said Julia, after the woman's snapping fingers brought her back to the coffee shop.

"How do you take your coffee?"

"Three sugars, thanks."

"They *can* talk from the beginning, ma'am. You just have to listen to what they're saying." Julia's savior shook three sugar packets, shifting the granules to one side before ripping the packets open and dumping their contents into the steaming liquid.

"Excuse me?" Julia moved the baby to her other shoulder to give her right ear a break and to get a better look at her benefactor. The bouncing and the back patting weren't working. Tallulah was only crying louder.

"The kid's got colic. She doesn't need to tell you verbally. The crying and the leg kicking are a dead giveaway. And as we all know, there's only one sure cure for colic. Care to give it a try?" She picked up the tray and pointed to the seating area.

The smile she shot Julia made her reciprocate with her own, lifting the tiredness she could feel sagging her face. "At this point I'm willing to try anything. Poor thing's been crying like this since yesterday."

Poppy put their tray down on one of the empty tables, set Julia's baggage aside, and pulled a chair out for her new friends. She sat across from Julia and held her arms out. With a little apprehension, Julia handed Tallulah over and sat back, watching expectantly.

"How old is she?" Poppy asked, aware that she was now expected to deliver a miracle cure and hoping she could.

"Four months," Julia replied.

Poppy immediately felt how hot the baby was from crying and noted how her little legs were drawn close into her stomach in an effort to comfort herself. Putting one of her hands behind Tallulah's head, Poppy faced the baby toward her and laid her in the well that her crossed legs formed. Slowly, she rubbed Tallulah's stomach with her other hand.

With the warm, comforting hand massaging her, the baby opened small forest green eyes and focused on Poppy. Both Tallulah and her mother listened as the miracle worker started singing softly. The song was a slow lullaby Julia was unfamiliar with, but the deep, rich voice made it sound timeless, and Julia noticed some of the patrons sitting close to them stopped talking and listened to what sounded like a fairy tale woven to music. For the first time in what seemed like days, Tallulah fell sleepily silent, and Julia relaxed back in her chair and closed her eyes, feeling as drowsy and content as her baby.

Poppy ended the song gradually and moved the sleeping infant to her shoulder. She inhaled deeply to take in the essence of the innocent life she held. Seeing the shade of green of the baby's eyes had left her temporarily shocked. It had been like finding a memory trapped in the small being she cradled. Having children had never crossed her mind, but Poppy did enjoy the feel of them in her arms, and she'd always liked to play with those who were part of her life through her friends.

Julia marveled as her tempestuous daughter lay curled on the broad shoulder, asleep for the first time in twenty-four hours. Whoever this woman was, she was a godsend, and Julia's nervousness about having a stranger hold Tallulah had evaporated.

She leaned over the table and extended her hand in greeting. "I know I'm kinda late but I'm Julia, and that young lady you're holding is my daughter, Tallulah."

"Heck. Maybe I was wrong and the kid doesn't have a stomachache. She's just protesting getting stuck with the name Tallulah." Poppy looked into another set of green eyes, only these didn't look all that happy with the comment she had just made.

"For your information, Tallulah is my grandmother's name. My grandmother who raised me from the time I was as old as the baby you now hold, so no cracks about her name." Julia stated her case a little more forcefully than she really meant. Poppy's reaction struck a nerve after almost everyone she knew had tried to dissuade her from saddling her daughter with the old name.

"I'm sorry, I was joking. Tallulah's a beautiful name. You just don't hear it very often these days. May she be as unique as her name, and as special as your grandmother obviously is to you. I'm pleased to meet you both. My name's Poppy." Poppy smiled again and noticed she was still holding the hand Julia had extended.

"Your name's Poppy and you're making fun of Tallulah?"

"Actually my name's Raquel Poppy, but people call me Poppy," she answered, adding an arched brow to her comment.

"But don't you think Poppy's a stranger name than Tallulah?" Julia was enjoying the teasing banter so much, the thought of having heard the unique name before was a fleeting one.

"For *your* information, Poppy is my mother's name. The mother who raised me from the time I was born. So no cracks about her name."

Whoever this woman was, Poppy found her delightful. And considering life had lost so much meaning for her in the past two and a half years that she hadn't found delight in anything or anyone, Poppy was surprised to discover it in a coffee shop in the form of a small child and her mother.

"I thought you said your name was Raquel?" Julia kept her hand where it was, enjoying the warmth of the larger one it was encased in.

"It is. I'm named after both my parents," started Poppy, before she was interrupted again.

"Your father's name is Raquel?"

"No, it's not, smart-ass. My dad's name is Raphael, and, as you already know, my mother's name is Poppy. Only no one calls her that." Poppy cocked her head to the side, making no attempt to continue, somehow knowing Julia couldn't keep quiet.

"What's she called?" Julia chimed in with her next interruption.

"If you'd sit there quietly, I'd have the opportunity to tell you. Her middle name is Isabelle, and that's what she goes by. Poppy, which is an old family name on her side of the family, got passed to me. And since my mother didn't think I could go comfortably through life with the name Raphael, she decided on Raquel as a close second. So, now that you know my whole name history, Miss Julia, is there a car seat or stroller I can put Miss Tallulah in so she'll be more comfortable?"

"Actually her car seat's up in the hotel room, but I'm sure I can manage if you give me my stuff back. We're heading to the airport, and we're running late."

"Then let me help you."

"I can't let you do that," said Julia.

"We've had this conversation already."

The elevator headed to the third floor where the lobby was located. Poppy was aware that Julia stole a few looks at her when it seemed she wouldn't notice. She did the same and immediately observed something important that made her decide to carry out her good deed for the day, then be on her way. A diamond engagement ring and wedding band occupied Julia's left ring finger. *About two and a half carats. At least the bastard's not cheap, and he certainly has good taste in women. Even though he's left her stranded here with no one to help her.*

From her side of the elevator, Julia noticed the wide platinum wedding band on Poppy's left hand. It was plain but seemed to suit the wearer, who with her height and good looks didn't need much adornment. They walked through the elaborately decorated lobby to take another set of elevators to the eighteenth floor to Julia and Tallulah's room. After seeing the pile of luggage, Poppy picked up the phone and called for a porter to help them. While she was on the phone, she watched Julia strap the baby into the car seat carefully so as not to wake her, then walk around the room checking to make sure she hadn't forgotten anything.

"Yes, Ms. Valente, someone's on the way up now. I apologize for not realizing you were in the building, ma'am."

"I'm just helping someone out. Could you also arrange for a car as well?" Poppy hung up and, when a knock came shortly after, headed toward the door to let in two porters who'd arrived to load up Julia's possessions.

Amazed at the quick response Poppy had gotten out of the hotel staff and how quiet they were being because of the sleeping infant, Julia whispered in her daughter's ear, "I don't know what her secret is, but she must be a dream to travel with. It's a shame she can't come the rest of the way with us."

Once downstairs, Poppy oversaw the porters strapping the baby's car seat into place in the black limo waiting to take them to the airport, and they thanked her for the generous tip she had evidently given them.

While Julia was still trying to find the right words to thank her, Poppy said, "It was a pleasure meeting you and your daughter this morning. I hope you have a pleasant flight wherever you're going."

She took possession of Julia's hand to shake it in farewell, finding she liked the way it felt in hers.

For the first time since they met, Julia looked up and saw that Poppy's eyes were Caribbean blue. It was the only color she could think of to describe them. They were the same shade as the water in all those travel brochures that showed the blue-green vistas around resort locations. It was a striking combination when you put it together with the jet black hair that looked slightly curly even though it was pulled into a short ponytail.

"Thank you for all this," Julia said as she felt Poppy start to pull her hand away. Julia squeezed her fingers and tugged to not break the contact just yet. "I don't know if I would've survived the morning without you. It was a pleasure meeting you too, and thanks for your song. Can I pay you back for the coffee, or anything?"

"My treat, and you don't have to thank me for doing something I love. In a way, you and Tallulah just showed me there might be a song or two left in me. You take care of her, and yourself as well, and have fun on your trip. Maybe we'll run into each other again some time." On impulse, Poppy kissed the petite hand she had been holding before letting go and walking away.

Heading back up to the lobby of the Piquant, she allowed her mind to retrace the events of the morning and to flood with memories she'd found in the shade of Tallulah's green eyes. Memories that solidified for Poppy that no matter how much pain she was in now, given the opportunity, she wouldn't change anything about the past. The moment she'd watched Carly walk toward her that night was the turning point of her life, the moment she'd first seen the woman who had held her heart and taught her how to love. The memories were all she had left now.

Thirteen and a Half Years Earlier—The Royal Orleans Hotel

Poppy was playing the guitar in the corner of the crowded bar. A slow jazz tune that blended well with the whispered conversations going on around the room. This wasn't her usual gig, but there were two more semesters at Tulane and she had plans.

The groups who gathered every night at the Oak Bar in one of the French Quarter's oldest and grandest hotels never seemed to differ. They were the upper crust of what the city had to offer, most of whom liked to be seen out in places like this. To Poppy they were a group of people willing to pay eight bucks for a drink poured into the smallest glasses the hotel could procure.

Tonight was different though. Tonight in the corner opposite where she sat playing, a group of three women were on at least their fourth round, and laughing louder than anyone had in this stuffy establishment for a long time.

The brunette in the middle sat flanked by two blondes, one short and one tall. Both had their heads thrown back, laughing at something she'd just finished telling them. The other older patrons scattered throughout the bar would look their way disapprovingly every so often, but every scowl thrown in their direction only seemed to drive the volume of the laughing up a notch and the waiter over with another round.

Poppy watched as the brunette retrieved a large purse off the floor by her feet and pulled out her wallet. Removing something, she got up and strolled toward Poppy. Watching the roll of the woman's hips and the ease of her smile, Poppy forgot the next notes of the song she had been playing and just sat there with a loose grip on the neck of the guitar until the woman halted in front of her.

Leaning over slightly and holding her hands behind her back, the woman asked, "Do you happen to know any Buffett?"

"Buffett?" Poppy could feel the blush running up her face and the beginning of the nervous tick that made her leg bounce. This woman was making her sweat and she had asked her something, but a fog had settled in Poppy's brain, making her unable to answer.

"Jimmy Buffett." The woman smiled as if enjoying the effect she was having. She leaned further over and stuffed a twenty-dollar bill into the pocket of Poppy's shirt before continuing the one-sided conversation. "'Margaritaville,' 'Pensacola Run,' or anything else along those lines?"

Poppy sat there mesmerized. The heat that radiated off her ears assured her she was blushing. "Sure, I know some Buffett tunes," she replied awkwardly. "They don't let me do them in here."

"Well, one of the patrons has made a request...um?" The woman left the question hanging.

"Poppy, my name's Poppy." The way Poppy answered made it sound like she was trying to convince herself it was the correct name. Before extending her hand for a more formal introduction, she wiped it on her black pants.

"Nice to meet you, Poppy. My name's Carly Stevens, and those two wild women sitting over there with me are Sabrina Thorenson and Matlin Moore." Carly pointed toward the table where her friends sat waving back at them.

To be polite Poppy smiled and waved back, then her eyes and attention were riveted on Carly once more.

"Now that you know who we are and we know who you are, we'd like to hear some Buffett, if you please."

As Carly walked back to her seat, Poppy could have sworn she added some extra sway to her hips. She certainly looked like she knew Poppy's eyes were glued to her. Hooking the guitar strap on and standing, Poppy gave the ladies their wish by performing all of the Buffett songs she had in her repertoire. She made enough tips that night from some of the other Buffett enthusiasts in the audience to pay for her next semester's books, which she had to purchase the following day.

The college education she was working on was something Poppy's parents, Raphael and Isabelle, wanted more than she did. They weren't poor, but the Valente family had what her mother called "a healthy respect for the dollar." Luckily Poppy had an excellent academic record as well as a natural musical talent, and a combination of scholarships and help from her parents had paid for the education Tulane provided for a premium price. This accomplishment was her mother's favorite subject when she sat for a visit with her friends. Not the part where Poppy was out in bars all night making a living, but the my-kid's-going-to-graduate-from-Tulane part.

A little bleary-eyed the next morning, Poppy went up and down the aisles of the campus bookstore. She had scheduled an extra class for the spring semester, which would allow her to take the summer off to work and finish up in the fall. After she walked across the stage in December, she would embark on the plan she had formulated two summers earlier, when she had worked on the island of Aruba.

Caught up in a dream of swaying palm trees and thick-cushioned chaise lounges, Poppy didn't see the woman standing behind her. Only after she'd backed into her and saw her sprawled on the ground did she realize it was Carly Stevens.

"I'm so sorry, I didn't see you standing there." Poppy dropped to her knees to pick up all the stuff now on the ground. In the light of day, she found Carly's delightful smile just as enchanting as she had in the bar. And to Poppy's surprise, her own blush from the night before was back in full force.

"What a surprise bumping into you here." Carly laughed at her own joke. "Don't worry, no harm done. I may be older than you are, but I'm far from fragile."

"It's just that I'm usually not so clumsy and dumb-witted. How about I pay for all my stuff, and then I'll treat you to breakfast down the street to make it up to you?" Poppy sat on her heels waiting for Carly's reply.

"That, my dear, is the best offer I've had all morning. Lead on, oh clumsy and dumb-witted one." There was a clear teasing tone in Carly's voice as she held out her hand to be helped up.

They headed to the registers together and paid for their selections, then walked to Carly's car to drop everything off. "There's a good café about four blocks from here, Ms. Stevens. Do you mind walking?"

"If I'm going to have breakfast with you we have to be clear on two things. One, you have to call me Carly, and two, you have to tell me your last name. Or are you one of those musician types who only goes by one name?"

"No, ma'am. I mean, Carly." Relief flooded Poppy that she hadn't struck out before the game even began. "My name's Raquel Poppy Valente, but my friends all call me Poppy."

"Fine. Now take me to some food before I pass out."

They spent the morning next to each other at the counter of the Camellia Grill, one of New Orleans's oldest traditions, talking about a whole slew of topics, starting with the chili drowning Poppy's omelet and moving to the problems of current politics.

The morning ended too soon for Poppy, and she found herself reluctantly escorting Carly back to the car to retrieve her purchases. It didn't help that they had walked past four different young women on their way back, and each one had greeted Poppy with a firm hug and a kiss and the suggestion that more was on offer. Or maybe Poppy was just imagining it must seem that way to Carly. She was sure she'd detected increasing irritation in the deep green eyes and the set of her full mouth.

The last block of their walk passed in silence and with no eye contact, and by the time they reached Carly's car, Carly seemed angry. They stood next to the BMW sedan, the ease of morning entirely gone.

Poppy shifted awkwardly. "Look, Carly, I'm not real sure what happened between the omelet and now, but if it's something I did or said, I'm sorry." New Orleans uptown women were in general a liberal, progressive bunch, Poppy realized, but there was a limit to their acceptance of different lifestyle choices. Maybe Carly's fairly palpable anger had to do with her figuring out Poppy wasn't a sorority girl. "I wasn't trying to make you uncomfortable, but I can't help who I am. I'm gay and I don't hide that fact from anyone. The girls this morning were all just friends of mine, as in just friends."

"You don't owe me any explanations," Carly said. "And I have no problem with who you are, just so you know."

"Does that mean you'd like to see me again?" The words were out before Poppy could run them through the common-sense test. In a hurry, she added, "You probably have an address book full of friends, but I'd like to see you again."

"Why would you want to spend time with me, when you obviously have the pick of the litter?"

Several different emotions played across Carly's features. Poppy thought she glimpsed uncertainty, even vulnerability, but she couldn't be sure. She wondered if Carly suspected her of looking for a free ride. There was something about the woman, who was at least a foot shorter than she was, with her brown hair and green eyes, that spoke to Poppy's heart, and she didn't want to stop listening just yet. And she didn't want her to walk straight out of her life.

"I don't want anything from you, Carly," she said, leaning against the side of the black sedan. "Except maybe to be your friend. You look like you could stand another one in your life, and I can always use one."

When she heard the beep of the car's alarm system, Poppy thought she had her answer.

"Where're you playing tonight?" Carly asked as she opened the driver's side door.

Poppy grinned. "A little dive in the quarter I've been playing for years. The tips are good and I get to play all the stuff I like, which would include, but will not be limited to, some Buffett songs. If you and your friends stop by, I promise to sing you something special."

"I'm usually not a little dive kind of girl, but life's too short not to try new things, so why the hell not. There's something about you, Poppy, that makes me want to—"

"Yes, makes you want to what?" Poppy leaned into the car a little.

"You make me want to sing, Poppy, and no one before you has ever done that."

CHAPTER TWO

As she walked back into the Piquant's lobby, Poppy rubbed the ring on her left hand. Engraved within the platinum band was a variation on those words: *You Make Me Sing—C.* The memories had gotten easier. The tears they usually brought no longer streamed down her face but were now held in her eyes, giving them a glassy look Poppy had grown used to. That meeting of two hearts seemed like an old cliché, and some days it felt like a lifetime ago. It almost seemed funny, looking back, that it had taken them so long to figure out that they belonged to one another.

Immaculately dressed in a dark gray suit, Elizabeth Stevens was standing at the front desk waiting for her. She concealed her surprise well, but Poppy guessed she hadn't expected to see her standing there looking very much like the CEO of Valente Resorts. The Piquant was their newest acquisition and restoration project, but Poppy hadn't been too interested once the papers had been signed.

Her business was vacation resorts. After she had worked her summers in the Caribbean playing some of the outdoor bars, she had fallen in love with the way of life the getaway locations provided to those lucky enough to visit. With the money she saved from those summer jobs and all the nightly gigs, she had purchased her first property ten years earlier in Cancun, renovating the place for college kids who wanted a cheap vacation before school started again. In the winter she'd catered to low and middle-income mature patrons who wanted some time in the sun.

With the right marketing and the help of Carly, Sabrina, and Matlin, who became Vice Presidents of Customer Relations, Villa Valente made enough money to finance the purchase of a second property that, in a domino effect, bankrolled the rest of the purchases Poppy had made since.

The business Poppy had built was so much more than she first had planned, and she owed her success to combining her dreams with Carly's and her friends'. Valente Resorts now owned six locations, and by expanding her dreams far beyond what she'd originally intended, Poppy had finally been able to build the one place that would, in a way, serve as a tribute to the woman she loved.

The culmination of ten years of work was near completion off the coast of Venezuela, close to Aruba. The land purchase had been the easy part; the hard part came in carving out one of the world's most exclusive resorts on the wild island paradise, but they were close to opening Carly's Sound.

❖

The top management crew for the new property had been at the headquarters of Valente Resorts, located in the Piquant, for the past three months getting their final training. Poppy's success came not only from the structures themselves and their exotic locations, but from the top-notch service everyone received during their stay in one of her properties. By paying close attention to what other places thought was minutiae, she and her staff made sure a Valente Resort formed part of every client's most desirable travel itinerary for future vacations.

As exciting as it had all been, when Carly died, Poppy had retreated back to their house and mourned. She was tired of the overwhelming sadness, but until now she hadn't been strong enough to lift the weight off her soul.

Walking up to her, Elizabeth pressed her cheek against her starched white shirt and embraced her. "Welcome back. You've been missed."

"Thanks, kiddo. I'm here to take a look at the place and the new offices. Then I have something I want to discuss with you."

"Whatever you want. There's a slew of things I need to cover about Carly's Sound, then I'm all yours. Are you feeling up to it?"

They took the elevators up two floors to the new offices, Poppy following Elizabeth to a large corner office with a nice view of downtown. Susanna Hebert, Poppy's administrative assistant, gave her a hug as well before following them in. The redhead was slightly taller than Elizabeth and had joined Poppy's team shortly after finishing college.

With a nod from Elizabeth, she said, "Miguel flew down last week to check the flow from the airport to the boat shuttles onto the island."

Miguel Flores was the general manager of the new resort. "His new assistant, Rayford Johnson, will be flying out this morning with Mrs. Johnson and a child. Hopefully Mr. Johnson will be available to help with any glitches between the Venezuelans and the shuttle captains."

"Rayford Johnson?" Poppy turned from the view, struck by the unusual first name. "Where's Mr. Johnson from?"

"The Houston area," Susanna replied, going to her desk for the appropriate file. "Just graduated from UH in hotel and restaurant management, but his father's an old acquaintance of Matlin's, a New Orleans native transplanted to Texas via the oil field. Apparently he called Matlin when the kid got out of school."

"I wonder if his son realizes how lucky he is getting a position like this right off, considering the ink on his diploma isn't even dry yet?" Poppy accepted the file and sat back to read it.

Unlike most corporate heads, she took an interest in who was on her payroll, especially when their position was garnered by family connections, not by experience. It wasn't that she mistrusted Matlin's decisions, but this project meant a lot to her, and Miguel had enough to deal with without having to act as a babysitter to some friend's kid as well.

According to the file, Rayford had requested family accommodations in the residents' quarters. Poppy's heart jumped at the name of the person accompanying him. Julia Johnson with a child named Tallulah. She was also a graduate of UH in landscape architecture, but would not be employed by Valente Resorts, Inc. Parts of the bio sheet were left blank, but Matlin's signature of approval was clear at the bottom. There was either a story behind the missing information, or Matlin the dealmaker was up to her old tricks again.

Everyone who worked for Poppy had their own unique abilities or talents, and those she depended on, like Matlin, enjoyed a healthy dose of her trust to make decisions on her behalf. There were no real written rules of procedure, but no one had ventured into the unexplored territory of betraying her trust.

Poppy, herself, possessed a little of each of the qualities that made Valente Resorts so successful, but she had surrounded herself with people who added to her talents and who had an innate ability to know exactly what she wanted without a lot of hand-holding on her part. With an operation as large as Valente Resorts, she had no choice but to give her team ample room to get the company's business done. All of the people she spent the most time with had an area they were responsible for.

Elizabeth was her own personal voice of reason. Any contract or legal issue they were involved with, Poppy gave her free rein. Sabrina Thorenson was Executive Vice President of Customer Relations, a title she shared with Matlin, and lorded over the day-to-day things that set Valente apart from their competitors. The quality of amenities, the excellence of room service, the firmness of a guest's massage were always up to standard because of Sabrina's vigilance. Susanna's responsibility was to keep them all on schedule and up to date on any issue of concern. But mainly, she was Poppy's link to Valente Resorts whenever she was busy with projects or unavailable.

Then there was Matlin Moore. She and Sabrina shared the same coloring, with big blue eyes and blond hair, but that's where the physical similarities ended. Sabrina was tall and slim with a style that often reminded Poppy of Carly. The one thing all three women had in common aside from a fabulous taste in clothes and a panache for decorating was to have chosen men who had no concept of fidelity. Matlin, though, out of the three, was all spirit and fun. More often than the other two, she was the reason for all of them spending so much time in after-hours detention when they were in high school together. A short, curvy spitfire who often kidded that the worst mistake of her life was not wrestling Carly to the ground so she could have beaten her to Poppy to request that song, she was Poppy's wheeler-dealer.

Matlin felt most rules were meant not to be broken, but bent just to the point where they were about to snap. Life was much more interesting with her around, but looking at the half-empty form in her hand with Matlin's signature at the bottom made Poppy shake her head. All the properties in their chain were important, but the opening of Carly's Sound was not the time for repayment of favors to old friends.

It was time to go fishing. "Mr. Johnson was here with the rest of the management team?" asked Poppy, not looking up from the folder in her hands.

"I assume he was. I spoke with him on a couple of occasions when they were in training. Want me to check it out for you?" Elizabeth tapped her manicured fingernails on the arm of her chair in sequence as if counting down from five, waiting to see why Poppy had asked the strange question. With all the other things going on in their lives, where some kid from Texas stayed during his training wasn't likely to be high on her priority list. She flipped her cell phone open so that she could check with the business office. "Hey, Joe, fire up the computer for me and look up Rayford Johnson's guest files. Should've checked out today."

Joseph St. Thomas, the man accessing the files, was the business manager of their New Orleans property, The Piquant, and one of the very few people in the city who knew that Poppy owned the hotel. She had purchased the building that housed it for two reasons. It was, in her opinion, the prettiest building in the downtown area, and the Herculean effort it took to renovate it had helped Elizabeth through her own period of mourning. After two years of round-the-clock restoration, it had opened to a brisk business six months earlier.

The venture in their hometown was something different from the rest of Poppy's properties, but it was something she'd been willing to try. There was no beach, and the tropical foliage was for the most part potted, but the five-star hotel offered everything else they were known for. Poppy also thought that their main offices should be located somewhere that centered on the company's main mission. Managers couldn't effectively manage a company focused on leisure and service if they weren't reminded of these aspirations by talking to the guests roaming around the building. A disgruntled customer was the best training tool Poppy could think of to keep her staff at the top of their game.

The only real hint of the identity of the owner hung on one of the pillars of the lobby. The picture showed the back of someone sitting with her legs crossed in an old rocking chair overlooking the city skyline, and had a brass plate at the bottom that read: "We hope you enjoy your stay." The only thing that changed from resort to resort was the view the same person looked out on.

The long legs in each photograph belonged to Poppy, and the reason they were all taken from the back was to commemorate her motto of always looking forward and not dwelling on the past. Even though she had failed to follow the motto after Carly's death, she still aspired to it, and the forward-looking pictures reminded her of that goal.

"Johnson was here alone for the three months of training. Shipped out this morning with the rest of the trainees and should be there by this afternoon," reported Elizabeth.

"No record of his wife and child?" Poppy took off her reading glasses and pinched the bridge of her nose, which prompted Susanna to get up, pour a glass of water, and take two aspirin out of the bottle sitting next to the pitcher. Poppy swallowed them without comment and waited for Elizabeth to answer her question.

"His wife and child?" Elizabeth asked the question almost to herself and without a verbal request from Poppy pulled out the phone again and subsequently clarified, "She checked in three days ago with the baby, in a different room, and a Mr. Frederick Johnson with a credit card that had a Houston address settled the bill. Room service records showed a dinner delivery for every evening she was here, but only for one. She also drank a juice out of the wet bar every day. Anything else you need to know, Dr. Evil?"

"No, Austin, that'll be all for now," said Poppy. Turning her attention back to the view, she thought of something Carly used to tell her. *Nothing is a coincidence.* How that statement applied to Julia Johnson and her daughter was something she would have to ponder later.

CHAPTER THREE

They sat together on the charter flight down to Venezuela to start on their new life. Julia just wanted the opportunity to get away from her family for a while and was glad Rayford had given her the chance to tag along. Her twin brother had wanted to stay in the Houston area with his friends, but the opportunity to help run something like Carly's Sound was too good to pass up.

Julia would miss her grandmother most of all, but the pressure her parents had put on her after the birth of Tallulah was too much to handle at the moment. Julia refused to believe, as her parents did, that the unplanned birth of her daughter was a mistake that would ruin her life.

She smiled at the thought of her grandmother. The old woman with compassionate eyes, whom Tallulah had been named for, had been her champion, as always. Julia and Rayford had lived with Granny Tallulah almost from the time of their birth. Her parents had been too busy with her father's career and social life to be burdened with children. The elder Tallulah had given her love and a stable home life, while her parents traveled the globe working in one exotic place after another as her father climbed the corporate ladder. While he had shirked and forgotten most of his responsibilities as a parent, Fred liked to flex his authoritative muscle every so often.

She looked at the man sitting next to her and wondered what their future held. They both deserved happiness, and maybe this job would bring an iota of it to Ray. A party boy, he'd always fallen short in his father's eyes, and Julia knew Fred cursed the fates for giving him a son with so little ambition. Rayford wasn't a bad person; he just liked the lighter side of life more than the mad rush for money and power.

Julia allowed her mind to drift once more to their destination. From the brochures she had seen, Carly's Sound didn't have the look of an average large resort. There were bungalows instead of a large building with suites, and the way they were arranged on the island gave every guest his own piece of private beach if that's what he desired. There was another beach area with a large collection of chaises and a bar for those seeking company and a livelier atmosphere. Four different restaurants served various types of food, and another bar would host live music every night for guests who wanted a little entertainment.

The whole resort was located on the lee side of the island, which faced the Venezuelan coastline, because the other side was almost barren of vegetation. Julia had read that the constant winds, which made the beach areas pleasant all day, made for monster waves on the northern shore. The island was almost a study in different habitats for the landscape architect.

"They've given us a bungalow with three bedrooms in the employee village," commented Rayford, without looking up from the girly magazine he was reading. "I figured you could put the kid in one room and you in the other. I won't be home much, so you can have the run of the place. Miguel says if you don't like the color schemes, or if you want some other appliances installed, to let him know. Your satisfaction is our first concern." Rayford said this with a laugh. Evidently the slogan had been beaten into his head in the conference rooms at the Piquant. He'd repeated it to Julia at every possible opportunity since they'd set off.

"Who's Miguel?"

"Miguel Flores is my boss, sweetheart, so make sure to talk me up when you meet him. I figure a couple of years of ordering the staff around and I'll be able to move to a better place." Rayford flipped to the next page and frowned when there were no pictures.

"Won't you have the best opportunities here? I thought this was the crown jewel in the Valente Resort Corporation in the Caribbean?" Julia said.

"To the idiot who built it, maybe, but I'm more interested in a hotel where younger, livelier people go instead of one on some rock out in the middle of nowhere. No, ma'am, this is a temporary situation. Once Matlin comes for a visit I'll start working on her for a transfer. You and the kid can come with me if you want."

"Ray, the baby's name is Tallulah, not the kid. Try and remember that." Julia kept her voice low so the other passengers couldn't listen in on their conversation and also not to wake Tallulah, who, thank

God, had done little but sleep since her encounter with the singing businesswoman three hours earlier.

"How can I forget? I can't believe you saddled that cute kid with that name, Julia. I was more partial to Rayanna."

"Let's not get into that conversation again, shall we? And I hope once she's old enough, you'll be able to give up this nasty habit of yours." Julia pointed to the magazine he was reading. "Just in case I've never told you, you're a pig, Rayford."

Her laugh took the sting out of the reprimand. Julia knew he was only waiting for her to shift her attention from Tallulah to the window and the water they were flying over. From the corner of her eye, she saw Miss March smile up from the centerfold he unfurled. He'd been ignoring the pig comment their whole lives. Why would she expect that to change now that he had a job and some adult responsibilities?

❖

With the special set of keys Elizabeth had given her, Poppy took the elevator to the penthouse suite, smiling when the doors slid open to reveal an extraordinary space. The picture in the lobby had been taken from the balcony outside the bank of windows, but the suite hadn't been finished when Poppy had come up to snap the shot. It was now an elegant mix of marble floors and cypress wood panels, sprinkled with antique pieces that Poppy was partial to.

After taking a tour, Poppy chose one of the comfortable chairs on the balcony, lifted her face to the sun, and closed her eyes as another of her favorite memories played in her head.

She was wearing a loud Hawaiian print shirt and khakis. It was ten years earlier, and she was working the crowd in a small bar in the heart of the French Quarter right off Bourbon Street, getting them to join in on the songs they knew and to clap along with the ones they didn't. For a Thursday night, the place was packed. Every so often someone would pass around a five-gallon water jug to collect tips for the performer, and from the look of it, Poppy would be able to afford new tires on her car.

As hard as she forced her eyes to keep moving around the room, they were tugged constantly back to the table right next to the stage where Carly and her best friends smiled up at her.

At midnight Poppy took a break and hopped down from the stage to make her way over to their table. She sat next to Carly and across from her two friends Sabrina and Matlin. All three women told her how much they liked her style, saving her from having to join in on the conversation. On the last two songs, her voice had cracked a couple of times from overuse.

Years later, Matlin had told her she and Sabrina were surprised that Carly had been so enthusiastic about spending another evening in a bar. She had practically dragged them out of their houses that night to make it on time. Carly's twenty-four-year marriage to Thomas Stevens Jr. had been shaky for some time, and finding out that he was having yet another affair, this time with his secretary, wasn't helping matters.

No matter how unhappy Carly was, though, she was financially tied to Tom, and he took great pleasure in reminding her of the fact. Matlin and Sabrina had thought it was unfortunate that the first sign Carly showed of being interested in someone, it had to be a poor college kid with a questionable future.

"Well, let me get back to work, ladies. Thanks for the water and the stories. They were much appreciated. Walk me back?" Poppy asked Carly. She held out her hand to help Carly off the stool and didn't let it go for the ten-foot walk back to the stage. "Want to have lunch with me tomorrow? As you can see from the bottle over there, I can take you some place nice."

"Will you wear a real shirt?" asked Carly with a smile.

"I'll see what I can do. I've got a ten-thirty class, but after that I'm all yours." Poppy waved off the bar manager pointing to the empty stage.

"I'd be honored to have lunch with you, Poppy, and you can wear whatever you like."

The three friends had left in the middle of the second act, noting it was well after two in the morning. Matlin had recounted Carly's version of events that evening more than once. When she pulled up to the large house in the Garden District, Tom was still awake and reading in his study on the first floor.

"Out barhopping again, Carly? Two nights in a row—what will the society columnists say? Try and remember we have an image to uphold, darling." He'd put as much sarcasm into his voice as he could muster for the late hour.

"Yes, dear, I'm sure you and your pet Rita can discuss etiquette and social decorum tomorrow, after you finish fucking her on your desk. Pleasant dreams, Tom. I'll be in the guest room if you need me. My suggestion to you is that you don't," said Carly with equal sarcasm.

Being stuck with the man for money was one thing, but being stuck with the man along with some STD was quite something else. Matlin's equally flawed marriage had taught both women that.

The next morning Poppy sat in the first row of the class and tried to ignore the grumbling coming from behind her because of her height. "Just how tall are you?" The familiar voice was so close, and the warm breath in Poppy's ear made the hairs on her neck stand on end.

"Six foot two, but who's asking?" Poppy replied with a smile and a question of her own.

"A fellow classmate," answered Carly. "Mind if I join you?" She was wearing a pale green linen dress. Not usual campus wear, but then Carly wasn't the typical student. She had decided a few years earlier to return and finish her degree, if just for her own sense of self after her child-rearing obligations at home had eased.

Poppy looked like every other preppy student attending Tulane, with her button-down cotton shirt and a pair of navy blue pants. "You don't ever have to ask me that. You'll always be welcome at my side," Poppy told her softly. "Fancy meeting you here. Are you taking this class or are you just stalking me?"

"What would you do if I said I was?"

"Wear brighter clothes so that you can find me easier?" Poppy made it a question.

"I'll keep that in mind." Carly sat next to Poppy when the professor walked in.

For the next hour Poppy couldn't have told anyone what the man said about advanced management concepts if her life depended on it, but she could still describe the smell of Carly's understatedly elegant Chanel perfume years later.

After class Poppy treated Carly to lunch at Commander's Palace, laughing at the shocked expression on her face when they were seated at one of the best tables in the restaurant. "I play the jazz brunch here every so often when they're short a player," was her only comment before turning her attention to the menu.

It was to become their routine for the next three months until the end of the semester and Poppy's time to leave for the summer. In those stolen hours they were able to carve out from their very separate lives, the two fell in love. Poppy's constant worry during that time was that Carly would forget her during the summer break, and Carly fretted aloud that Poppy would come to her senses while she was away and decide that Carly was too old.

They were studying for finals in the library on one of Poppy's evenings off, when the talk turned again to the upcoming summer. "You could take a week off and visit with me," said Poppy. Even though they hadn't done anything that could be called sexual, the thought of leaving Carly behind was becoming physically painful.

"Come and walk with me." Carly stood and gathered her books and held her hand out in invitation.

She smiled when Poppy readily accepted it and took her books away from her. They crossed the street to Audubon Park and sat under one of the oak trees. Sitting between Poppy's long legs, Carly relaxed back against her and they both gazed up through the branches at the night sky.

"I don't know if I'll be able to make it down there this summer," Carly said. "Even if I don't, I want you to have a good time and try and find some time to write and tell me how it's going. No matter what, I want you to know I'll miss you."

Poppy slid her arms around Carly's waist, and a small thrill ran through her as she felt Carly's hands run back and forth along her forearms over the bands of muscle just under the surface.

"You won't forget about me, will you, Carly?" The question came out in a whisper with a large dose of uncertainty.

"Oh, honey, how could I forget you? You're the best thing in my life aside from my children. For the past twenty years or more that's all I've concentrated on, and they helped me forget about everything else missing in my life. Things like romance and a healthy relationship. But now all I have is Elizabeth left at home, and next year she'll join Tommy and Josephine at college. What I want is the chance to be happy. You make me happy, Poppy."

"I love you, Carly." Poppy was almost hesitant in the admission, not sure how it would be received. Carly stopped the motion of her hand on Poppy's arm and turned to face her. Poppy's heart sank when she saw tears in Carly's eyes.

"What did you say?" The tears spilled down Carly's cheeks, but she made no move to wipe them away.

"I said I love you," Poppy repeated. She brushed the soft skin of Carly's face with her thumbs to remove the moisture and fought the urge to cry herself if her feelings weren't returned.

"God, that's so wonderful to finally hear. I've been in love with you, Poppy Valente, for so long I can't remember not being in love with you."

"Yeah?"

Carly just nodded, and when Poppy pressed her lips to Carly's, the kiss conveyed all that she was feeling in her heart.

When she pulled back she could see that Carly still had her eyes closed. "Are you all right?"

Carly's eyes finally blinked open but she still looked dazed. "I'm not sure," she admitted, then explained her hesitation stemmed from fear that Thomas would see the love she had for Poppy and use it as an excuse to get rid of her and install someone else in his life. That wasn't important to her, but she did want to have some means to take care of herself. She was old enough to know that sometimes love wasn't enough to get you through. She and Tom had proven that.

"Look at me, Carly." Poppy put two fingers under Carly's chin and pushed up gently. When the green eyes Poppy knew so well focused on her, she went on. "I don't want to push you into making any rash decisions. There should never come a time you have regrets about the path you choose. I want a partner, Carly, not someone who's beholden to me. What I want is to give you the freedom to be just you. What do you want?"

"Honey, I just want to be happy with you and for you to be happy in return. At this point in my life I would be happy in a two-room shack if it means seeing you come through the door at the end of the day. My question is, do you want a woman with three grown children? They are a part of me, and for all I'm willing to leave behind, my children are not negotiable."

"When I said I want you, Carly, that means all of you." Poppy kissed Carly one more time before she stood up and pulled her up after her. As alluring as Carly was, they were in the middle of the park, and that wasn't Poppy's idea of a perfect location for their first time making love. "Come on, enough serious talk for one night."

A week and a lot of kisses later they said good-bye at the airport before Poppy boarded a plane bound for Aruba. Two months had seemed like a lifetime to them, but Poppy needed the time to put the final pieces of her plan in action.

She slept her days away and worked nights for three weeks solid before she set up her meeting with Gloria Guiterrez to finalize their ongoing negotiations. Gloria's husband had been one of the first to build a resort in the area known as the Mayan Riviera, or Cancun. Roberto Guiterrez had died, and his widow had no interest in running the small, old Spanish-style hotel he had left her, so when the young, charming American came to call on her, Gloria was more than willing to listen.

The aging Mexican native had expressed amazement that Poppy spoke fluent Spanish with no American accent, almost as if it had been her first language. After their second dinner in Aruba, Poppy admitted that her family, while naturalized citizens of the United States, was originally from Cuba. Raphael and Isabelle had insisted that their only child speak the language of her heritage, and in this case, the child was glad they had been so hardheaded about it.

By their third dinner, they had arrived at a price and terms they were both comfortable with, and Poppy wrote a check for the down payment that would give flight to her dreams. The money Gloria walked off with represented thousands of hours spent in dimly lit rooms in front of microphones for Poppy, but it had been worth it. Now she would get to sing in her bar, for her customers, in her hotel.

Her parents would wonder where the large sum had come from, but frugal living and persistence of her own had paid off. The payment wiped out most of Poppy's savings, but there was still enough for some fresh paint for the rooms and three months of operating expenses. After that it was a gamble, but it would be an interesting roll of the dice.

After putting Gloria in a cab, Poppy walked to the nearest mailbox to post the letter she had written that morning. She hoped Carly would accept her invitation.

A week later Poppy waited at the airport for the plane Carly was supposed to be on, if she had decided to use the ticket Poppy had sent. Poppy waited until every passenger got off and the plane took on new passengers for its return to Miami before throwing the orchids she had bought in the nearest trash can and heading back to the hotel to get ready for work. The experiment of a young lover and an older woman obviously didn't stand the test of time and distance, she surmised, but the admission didn't come easy to her heart. Neither did the prospect of heading alone to Mexico in January.

Poppy fell into bed and slept until it was time to go to work, even though singing for happy tourists was the last thing she wanted to do that night. An hour into her night, Poppy put down her guitar and sat at the piano and started to play an old song for a couple in the audience who were celebrating their fiftieth wedding anniversary. In the middle of the chorus she looked up and saw her.

Carly stood at the foot of the stage wearing a green dress that matched her eyes and an orchid in her soft brown hair. In one hand she held the letter that Poppy had sent the week before, and in the other a card that said simply "Yes." For the rest of the night Poppy sat at the piano and played slow love songs for the anniversary couple, but the woman in the green dress sat and listened to the words she knew were being sung to only her.

Carly sometimes talked about the way Poppy had been slow and methodical in her courting techniques. From the first song all those months ago in the bar of the Royal Orleans, Poppy had swept her off her feet until Carly felt she would die without her touch or the sound of her voice.

When the set ended they didn't say anything to each other at first. Carly just followed Poppy out of the bar to the beach. At the shore, they looked out at the distant lights of the Venezuelan coastline, and as the gentle waves came up to caress Carly's feet, she felt the arms she had dreamed about for weeks come around her waist and hold her close.

"I missed you, baby," was all Poppy said before turning Carly around and kissing her.

"I love you, Poppy, and I missed you too, honey," Carly said.

She would tell Poppy eventually that the stifled feeling that had plagued her in New Orleans was gone. Poppy made her skin hot, her emotions raw, and Carly found it an exquisite feeling.

They sat on one of the chairs under the palm trees and enjoyed the star-filled night and the feeling of being close again. What didn't go as planned in Carly's mind was that she found herself deposited at her room not long afterwards, with Poppy kissing her good night.

The next morning they sat in the large outdoor café having breakfast. Poppy sat with her legs propped up on one of the empty chairs at the table, and Carly took the opportunity to give her a thorough appraisal. She noticed the darker coloring of her skin made the blue of her eyes stand out even more than they usually did, and Poppy had also lost weight, which made the muscles she possessed more obvious. Her hair was also longer than she normally kept it.

"What?" asked Poppy as she consumed a piece of mango. She could feel Carly's eyes on her, so she turned her body to face her.

"Nothing, just admiring the view. I haven't been able to look at you for a month, so I'm entitled." Carly returned the smile Poppy sported and entwined her fingers with Poppy's for their talk. "Before I got your letter, I formally and legally separated from Tom, and rented a small house in the French Quarter. I went to Tulane and arranged for a student loan to get me through the fall semester, and then I'll be heading out into the working world with you. You should know I want certain things out of life."

Poppy lifted their hands and kissed the back of Carly's. "What do you want, baby?"

"I want a life with you. I want to live with you and wake up with you in the mornings. To love you and be a part of your family for as long as you'll have me." This step was obviously scaring the hell out of Carly, but she liked to say that gazing into Poppy's clear blue eyes that day and seeing nothing but devotion meant poverty didn't sound all that bad.

"Are you sure about this?" Poppy asked. "Because I'm talking about forever. This isn't a passing phase for me, and I have to know you want the same things. The letter I sent you asked if you wanted to join me on a journey, and the card you held up last night said yes. It isn't a vacation trip I'm talking about, baby. It's a life's journey," Poppy explained.

"I want the same things as you do, darling, and no, this isn't a phase. Whatever you do, and wherever you go, just look to your side and I'll always be standing there. What do you want to do?"

"Love you and make music in the sun."

"Perfect."

Poppy told Carly, then, about the purchase and her plans for the future. After graduation they would head down to Mexico and go into the resort business. She laughed at the look on Carly's face when she found out exactly how much Poppy had saved.

With balled fists on her hips, Carly started fussing. "You had that much in the bank and you drive that death trap of a car?"

"Yes, that's why I have so much. I'm cheap. I got used to being frugal when I was young, and considering that I've worked almost every day since I was a junior in high school, it adds up."

"Listen to you, 'When I was young.' Compared to me you're still a baby. I want to celebrate."

Poppy loaded Carly on a sailboat she had borrowed from one of the managers of the hotel and set off to show her a treasure she had found while working on the island the year before. Carly kept her arms wrapped around Poppy's waist for the forty-minute sail, relishing the spray of the blue-green water as they cut through the waves. When Poppy dropped anchor a little way out from one of the most perfect beaches she had ever seen, Carly turned and kissed her.

"One day, baby, I'm going to buy this whole piece of the world and build a resort, and I'm going to name it Carly's Sound. After a lifetime together we're going to walk along that beach right there," Poppy pointed to the expanse of land before them, "and relive the memories we made here, starting today."

"What memories are we going to make here, my love?" Carly looked up at her, full of adoration.

"It'll be the place we first make love, and it'll be the place we gift the world with when we're ready to share it." Poppy leaned down and kissed the tip of Carly's nose, then moved to put on a backpack. "Wait here a second, baby," she told Carly, before jumping over the side into the crystal clear water, motioning for Carly to join her.

On the white pristine sand, under the large majestic palm trees, Poppy took the blanket she had brought out of the backpack. She ran a shaking hand reverently over Carly's face. "I want to touch you."

"I want you to." Carly smiled up at her with reassurance, like she was trying to help settle Poppy's nerves. "It's okay, honey, we'll take this nice and slow. I'm the one who should be nervous here. I've never done this with a woman, and compared to yours, my body may be a little lacking."

"I've never done this before either, with anyone, so quit worrying," laughed Poppy.

"You're a—"

"I believe the term is virgin, baby."

"Thank you for sharing this with me, Poppy." Carly had tears in her eyes. She pulled up the wet T-shirt Poppy was wearing, revealing the contrast in color where clothes had protected the skin from the sun. When Poppy went to do the same, Carly stiffened a bit, causing her to stop.

"It's silly, honey, but three pregnancies and forty-two years haven't exactly been kind to me. I don't want, well, I don't want to turn you off."

Poppy reached for the shirt again, and with slow movements, she removed it and peeled the straps of Carly's bathing suit down before helping her step out of it. Then she just knelt before Carly, and alone on their island in the late morning light that hid nothing, Poppy added lust to the love she felt when she looked up at the woman who stood naked before her. Carly was right. Her body wasn't perfect, but to Poppy's eyes it was. She saw past the little bit of sagging and the stretch marks, taking in every curve and every imperfection Carly was worried about and replacing doubt with passion. Needing to satisfy a deep hunger, she touched Carly.

Her skin was creamy white, soft, and smelled like coconut cream from the sunscreen Poppy had helped her put on. Poppy couldn't help the moan that escaped when she put her hands on Carly, making the standing woman lean against her for support. Having Carly's naked body pressed up against her was the most wonderful thing Poppy had experienced in her life. Any fear or feelings of inexperience melted away when Carly leaned over and kissed her. The look of want on Carly's face followed by the touch of just her fingertips made rational thought impossible.

Carly said, many times in the years that followed, that in that moment, for the first time ever, her identity was not wrapped up in being someone's daughter, or wife, or mother. Instead she knew herself as a woman who was desired.

❖

A sound from the street below intruded on Poppy's memories, and she stirred in her chair. Rubbing the ring on her finger, she scanned the buildings in downtown New Orleans and smiled at how much more comfortable Carly had gotten in shedding her clothes once she knew how Poppy felt about her in an intimate way. Carly had told her that no one could fake that kind of passion, and that was the best way to describe their relationship, passionate.

With the help of Matlin and Sabrina, Carly had polished Poppy like a jeweler would a rough diamond. Gone were the shorts and the sweatshirts. In their place were tailored suits and starched pinpoint cotton shirts that were custom made. Her shoes were Italian, and her hair was done by one of the exclusive salons in New Orleans. But some of the rough edges would always remain, and Poppy knew that was all right with those who loved her.

She had been transformed into the CEO of Valente Resorts, but she would give up the title in an instant in exchange for getting Carly back. She would've been happy playing her guitar in the French Quarter bars for that chance.

"Oh, honey, I miss you so much," she whispered.

CHAPTER FOUR

The plane taxied to a stop on the tarmac a few hundred feet from a terminal that bore the Valente company logo, which comprised a cluster of palm trees with a guitar leaning against one of them. Jeeps were lined up to take the passengers to the docks as soon as they had collected their luggage and cleared customs. The island they were headed to was a part of the old Dutch Antilles chain, and was located south of Aruba near the coast of Venezuela. Incoming Carly's Sound tourists flew into the Amuay Regional Airport, rather than making the scary landing at Oranjestad. The Venezuelan authorities had agreed to process the arrivals on behalf of the Arubans, provided the Valente Resorts' guests were immediately transferred to the boats that would shuttle them to Carly's Sound.

Julia paused at the top of the steps and tilted her head back to the sunshine and fresh air. The wind, though tinted with a scent of salt water, was hot and reminded her of Texas. She took one more deep breath before she started down toward the tarmac with Tallulah.

A middle-aged, tall Mexican gentleman met her at the bottom, greeted her by name, and offered to carry the baby for her. He introduced himself as Miguel Flores, and Julia found herself charmed by his thick Spanish accent and snow-white hair. When her luggage had been loaded by one of the porters, and Tallulah was secured in the backseat, Miguel had one of the customs officials come to the Jeep and stamp both her and Tallulah's passports. When the man was finished, Miguel drove the Jeep toward the helicopter that waited for them on the other side of the terminal. It, too, had the Valente logo on it.

"I thought we were taking boats to the island." Julia looked back to see Rayford standing next to a Jeep, pointing in their direction. He seemed to be screaming at the driver, but the man was doing a good job of ignoring him.

While Miguel had been tending to her and the baby, Rayford had been standing around talking to some of the women he had met during training. Julia laughed at his belated attempt to catch her attention, then turned back to Señor Flores. Rayford had, after all, asked her to be nice to the man he was working for.

"The owner, she say all the waves not good for the baby," was Miguel's only response. "This is better, no?"

"Yes, it is. I'll let you in on a little secret, Señor Flores. I get seasick in the bathtub, so I wasn't looking forward to that boat ride." Julia watched as the pilot loaded their luggage in the compartment under his seat, then turned for Tallulah's baby seat. It sure was observant of the resort owner to know she had a baby and arrange special transportation.

"Please call me Miguel, Mrs. Johnson. Señor Flores makes me feel too old." Miguel helped Julia up into her seat and walked around to the other side. "Okay, Juan, vamanos," he said, and made a circle with his finger, then handed Julia a set of headphones.

After Juan, the pilot, went through his preflight checklist they lifted off for Carly's Sound. Along the way Miguel kept up a running dialog as to the different sea life visible from the air, pointing out some of the moose head coral reefs that were just below the surface as they neared the island. Through the microphone he explained it was called that because the coral looked like the antlers of a moose.

The helicopter touched down on a natural rock formation that, with a little obvious help from a construction crew, was now a flat-topped helipad. Stairs fashioned from the same rock led down from the helipad to the trail that approached the resort area.

Several porters loaded Julia's luggage onto a golf cart with a bench seat across the back, and they headed to the bungalow where she would be living during her time on the island.

The sturdy-looking structure was bigger than the ones close to it, and Julia took note that, despite the rustic appearance, there was an air conditioning unit hidden in the foliage planted along the side. A distance away stood a lone bungalow with a much larger back porch that overlooked the water.

When Miguel saw where Julia's line of sight was trained he said, "That one is not available, Mrs. Johnson. It belongs to the owner, but I don't think she'll come very often so it'll stay empty most of the time."

"Please, Miguel, call me Julia. Mrs. Johnson is my..." She hesitated, not sure how to complete the sentence. "Let's just say that's someone else."

Miguel looked at her like he didn't understand but let it go, no doubt assuming a language barrier problem. Bowing slightly at the waist, he waved his arm in the direction of the bungalow and said, "You and the baby come with me into your new home."

Julia wondered why he wasn't sweating with the dark blue slacks he had on, and how he kept the white linen guayabera shirt he was wearing so crisp.

They entered the mutely decorated front room that led into the kitchen area. All the other rooms were similarly decorated, and all had large windows that looked out to the vast gardens outside. Because the colors of the rooms didn't compete with the flora outside, the natural colors on the other side of the windows were that much more vivid. Whoever had designed the living areas had kept as much of the beautiful surroundings as intact as possible, only cutting into the dense vegetation when necessary and accentuating the gardens so they looked well balanced.

Because of her background and education, Julia knew what kind of planning had gone into the natural-looking spaces around the bungalows. No plants grew in the wild in those perfect proportions, so while they looked untouched, the gardens were actually immaculately kept and well thought out. Just the view out of the kitchen window was a mark of genius.

Tallulah's fussing brought her attention back toward the living room, and Julia headed in that direction to give the baby her afternoon meal. Miguel beat it out of the front door when he saw that she was about to breast-feed, but promised to check on her again to make sure she had everything she needed.

With Tallulah cradled in her arms, Julia sat on the plush couch and offered her a nipple. As the little girl started suckling, Julia ran her index finger over her head and began to hum to her. It took her a moment to realize it was the melody of the song Poppy had sung to Tallulah back in New Orleans.

Just as quickly, Julia found she missed the woman. *I wonder what she's doing?*

The soft ring brought Poppy back, and she smiled as soon as she heard Miguel's voice. "She wants to live on an island and she gets seasick?"

"Si, she does. So I think the helicopter was the best idea you could have." Miguel had been part of the initial grounds crew when Poppy had bought her first place in Cancun. The son of a poor farming family, he had been a laborer at the old resort and had introduced himself to Poppy after watching her charm guests into parting with extra money for a couple of months.

At first, when he saw Carly and her friends, he had wrongly surmised she was the rich, older woman financing the operation. He had admitted to Poppy with some embarrassment that it took him a while to figure out that the woman who looked like a beach bum was actually the new owner and his employer.

Both Carly and Poppy saw his potential and promoted him from laborer to junior management. The day Miguel put on his new uniform and collected his new higher wage, he had promised he would follow wherever Poppy wanted to lead him. Poppy knew it wasn't the money or the clothes that were the best part of what she had given him, but the look in his children's eyes when he left every day for work. She knew exactly what it meant to Miguel that they would be able to stay in school and have more opportunities in life.

Now, his oldest son had one more year at Poppy's alma mater in New Orleans before he graduated. Then he would begin his career with Valente Resorts. The other two children, twin girls, were still in high school, but had already been accepted into Tulane. Leaving his wife and daughters behind in Mexico, not getting to see them except for summer vacations and frequent trips home, was the only drawback to taking the job at Carly's Sound. Poppy had promised that as soon as the other assistant managers could run the place without problems, Miguel could start making trips home more often.

"Did everyone like their accommodations?" Poppy asked.

"Si, they like that it is like a home instead of living in a hotel room. When we get to see you? Gisella and the girls will be here soon and they want to cook for you." His family had adopted Poppy and Carly into their fold, and loved Poppy's huge repertoire of silly songs.

"Sooner than you think, amigo."

"We'll be waiting, then. Adios, Poppy, que Dios te bendiga." *May God bless you.*

"Gracias." Poppy snapped the phone closed and shut her eyes again.

She thought about getting up and going to meet Elizabeth, but the months of inactivity had left her with a fatigue that sapped her just as much as the depression. With a sigh, she stayed where she was and wondered how she would ever get through day after day alone. What was the point?

The sound of the sudden voice sent a bolt through Poppy as if someone had touched her with a cattle prod.

"Mind if I sit down?"

Poppy's eyes flew open. There, next to her, sat Carly. Not the sick Carly she remembered from just before the cancer finally won the battle, but the Carly she had first met. Back was the wavy, shoulder-length, brown hair and the beautifully tailored clothes. The only thing out of place was that Carly was barefoot.

"Hey, I'm dead. Don't need shoes for that, believe me."

Poppy stared at the woman she had grieved over for what seemed like an eternity, and felt a fat drop of sweat run down her face and drop off the end of her chin onto the white cotton shirt she was wearing. When she found her voice, it came out awed and cracked from emotion.

"Oh, my God, it's you. It's really you."

"It's me."

"I can't believe it. I've missed you so much. There hasn't been a day I didn't think—" Poppy brought her hand up to touch the side of Carly's face, coming to an abrupt stop when something clicked in her head. "Holy shit, I've gone off the deep end."

She had read about things like this. People in intense pain just snap one day and lose touch with reality.

"What have I told you about cursing?" Carly pulled one leg up to her chest and leaned back into the soft cushion.

"Not to."

"That's right, no cursing, honey. So how've you been?"

Poppy was amazed to find that her overactive mind added even the smallest detail to the image it had conjured up. Like the way Carly had cocked her head after she had asked the question. The move had always meant she was waiting for an answer, and the smile just put you at ease enough to give her one.

"You can talk to yourself, but if you find yourself answering questions it means you're crazy," said Poppy, ignoring Carly's question. She turned to the front in hopes the world would shift back on its axis and the woman next to her would disappear.

"Poppy, snap out of it. I'm here, so deal with it. Think of it as a gift from Satan." Carly waved her hands as she explained the situation.

"You're in hell?" Poppy snapped her head around again to the apparition sitting next to her. It looked so real, almost like she could reach out and touch it.

"At the moment, yes, if you don't stop babbling like an idiot. But technically, no. I'm not in hell, just a little dead humor. I thought it'd get you to calm down. Now that I have you focused, we have to set some ground rules for our visits."

"You're sticking around?" As scared as Poppy was from seeing Carly again, she couldn't take her eyes off of her, more afraid that she would vanish.

"Why, don't you want me to?" The pout Carly sported reminded Poppy of exactly why she hadn't won an argument with the woman since they'd met.

"Of course, baby, but unless everyone else can see you, people are going to think I'm certifiable." Poppy's pulse raced as she allowed her eyes to rake over the woman sitting next to her. Even death hadn't changed what she'd always referred to as "The Carly Effect." In all their time together Poppy always got sweaty palms when Carly looked at her with the smile she wore now.

"Sorry, slick, only you can see me and only you can hear me, and get your mind out of the gutter." Carly placed the tip of her finger on Poppy's nose to let her know she was wise to where her thoughts had strayed. "Not that it's not flattering, but let's stay on subject, shall we? As for the certifiable part, we both know that to be true without the benefit of seeing dead people. Now answer my question. How have you been?"

"You went and died on me, Carly. How in the hell do you think I've been? You left me here alone and I feel so dead inside. It's like I'm sick and there's no cure for what I have."

The tears Poppy almost never cried except when she was alone pooled, but didn't fall until she leaned over and rested her elbows on her knees and started crying, which quickly turned to sobs. The hand that rubbed her back to try and soothe her seemed so real and so warm.

"I've just missed you," she went on. "I loved you so much that I can't quite figure out how to go on without you, or even if I want to."

"You're going to be all right, honey, I promise."

The crying jag slowed, and as Poppy gained control, she laughed with a weird mix of shock and irrational happiness. "Of course I'm going to be all right. Now I'm seeing things. I should've listened to Lizzie and seen a therapist."

"Told you there's no hell, and you're the most mentally balanced person I know, sweetie. You don't need a therapist." Carly touched the side of Poppy's face.

Heck, maybe being crazy wasn't so bad after all, thought Poppy, if her mind was able to conjure up such realistic pictures.

"I'm here to help you, honey. Sorry it took me so long, but it seems like just yesterday to me that I closed my eyes with you holding me on our beach. I don't know how I got here, and I don't know how much time we have, but I'm here because Lizzie asked me to be. All those prayers were hard to ignore, and she sounded so worried about you. That kind of selflessness deserves an answer, don't you think? We did a good job on that one, didn't we?"

"Yeah, Lizzie's a great kid. Best attorney on my payroll and the best friend I've had since you've been gone." Poppy reached across the space between them again and touched Carly's face. It felt so good to have that beautiful head lean into her hand, and to see that smile she had only seen in her dreams and her memories for the past two years.

"So you've managed to watch the tape and get out of the house, huh? Are you ready to head back to Carly's Sound?"

"That's why I'm here. I think I'm ready to try something familiar again. I'm going back to my lounge lizard persona. It's the least stressful way of trying to ease back into work."

"I fell in love with that lounge lizard, so don't knock her. It was a thrill to have some good-looking young thing singing to just me night after night. I could see why my ex always went for younger women." Carly stood up and straightened her long skirt. "I'm here to help you, but I want you to promise me something."

"Name it."

"I want you to try and find that part of your heart that was always brimming with hope. It's time to start over and find something worth waking up for."

"I had that, then you left me."

Carly held her hand out to Poppy and waited. "Then trust me when I say that I've come back to guide you to that again. Come on, honey, let's walk and take a look at the wonderful job our little girl has done around here. Keep a girl locked away in an urn all day, and she's got to stretch her legs."

Poppy took Carly's hand, and it felt so solid goose bumps rose on her arms.

The woman she loved gazed down at her and laughed. "It's time, my love, so let's get going. Poppy, would you like to join me on a journey?" Carly asked the same question Poppy had posed to her in Aruba years before.

It sounded so easy, a laugh bubbled effortlessly from Poppy. She had lost her mind, but so far it was a big improvement. "Yes," she said, without reservation.

CHAPTER FIVE

L ate afternoon light crept through the blinds in Julia's room. The breeze coming off the water had been so cool she had forgone the air conditioner and opened the wall of windows in the bedroom that faced the surf.

It was different waking up in the bungalow than at home. Lying next to her was Tallulah, who had woken up an hour before, ready for her afternoon feeding. Once she had eaten and been changed, the little girl had rolled into what looked like a soccer ball and gone back to sleep. Julia had heard Rayford stumble and crash into a smaller room down the hall with all his gear, but she was too tired to get up and check on him.

After her nap, she felt energized enough to go out and see what there was to do on Carly's Sound and how she could occupy her time so that she wouldn't go mad during their stay. She got out of bed and walked into the large bathroom on the other side of the room. Whoever had designed these facilities had gotten the proportions of the rooms just right, she noted as she snapped the lights on. Someone who obviously loved to spend time in the bathroom had laid out the room she was standing in. From the large claw-foot tub by the bay window, to the large shower stall, it was the vision of perfection.

Having lived with her grandmother in a house with small bathrooms and then in a dorm room at the university, Julia was in heaven when she adjusted the temperature of the water coming out of the large rain type of showerhead. Pulling her T-shirt up and over her head and untying the drawstring on her pajama pants, she spent twenty minutes soaking up her new surroundings in hedonistic fashion.

I'll call Granny today and tell her about this. With any luck she can come down for a visit before we get thrown out. It would be nice to explore the island with a friendly face. She would have to check with

Miguel and see what the policy was on family visitors to the employees' facilities.

Once she was showered and dressed, Julia changed Tallulah's clothes so they could go out and have a late lunch. Miguel had told her to leave a grocery list at his office, and it would be filled on their next trip into Venezuela. Despite not knowing what they liked, the staff had stocked the refrigerator with an ample supply of soda, juice, and milk, and there was fruit and bread on the countertop.

Since the facility wasn't expecting guests for at least four more months, the employees were allowed to dine in the areas usually reserved for paying customers. There didn't seem much point, Julia thought. The staff areas she had seen seemed every bit as nice as those for the clients. She sat by the large pool and ordered from a friendly young man with a thick Spanish accent, who cooed at Tallulah the whole time he was at the table.

"Mind if I join you, Señorita?"

She looked up and smiled to see Miguel. The pants and pressed shirt from the morning had been replaced with a resort T-shirt and shorts. "Please, I'd love the company."

"How are you two enjoying our fair island?" He sat down and the waiter ran over to take his order.

"I haven't really gotten the opportunity to walk around, but that's on my agenda for today. Things will be different once guests start to arrive so I want to see how the other half lives before I'm sent back behind the bushes," teased Julia.

Miguel laughed at her joke as the waiter put down a basket of bread and poured them both a glass of freshly squeezed fruit juice. "I would love to show you around, but I'm helping the staff stock the resort for the rest of the day."

"Stocking the resort?"

"The things for the bars and the maids' carts have arrived and need to be put away so we may see what's still missing. Time, she is running short, and I want to be ready." Miguel paused to drink the glass of juice. "If you like, I'll be free later to show you around."

"That would be great, Miguel, but I don't want to keep you from your duties. I'm pretty good at putting things away, so if you need any help Tallulah and I'd be happy to be of service to you and the staff." She could see he was getting ready to protest so she went on. "Please,

Miguel, it'll give us something to do and we won't be in the way. It's the least I can do to repay the owner for the wonderful bathroom in my bungalow."

"Well, okay, but don't tire yourself out. You just have a baby and I don't want any problems with that."

"You have yourself a deal." Julia shook his hand and smiled at his overprotectiveness.

They finished their meal together with Miguel telling her more about his family and his beginnings in the resort management business. When he found out she was a landscape architect, he promised to introduce her to the groundskeeping staff responsible for the beautiful plant life on the island.

Her first stop after Tallulah's feeding was the front lobby. Miguel put her in one of the coolest spots in the resort to fill the caddies along one of the walls with the brochures that explained all the special amenities available on Carly's Sound.

As she was going for more parasailing brochures, Julia noticed the picture hanging in the lobby. The scene the person overlooked was a section of the beach Julia guessed was located on the island. The long legs were covered by navy blue, what looked to be linen pants, the feet were bare, and the fingers of the left hand were the only other clue as to the identity of the person in the image. They were strong looking and sported a wedding band on the ring finger. The reason Julia studied the hand for so long was that it looked familiar, so familiar, she expected to see it lifted and the person in the chair offer her a seat.

"It is the owner, Señorita," said one of the girls behind the counter. "I never meet her, but I hear from the others who have, that she's nice. She can sing like the birds and looks for her lover in the sea."

"Celia, do I have to find you something more to do since you have so much time to spin tales for Señorita Julia," asked Miguel from the arched entryway.

The lobby, like the rest of the public areas on the island, was open. With the area reputedly receiving only two inches of rain a year, Julia supposed there was no reason to shut out the beauty that surrounded them.

"Perdonar me." *Forgive me.* "I did not mean to talk about the boss behind her back."

"It's okay. The boss is used to such romantic stories about her, I think. Come, Julia, it's time for dinner and that tour I promise you," said Miguel.

The beehive of activity continued without them as they sat under one of the umbrella tables by the pool. Julia found herself pensive, the image of those fingers still playing in her head as she held Tallulah to her breast with a light blanket covering her open shirt. Eventually, she asked, "What did she mean, she looks for her lover in the sea?"

"It's idle talk among the women. It means nothing. The love those eyes search for is gone for good, and it's a shame, it is. Ms. Valente is my friend, so I don't like, as you Americanos say, to talk out of the schoolyard about her business."

"Her story sounds sad," Julia mused.

"Her story is not complete yet. I refuse to believe that so good a heart will die broken." Miguel hesitated but seemed unable to resist a final comment. "Her love waits still. Perhaps she will find it again here by these blue waters."

They ate the rest of their meal in silence, Julia wondering why a stranger's tale had touched her so much.

❖

Waiting for Elizabeth, Poppy couldn't help but admire the lobby, even though she was still in shock from what had happened upstairs.

It was done in white marble, with one wall of arched windows that reached part of the fourth floor to let in an abundance of natural light. The last time she had done a walk-through, the old walls had been ripped out, and she could see through the studs how large the lobby was. The courtyard that it looked out on served as a café during the morning and lunch hours and a bar at night. Two huge ornate wrought-iron gazebos were placed side by side in the center, serving more as a point of interest than for shade. To Poppy, the people sitting at the tables under them looked like birds in a fancy cage without sides.

"You haven't been waiting long, have you?" asked Elizabeth.

"You're worth waiting for, no matter how long it takes."

Poppy took Elizabeth's hand and followed her outside to a table where a waiter was already setting down a teapot and a basket of freshly baked bread. Poppy pulled Elizabeth's chair out for her and pointed to her coffee cup, getting the server to go for the pot at his station.

"Thanks for meeting me this morning, Lizzie. I made a decision and I wanted you to be the first to know. I'm going to take off for a little vacation and see if I can't get going again. I don't want you to worry about me. I just want you to keep an eye on the shop while I'm away."

Elizabeth had entwined her fingers with Poppy's and squeezed a little harder when she mentioned leaving. "For how long and where're you going?"

"To Carly's Sound. For how long, I don't know. However long it takes me to get my head screwed on straight again, I guess. I'm tired of feeling sad." Poppy didn't need her approval, but she didn't want to upset Elizabeth any further. She hadn't been so absorbed in her own grief not to notice how Carly's death had affected her daughter. They had been each other's comfort ever since, but also a constant reminder of what the other had lost.

"Are you going to help Miguel run the place?"

"Nope."

"No? What, you're going as a tourist?"

"No, I'm the new nightly bar act. Just a guitar, the piano, and me to entertain the folks and the wildlife after sunset. I thought I'd go back to the basics and see where that takes me." Poppy rubbed her thumb along Lizzie's hand when she saw the tears in the green eyes that looked so much like her mother's. "I had Miguel promise to hide all the rotten fruit since I haven't played in so long. I might actually suck, but I'm willing to give it a try."

"That sounds like a great idea, Poppy. I'm just going to miss you. Can I call you?"

"You'd better, or else. I wanted to take the time to say thank you."

"For what?"

"For helping me through this, sweet pea. I don't know what I would've done if I'd lost both you and your mother." Poppy lifted Elizabeth's hand and kissed the back of it. "I love you."

"I love you too, and you don't owe me any thanks. The time I spent with you and Mom was great. You always valued my opinion and cared about what was going on in my life. I'm glad you're going back to singing. It's your gift, Poppy. You make other people happy when you do. But just because I'm glad doesn't mean I'm not going to miss you."

"I'm going to miss you too, kid. Don't think I don't appreciate all that you've done while I've been trying to get out of this pit. It's just that your mom wanted today to be a beginning and an end for me, so I guess now I start on the beginning part of the equation, ready or not."

Elizabeth let out a breath. "She just wanted the same things for you that you always gave us. And that's for you to be happy. I've watched you all this time, Poppy, and you've scared me."

"I didn't mean to. I just didn't know how to move on. The truth is, I didn't want to move on, and if I'm totally honest, I'm not sure I do yet." With the admission Poppy had a hard time keeping eye contact with Elizabeth.

"Why? Mom died, not you. If you allow yourself, I'm sure you can find a life again. But you have to be willing to let go just a little bit. It's what she wanted, and no one's going to think any less of you for trying. I think she'd be disappointed in you if you just gave up."

"Thank you for caring. You're so much like her."

"That's the best compliment you could ever give me." Elizabeth leaned back a little and for once looked a little unsure of herself. "What do you think?" she asked, waving a hand to the area around them.

"Does it matter, what I think?" asked Poppy.

Elizabeth let go of Poppy's hand and lifted her napkin from the table, picking at the corner before putting it in her lap. "You own the place, so I'd think your opinion would mean something."

"Lizzie, you don't need me to tell you that you did a wonderful job."

"Yes, she does."

Elizabeth had to get up and pat Poppy on the back when the sip of coffee she had just swallowed went down the wrong way. "You okay?" The coughing stopped and Poppy nodded to Elizabeth's question, still not sure of her voice. "Drink some water. It will make the burning go away."

"Go on, tell her," Carly insisted. "I mean, look at this place. I would've demanded to sell the house and move into the suite we were just in."

Poppy took a deep breath and reached over the table to take hold of Elizabeth's hand before she went on. "With all you've achieved here, I see the pupil has come into her own. You may have wanted more time with your mother, but you spent the time you did have very wisely. From the torn and tattered canvas you started with, I'm awed by what I see. You didn't just imitate her style, you took what she taught you and improved on it." Poppy turned to the smiling, teary-eyed Carly before adding one more sentiment. "In fact, I'm sure she's looking at you now with a big smile and a heart full of pride at the job you've done."

"You mean it?" All pretense of confidence was gone, and the question sounded like it was coming from the teenager Poppy had met years before.

Poppy was sincere when she told her, "The Valente chain has a new crown jewel, Elizabeth, and it's the Piquant. I love it, thank you."

Poppy watched the little girl recede back and the counselor and president of Valente Resorts return instantly when a tall young man wearing a charcoal gray suit with a small stickpin with the letter P in his lapel walked up and waited to be addressed.

When Elizabeth followed him back inside to deal with whatever crisis was happening behind the scenes, Carly said, "Thank you. I sometimes thought she craved your approval more than she did mine. But you didn't exaggerate. She did a wonderful job with this place." She had taken the seat beside Poppy.

"I had every confidence. She's your daughter so I was never concerned about her doing a good job. It's all in the genes." Though slightly freaked that she was seeing things, Poppy felt it would be rude not to answer.

"Ah, and here comes the shallow end of that genetic pool now."

Poppy still had her eyebrows bunched together, trying to decipher what Carly's statement meant, when a shadow darkened the table.

"Talking to yourself now? Come on, Valente. Carly was good, but don't go losing your head over her death." Thomas Stevens, Carly's ex-husband, stood glaring at her with a folded newspaper under his arm.

No amount of time would change the animosity between them. As happy as Poppy had made Carly in her life was as miserable as Thomas had tried to make her once she'd told him she was not only leaving him, but for a younger woman. He had become downright venomous after that.

Poppy supposed the distinguished-appearing older attorney was surprised to see his nemesis sitting at one of the café's tables, and couldn't help but come over and give her a hard time. It was true that Carly had left him, and in his opinion turned Elizabeth against him, but he had done the same with their other two children.

At his insistence Thomas Jr. and Josephine had cut their mother out of their lives. The fact his first wife had died without seeing them again seemed to give him a perverse sense of satisfaction because of the humiliation Carly had caused him. Even now, he studied Poppy as if she were the bitch who had ruined his life, his own culpability conveniently forgotten.

Poppy looked up and kept her temper in check. "Thomas, gosh, and here I thought I'd never have to see you again. You should learn to talk to yourself. It's a sign of genius." The chair across from her scraped along the floor as Carly's cast-off husband pulled it out and took a seat. "Please join me," Poppy invited sarcastically.

"What are you doing here?"

"I'm having breakfast, and you?" Poppy bypassed the now-cold coffee and picked up her glass of orange juice instead.

Thomas lifted his hand to get the waiter to come back to the table. "I like taking a break here before work to have coffee and read the paper. This place makes me want to linger."

"Thank you. I'll make sure to tell Elizabeth you enjoy it." Poppy nodded to another cup of coffee when the server put down a fresh cup.

"Why would she care?"

"She was in charge of the building's restoration, and she's very proud of the final product."

"I thought she worked for you?"

"She does."

"You mean you own this place?"

"Your grasp of the obvious is astounding even to me, and I don't know you all that well. As simplistic as this next statement might sound to you, I urge you to listen to me. If you called your daughter just once a month, you'd know these things and maybe share in her accomplishments. Elizabeth will be an even more outstanding person than her mother, so don't mess up this relationship too with your pride."

"Of course she'll be better than her mother. Measure from that low a bar and you can't help but do better."

The sun felt warm on her face despite the chill of the morning air, and Poppy closed her eyes and enjoyed the contrast in sensations as she leaned back in her chair. The hate this man spewed was nothing new, but it didn't get easier to take no matter how many times she heard him.

"What'll take up your time now that Carly's no longer living and I'm leaving?"

From the expression on his face for one unguarded moment, Poppy could tell her question took him by surprise. He looked like a child who had built a castle of blocks and was displeased with the result of his effort. That's what Thomas's life had come to, but each block he had stacked had been placed with care and calculation. It was his own fault he had ended up with a twisted mess that held no warm places or beautiful views that, as he had said, made him want to linger.

"You can pretend you are better than me, but the truth is you are so much worse than I could even think to be." Thomas had lowered his voice, apparently not wanting to cause a disturbance that would bar him from returning.

"Thomas, you come here often like you said because this place draws you in and makes you want to enjoy what it has to offer. The next time you come here for coffee, put your paper down and take the time to look around. Open your heart for once and look at why you feel so good here."

His finger ran a constant circle around the rim of his coffee cup. Poppy could sense his irritation. He didn't want to listen to what she was saying, but it seemed he did not quite have the strength to get up and walk out.

"I come here only for the coffee and the quiet," he said.

"On every wall, in every guest room, in every color Elizabeth picked, you'll find her mother. That's what Carly taught her. It's what Carly created for you, but you could've cared less. You let it slip through your fingers so easily because you thought Carly was so beneath you, so unimportant. But that hasn't been the case, has it?"

"Don't pretend to think you know so much about me. You don't. My new wife loves me and my children respect me." All of a sudden Thomas started to squirm like his chair was uncomfortable.

"I'm sure they do, but consider this. Elizabeth spent hours here creating the space you find so inviting as a tribute to the woman she and I both loved. It makes you wonder what your legacy will be when you're gone. What'll the children you taught and nurtured build for you? Will it be a place where you see people having a hard time getting up to leave? You cannot know how happy it makes me that Carly Valente will never die away or be forgotten. Not because of places like The Piquant, but because of Elizabeth and all the extraordinary things she'll accomplish in her life."

She could see Thomas was about to dispute what she had just said, but she silenced him by summoning the waiter.

"Something you wanted, ma'am?"

Poppy looked at his name tag before she said, "Avery, I want you to put in an order for me and have Ms. Stevens sign off on it. Do you think you could take care of that?"

"Yes, ma'am." He put his pencil to the pad in his hand, waiting for her to make a selection.

"Whenever Mr. Thomas Stevens comes in here in the morning he's never to pay for a cup of coffee or breakfast again, even if he comes every morning until the end of his life. Tell her it's a gift from Carly Valente and sign the order Raquel Valente. All he has to do is show you this card." Poppy pulled her wallet out and extracted one of her business cards. On the back she wrote a synopsis of what she had told the waiter and then signed her name.

"Why?" Thomas looked at her.

"Because, Thomas, if you can't be grateful to Carly for what she gave you while she was alive and with you, you can maybe work up enough gratitude for a cup of coffee and a nice place to sit and enjoy it. Think of how much more pleasant sitting out here would be if you got Elizabeth to join you for a cup of tea. If you're lucky, you may find it's not too late for her to build you a legacy of your own when the time comes."

"I don't drink tea."

Poppy rolled her eyes and prayed for patience. "No, but Lizzie does."

❖

"These are palm trees, Tallulah," explained Julia, pointing up at the fronds they were sitting under. Mother and daughter were enjoying the late-afternoon breeze on the beach after their dinner with Miguel.

"What do you think this looked like before the resort was built?" Julia asked the baby.

The stretch of beach they were sitting on was deserted except for the occasional colorful bird that flew by. Julia thought that even at maximum capacity, the island would still retain a sense of peace. That was something she had known growing up with her grandmother back in Texas.

It was the elder Tallulah's love of flowers that had pushed Julia to get her degree. She had seldom felt lonely or isolated on her granny's ranch all those years. In the afternoons, she would get off her school bus, see her grandmother waiting by the ranch gates, and know there would be a snack set out on the porch for her. After recounting her day, they would step down into Tallulah's garden and tend the multitude of flowers they grew. On those afternoons Julia learned more than just about plants. Her grandmother taught her valuable lessons about love and how to raise children, since her son had abandoned his own so easily.

Looking at the baby asleep on her lap, Julia didn't understand what her parents had done. Tallulah was such a big part of her that the thought of giving her to someone else to raise made her nauseous. "Even if it's just you and me forever, Tallulah, I promise it'll always be enough. I'm never going to give you away to anyone for the promise of something better. My life was always so good because of Granny and Ray, and I'm going to try my best to always make you feel that way. Let's go and see if the big goof got something to eat, shall we?"

The sun was setting and the lights off the Venezuelan coastline were becoming more visible. Julia gazed at the twinkling spots in the distance, knowing that some represented homes full of happy families. She closed her eyes and made a wish on the lights that looked so much like stars from where she was standing, repeating the sentiment her grandmother had shared with her so many years ago. *I wish for the one person who'll love me like he did her.*

"If you're strong enough to face whatever life has planned for you, those wishes gonna come true."

Julia's eyes snapped open and turned toward the heavily accented voice in surprise. The smooth light brown skin gave no clue as to how old the woman was, and the completely white outfit gave no hint as to why she was there. Julia held Tallulah closer and opened her mouth to say something but didn't when the most fantastic laugh spilled out of the tall stranger.

"Don't be afraid, Miss Julia. I just like this spot too when all those lights come alive."

"How do you know my name?"

"What you looking for here, child?" The woman acted as if Julia hadn't spoken.

"Nothing, I was just enjoying the view."

"Then, what you hiding from?"

Julia tried to look away from the lambent brown eyes but couldn't find the willpower. "I'm just…" she found herself not being able to answer the question.

"I know, child." The woman moved forward and hugged her when tears started running down Julia's cheeks. Why she needed to cry was something else Julia had no explanation for. "You come to hide, but this island gonna surprise you if you let it."

That laugh came again, and Julia focused on how hot the hand pressed to the side of her face was. Whoever the woman was, she had the effect of a living security blanket that smelled like cinnamon. "What do you mean?"

"That's why they called surprises, girl. You keep wishing and they gonna come, and like the sun, they gonna blind you to everybody else."

"How do you know what I wished for?"

"Girl, you ask more questions than I don't know what. You wanna know what you wished for?" Julia nodded and the woman dried her face with two slightly callused thumbs before moving a little away from her and the baby. "You wish for love." She stripped the white bandanna off her head and fanned herself with it, even though the breeze had picked up when the sun had set. "Not long now."

"For?" Julia even had to laugh, acknowledging everything that had left her mouth had been nothing but questions.

"Can't you feel it? The wind carrying it here, that magic this place been missing for too long."

Julia watched the woman walk away, realizing when the vegetation had swallowed her from sight that she'd never said her name. "Weird."

CHAPTER SIX

What am I doing here, interfering with the living? They have not let go of me; am I equally attached?

Time has passed, and I have watched her moving dull-eyed through the world I've lost. Sometimes I stay close, compelled as I was from the very first by her beauty. Six feet tall and a handsome face with cheekbones to die for. Black hair a fabulous accent for her Caribbean blue eyes. She never had any concept of how stunning she is. Her looks are like the money; neither mattered in the realm of all things.

Her hands preoccupy me. Large and strong. Hands that owned my body from the first time we ever made love on that beach. And her voice summons me, that soothing, addictive baritone.

I can't leave her. I need to bring back the fire in her soul. It's time for her to move on to the next phase of her life, and to the young woman who waits there.

Like a fast-moving cloud obscuring the sun, a wave of melancholy swamps my soul. This is the first step in getting Poppy to let go, to loosen the stranglehold I have had on her heart. It is all I could do for her now. The last gift I can give.

❖

"Hey, Poppy, it's nice to see you again," said Huey. The old gruff-looking man was the mechanic for the marina in Aruba.

"Hey there, Huey, how's it going?" Poppy took a break from loading her stuff onto the *Pied Piper* to catch up with her old friend. They had met years before when he had taught her how to sail. When her first investment started to make money, Poppy had come back and bought the old boat she was now loading. Together they had restored the *Piper* to its original splendor.

"Getting older and crankier by the day. Loren and I were sorry we couldn't make it to Carly's services. Doesn't seem right for that to happen to someone so full of life," said Huey. He had twisted his hat into a ball while he had been talking and clearly wanted to avoid bringing up bad memories for her.

"You're right, pal, it wasn't fair, but you know what they say about life and fairness. Don't always go hand in hand, do they? And tell Loren she didn't miss the services because I haven't had any yet. Thanks for putting on a coat of shine for me. The old girl's never looked better."

"Are you sweet-talking me again?" asked Carly from the top of the storage cabinet on the dock.

Poppy, not expecting the sudden appearance, lost her balance and fell headfirst into the water. She surfaced with a scowl on her face and one of her sandals in her hand, and after throwing it onto the dock she had to dive to the bottom to retrieve the other one.

"Are you all right?" Huey asked, oblivious to the casually dressed ghost sitting right next to him.

"Yeah, just lost my balance. Maybe I'm getting on in years myself," Poppy muttered as she twisted the bottom of her T-shirt to wring out some of the excess water. "You shouldn't do that, you scared the hell out of me." The comment was directed to the storage cabinet, making Huey frown in confusion.

"I'm sorry if I scared you," he said.

"No, just talking to myself, don't mind me. I'll see you before I go back to the States. I'm going to take the *Piper* to Carly's Sound for a couple of weeks, but I promise I'll take good care of her. Say hello to Loren for me, and I'll see you soon, okay?" Poppy jumped on board and headed down to the cabin to get a fresh set of clothing.

Carly sat on the wide bunk and watched her strip off the wet clothing. "Honey, when I show up, you're going to have to act more cool or there'll be a competency hearing on your behalf. You've gotten obsessive about working out again, haven't you?"

"You're crazy if you think I can pass a competency hearing now." Poppy pulled on some fresh shorts and a polo shirt and shook her finger in Carly's face.

"Uh-huh, tell me, why haven't you had any services for me yet? Does that mean you're going to have services for me? I was never a big fan of the religious mumbo jumbo that went along with sending someone into the great beyond. I found the directions quite nicely by myself, thank you. Heck, I even found my way back."

"Yeah, lucky me."

"Be quiet. You know you love having me around again, admit it. Stop being such a sourpuss and take me sailing."

❖

Once she'd secured their course, Poppy sat next to Carly and opened a beer. The water smelled wonderful, and she looked up at a sky full of big white fluffy clouds. She had missed the freedom the *Pied Piper* had always given her to escape into the serenity of these waters, and wanted to explore some of the other smaller islands along the way before setting her final course to Carly's Sound.

A look at the underwater radar set Poppy's course toward what looked like a small stretch of beach, the closer they got. "This one looks a little different from the other two."

"More trees and something else waiting for you, baby." It was the only hint Carly seemed willing to give.

"Come on, then, let's go see what there is to see." Poppy eased herself into the water and started swimming.

Carly was waiting at the very edge of the surf. The water lapping around her feet made them sink and disappear. "Have fun."

"You're not coming? It'll be like old times, us finding the treasures the world has to offer."

The body Poppy was looking at dimmed for a split second. "These are new times, sweetheart, and what you'll find here is a gift."

"But," started Poppy.

"Honey, I'm asking you to take your time here looking around. Clear your mind and open your eyes. There's treasure here, and when the time comes and you're willing to open the part of yourself where you keep that trove, I don't want anything, especially me, to tarnish the shine of this gem for you. Please, baby, for me."

The whisper of Carly's voice in her head was enough for Poppy to give in and start walking. The beach was littered with fallen coconuts covered by wild orchids. The stretch of sand was shorter than Carly's Sound, and beyond it lay the volcanic rock that made up the majority of the islands in the area. What made this island different from all the others was at its center. There amongst the rock formations was a small waterfall.

It was salt water, but it was warmer than the water she had just swum through. When the sun hit the spray it made the most wonderful rainbow effect, reminding Poppy of a trip she had taken with her parents to Niagara Falls when she was ten. The roar of the water wasn't close, but the rainbow was the same. The setting filled her with a sense of peace that replaced the longing, if only for a heartbeat.

The sun was setting by the time she pointed the bow in the direction of Carly's Sound. She dropped anchor offshore from her house and dropped an inflatable raft over the side so she could transport her gear to shore. Hopefully Miguel had stocked the kitchen with something to eat, and the refrigerator with something to drink.

The last two waterproof bags Poppy lowered into the raft contained her laptop and other electronic leashes that were part of her life. In the morning she would check with Susanna and Lizzie on the status of the invitations they had sent out. Ready or not, the staff would be entertaining guests in two months. The trial run before the grand opening would be with guests who had frequented their properties in the past and were good customers, but hard to please.

They were the perfect patrons to put the staff through their paces. If they could handle a resort full of what Poppy liked to refer to as the guest from the pits of hell, their normal day after they left would be heaven.

She jumped into the now-inky black water and towed the raft to shore. The island was quiet and dark due to a lack of moonlight, but the bungalow on the end, away from all the others, still looked inviting. This was the spot she had brought Carly onshore a million years before, and it was where the first structure had been built.

Poppy dragged the raft as far up as she could before she started piling its contents onto the porch. The old wicker rocking chair used to take the lobby photos for each property sat facing the water a few feet from her. At one end of the porch was strung a hammock, and on the other side stood a concealed outdoor shower.

Comfortable with the fact the shower was far enough away from the other bungalows, Poppy stripped her wet clothes off and stepped inside to shower methodically before walking, dripping wet, into the house to get a towel.

The bungalow contained two large bedrooms. Rustic looking from the outside as all the others on the island, the inside of the structure was anything but. High quality Persian rugs covered polished hardwood cypress floors. The wood had been salvaged from an old plantation in Louisiana, and Poppy had spent weeks refinishing the floors she now walked over. Carly had always compared herself to the wide planks, saying that she, too, was slightly battered in places but still functional.

The furniture was a mix of modern comfortable with antique pieces sprinkled throughout. In the master suite was an antique sleigh bed Poppy had also refinished and modified to accommodate her height. She had refinished the four-poster bed in the guest room as well, and it was there she set all her things. She had no interest in sleeping in the room she had shared with Carly.

Once she had gotten dressed, she strolled into the kitchen, which was fully stocked with every cooking gadget she had collected from around the world, and found a note propped on the counter. Miguel had brought the cleaning staff in, expecting her arrival, and had stocked not only food but toiletries as well. She grabbed a beer from the fridge and read what Miguel had written as she walked slowly down the short hallway.

Poppy looked at the picture of Carly and Lizzie that sat on the desk of the small office in the front of the house and remembered the day it had been taken. It was the first summer Lizzie had spent with them, and that little taste had made her fall in love with the idea of following them into the business.

Poppy took her laptop from its case and fired off an e-mail to Lizzie to tell her she had arrived safely and would call her in the morning. She then checked on the status of the other properties to see if anything needed her immediate attention. Since Carly's death, she had left the day-to-day operations to Lizzie, Matlin, and Sabrina, but a part of her couldn't completely let go no matter what was going on in her life. It had nothing to do with not trusting the three women, just the anal part of her personality that balanced out the beach bum.

Once she was done, Poppy left the computer running and went in search of an old friend she hadn't seen in a long time. It sat in one corner of the spacious living room. Scarred from all the late nights it had spent with her from the time she was a teenager, it was still eager to please. No matter how many more guitars Poppy acquired through the years, this was the one that had built her bank account. It was time to see if there was any magic left in her and her old ally. Time to find if she could recapture part of her past.

Poppy started to play, not a ripping bar song or a love song, but a classical piece. It was something she didn't get to do often, since they weren't real inspiring to drink to. But the music she had learned first was Mozart and Piazzolla. She played Piazzolla's *Milonga Del Angel* now, getting lost in the passion of the staccato-like rhythm.

In the quiet of the night, the music carried to the open windows of the nearest bungalow, and Julia stopped pacing with Tallulah in front of her bedroom window and listened to what she assumed was someone's stereo. She hummed along and rocked from side to side, trying to get her daughter to sleep. When it stopped a while later, she was sorry but not completely surprised to find Tallulah sleeping contentedly in her arms.

"Maybe music does sooth the savage beast," she whispered as she placed Tallulah in her bassinet.

A few hundred yards away, Poppy set the guitar next to the wicker rocker and went to bed happy that she could still play.

When Julia retired, she felt happy for some reason, and the feeling seeped into her unconscious. She often felt, when she awoke from nights like this one, that she had spent every moment in the foreign landscape of her dreams looking for something. Happiness? A missing piece of her soul?

Julia couldn't say. She supposed everyone felt that way some time.

CHAPTER SEVEN

In the morning, after her shower, Julia got Tallulah dressed and ready to go out. On the way out the door to do some more exploring she ran into Rayford, who was just getting up.

"Where're you headed off to so early this morning, sweetheart?" he asked with a smile on his face.

He had seen her having both lunch and dinner with Miguel three days in a row, and Julia could tell he wondered what the manager found so interesting in her. She watched him take the juice container out of the fridge without a glass in sight.

"Don't you dare drink the juice out of the carton," she said, then continued in a softer tone when he reached for a tumbler. "I'm going out to do a little exploring and look at the rest of the landscaping on the island. Miguel's going to introduce me to the guys who maintain the gardens today, so I can ask some questions as to how they got some of this stuff to grow like this."

"Yeah, I saw you two by the pool while I was working my ass off. What in the world were you talking about, anyway?"

"He's been giving me a tour of the island. No need to work yourself into a frenzy over it. Don't worry. I talked you up every chance I got." Julia made little quotation marks with her fingers.

She decided to head away from the main facilities that morning and out to the thick foliage close to the lone bungalow by the beach. It would be time to feed Tallulah soon, and the palm trees would give her the privacy she needed to accomplish the task outdoors. At the same time she would also have the opportunity to look more closely at the back of the owner's bungalow for further clues about the person it belonged to.

A few minutes from her bungalow, Julia strolled around a corner and was surprised to find a patch of wildflowers cascading along the back porch of the empty bungalow. They were the kind of wildflowers you found back home, not on a tropical island. Growing up in Texas, Julia had loved the patches of highway the state planted every year with multicolored sprays like this one.

As she glanced up at the porch, Julia noticed an old wicker rocker that seemed vaguely familiar. Tallulah was starting to fuss, encouraging her closer. Since the place was empty, she supposed no one would mind if she sat up on the porch for a few minutes feeding her daughter. She was about to mount the stairs when she noticed a pair of feet stretched out in the front of the rocker, and a hand hanging off the side.

Julia froze and was about to head for the trees that had been her first destination, when a deep voice asked, "How do you like your new home?"

Julia swung her eyes up, startled. "Oh, my God, it's you."

The woman she had met in the coffee shop in New Orleans gazed down at her with a trace of amusement. The suit had been replaced with a white terry cloth robe, and the black hair was wet and slicked back. That's where she remembered the chair from, Julia realized in the same moment; it was the chair from the hotel lobby, and the hand was the one from the picture.

"Yes, it's me."

Tallulah voiced more displeasure. Torn as to what to do, Julia said, "I didn't mean to disturb you. I was on my way down to the beach to feed her."

"No need to keep her waiting on my account." Poppy got up from the rocker and walked to the edge of the porch. "Would you like to borrow my chair, Tallulah? I'm beginning to develop a complex since you're crying every time I see you." Her tone was teasing.

Feeling self-conscious over invading her neighbor's privacy, Julia climbed the steps onto the porch and sat down in the rocker. "Thank you. It's nice to see you again. Quite a surprise."

"Yes, isn't it?" Poppy seemed completely at ease. She lifted another wicker chair from farther along the porch and brought it a few feet closer to the rocker.

Tallulah was now in a full-blown tizzy, acting as if Julia never took the time to feed her. As Julia fumbled with the buttons of her shirt, her daughter was lifted out of her lap and the little green eyes that had been shut tight during the tirade popped open as a low voice began singing a silly song.

The morning serenade had the same effect as the first one Tallulah had coaxed out of Poppy. Julia finished unbuttoning her blouse as she watched her daughter interact with their new tall friend. The song about bugs got Tallulah's mind off her stomach until Julia was ready for her.

"I hope that isn't the theme song for this place," Julia said with a laugh.

Poppy was almost reluctant to let Tallulah go when the crying stopped and the dreamy face she remembered from the coffee shop was back. She handed the baby to her mother and watched as Julia lifted Tallulah to her exposed breast. When the baby started her meal, one little hand waved around as if trying to get Poppy to come closer.

"You didn't answer my question," Poppy said once Tallulah had settled.

Serious green eyes regarded her with an unguarded openness. "I love it here," Julia replied. "It's a real challenge to get out of that bathroom everyday. Whoever designed it must be a hedonist to the first degree."

"Well, I have a definite streak of pleasure hound running through me, I'm afraid. I'm glad you like it."

Poppy looked out across the water to a beautiful sailboat that bobbed a couple of hundred yards from the shore. She had been sitting on the porch watching the boat and enjoying a cup of coffee when she'd heard the footsteps coming up the path. The thought of getting up and screaming at whoever had decided to disturb her morning had crossed her mind until the whimper of a baby let her know precisely who was sneaking up on her. She found, then, that she didn't mind the interruption at all.

"How've you been?" Julia asked politely.

"Better." The melancholy of the morning was slipping away as Poppy watched Julia and Tallulah sitting in her chair, and she found herself moving closer and putting her finger out for the baby to grab onto. "Though, I'm not being a very good hostess, am I? Would you like a cup of coffee?"

Poppy gave Julia a genuine smile, which Julia readily returned. She was finding the more relaxed version of Poppy even more attractive than the one she had encountered in New Orleans. "I'd love a cup of coffee. Let's see if you remember how I take it."

Julia moved Tallulah to her other breast as Poppy returned and set the hot coffee on the small table next to the chair. The suckling had gotten slower, and Poppy could see it would be a matter of moments before the baby would go to sleep. To help the process along, she picked up the guitar and played an old Spanish lullaby her mother had sung to her as a baby.

"Want to put her down inside for a nap while you finish your coffee?" she asked when Tallulah's head drooped.

"That sounds like a great idea." Julia put her clothes in order, then got to her feet.

Poppy took the comforter off her bed for Tallulah and carried it into the living room. "Here we go. How's right here?" She spread it out in the middle of a thick floor rug.

"Thank you, this is perfect." Julia laid Tallulah down, barely disturbing her.

"I have to get dressed now and meet Miguel to review a few things, but you're welcome to stay as long as you like. As a matter of fact, you could take a nap in here on the couch while I'm gone."

"Are you sure you don't mind?"

"Nope, go ahead." In fact, Poppy liked the thought of the two of them sleeping in her home. In an effort not to be alone later in the day, she said, "When I get back maybe I could interest you and the bald one in some fishing."

"Maybe you could." Julia glanced at the soft beige sofa along the wall next to the door. "And since you mention it, I am kind of sleepy."

"Then help yourself. That way you'll be well rested and can bait my hooks," teased Poppy.

❖

"Where've you been?" asked Poppy as she and Carly passed one of the garden crew who was pruning a hibiscus plant.

"Having breakfast with Elvis."

"So he's really dead. *The National Enquirer* will be so disappointed."

"The real scoop for them would be to find out what really happened to Jimmy Hoffa," said Carly with a twinkle in her eyes.

"What, you're not going to tell me?"

"I could, but then I'd have to kill you, honey, so it's best you wait to find out. On a different subject, I'm glad to see you're mingling."

"Mingling?"

"You know, the mother and cute baby." Carly pointed at the bungalow behind them.

"I'm just trying to be nice. She's married, which makes her unavailable. Being blamed for the breakup of one marriage is enough for me, thank you. Her husband's our new assistant manager."

"What have I told you about jumping to conclusions? And you did not break up my marriage. Thomas and I did that all by ourselves, with no outside interference needed," said Carly.

Poppy held back an answer, spotting Miguel ahead of them sitting with Rayford.

"Poppy! I'm so glad to see you, amiga." Miguel stood up from the paper-covered table and embraced his boss.

"Hello, Mickey, how's it coming?" asked Poppy, using Miguel's nickname.

"We should be ready soon. We're just reviewing the inventory list now. After everything is stocked I'll let the staff take turns being guests to get them in the flow. It should not be hard to finish ahead of time when everybody knows Sabrina and Matlin will be among the first group arriving." Miguel waved a hand toward Rayford, who was standing, awaiting introduction. "Rayford, this is Poppy Valente."

"Nice to meet you." Poppy extended her hand to the young man. "I understand your father's a friend of Matlin." Seeing him reminded Poppy that she'd forgotten to ask Matlin the story on the mostly blank employment form. *So this is the sort of guy that Julia goes for*, she thought as Rayford shook her hand weakly.

From the blank expression on his face, it seemed obvious the new assistant manager didn't realize who she was. The training session he had just finished in New Orleans would have referred to her as Raquel Valente, not Poppy. He looked like he was trying to add two and two. Her last name could not have escaped his attention. Poppy didn't enlighten him. She wanted to get a sense of him, unguarded.

"Pleasure, I'm sure." Rayford extracted his hand from a firm, unfeminine grip.

The sun, and the fact Miguel had just sprung the news of guests' arrivals a month ahead of time, had not left him in the best of moods. His head was filled with the duties Miguel had just listed, which included some repairs. Carly's Sound had sat dormant for so long, it was going to take a tremendous amount of work to get the place back to the level expected of a Valente Resort. Now, it seemed like some relative of the boss was on-site, probably expecting instant results. He looked the woman up and down and wondered what was expected of him.

The blond man was shorter than she and much stockier, but quite handsome, with his slightly tanned skin and chiseled features. However, his good looks contrasted with a personality that seemed almost arrogant. Poppy was willing to concede that her first impression could be wrong, but so far, she didn't warm to Julia's husband.

"I need to borrow Mickey here for a moment," she said with a tight smile. As she moved away with Miguel at her side, she asked, "What's your feel for him?"

"He's young. Give him time," Miguel said as they occupied a table over at the other side of the pool. "The young, they think the world owes them sometimes, but he'll learn you must work for what you get in life. I keep my eye on him, so no worry."

"Anything else I should know about now that I'm here?" The smell of the pulp-filled juice permeated the air around her as Poppy lifted a pitcher from the table and poured a glass.

"No, I have everything under control except for a couple of new arrivals."

"What about them?"

"They listed some experience, but now that they're here we're having a few problems. Perhaps they took some liberties with the truth."

"No shortcuts this time, Mickey. If they lied up front, you and I know it's not going to get any better. Check them out, and if they don't, they're on the next shuttle out of here." She took a sip of juice and watched Rayford stroll to the bar and lean across to talk with one of the female employees. "Anything else?"

"Elizabeth and Susanna have ironed out all the problems that have come up. So you can enjoy your stay. But I'll keep you updated."

"Good. If Matlin and Sabrina call, tell them I'm here and doing fine. If those two queen bees think I'm wallowing in self-pity, it'll take dynamite to get them out of my bungalow. Oh, and while I'm here, I'm just another one of your employees. I'll be out by the pool bar as soon as I can. The vocals may be a bit rusty, but I'll try my best."

Poppy leaned back in her chair and tried not to appear distracted. Carly was perched on the table facing her, but not blocking Poppy's view of Miguel. "It'll be great if you're still here when the first guests arrive. It's something, to make people forget themselves the way you do. A gift. Remember that."

"Why do you think I made you name all the bars at the different resorts Poppy's?" Carly contributed.

Outnumbered, Poppy said, "I'll try. Now if you will excuse me, I have a date to take two ladies sailing this morning."

She walked back toward the bungalow, trying to ignore a sense of desolation as Carly waved good-bye before disappearing into a mist. Someone was waiting on the porch, and the sight of the visitor made Poppy smile and quicken her steps. As always, Marta Rojas was dressed from head to foot in white, including the scarf that was tied tightly around her head.

Marta had been a friend of the Valente family all Poppy's life and now worked for her as a chef. But she was also a mentor of sorts. For Poppy, her true talents lay in her special gifts. The women in Marta's family were clairvoyants. Poppy had seen grown men break a sweat when they talked with the perpetually jovial woman as she told them their innermost secrets.

"Poppy, mi amor, how are you? Marta's mad with you. You never call no more even though I love you. Come here and sit so you can tell me how you are." The old family friend pulled Poppy into a tight hug.

They caught up with each other for over an hour before Marta leaned over and told Poppy something she already knew. "I don't want you to worry, but Carly, she here. She got unfinished business, that one, and it got to do with you. The love she have for you, Poppy, it's stronger than even my magic, so you listen to what she got to say. She come to help you like Marta come to help you."

"Are you running the kitchens here?" Poppy was thrilled to see her friend but wondered why she had left her sister behind in New Orleans. The two were usually inseparable, and the restaurant at the Piquant had been built especially for them. It had been the only place Lizzie, Matlin, and Sabrina had not ventured into when the renovations in the New Orleans hotel were underway.

"For now, baby. So come to the restaurant before the wind blow me back to New Orleans. I come here to bring you lunch so you can feed Julia." Marta got up from the rocker and headed down the stairs in the direction of the main restaurant, but not before she cupped Poppy's face in her hands and kissed her forehead.

"You've met Julia?"

"Si, but I got no time to talk about that now. Enjoy the day, child." She blew Poppy a kiss before moving farther up the path.

"How'd you know I needed a picnic lunch, sister?" asked Poppy.

Her answer was a strong laugh as the woman dressed in white walked away. At the end of the trail, before the foliage swallowed her, Marta turned and shouted, "Carly, she tell me."

The picnic basket sat on the kitchen counter along with a cooler full of drinks. A quick look in the next room established that Marta's visit hadn't disturbed Julia or Tallulah. Mother and child were still sleeping peacefully. Every so often, the breeze coming through the windows ruffled Julia's blond hair. Poppy sat on the sofa to watch.

There was something about this woman and her baby that touched her; it wasn't so much attraction as the need to protect. Poppy had first felt it when she'd seen the other customers in the coffee shop turning a blind eye to their need. Helping Julia and her child had been instinctive. It was a strange feeling that she would have to think about later since up to now in her life, her protective nature had only shown itself with Carly and her family. As generous as she was, it wasn't her habit to play the knight to damsels in distress.

Poppy was so caught up in her thoughts, it took her a few minutes to notice the green eyes looking up at her. They were so much like Carly's that Poppy's misted. The little hands waved at her in a silent plea, and Poppy moved to pick the baby up.

She walked outside with Tallulah and sat on the rocker to talk to her. The baby was small for her age, but Poppy attributed that to Julia's being so petite. Tallulah's head was missing any substantial hair growth, but the wisps she did have were almost white. Poppy held one of her little hands in her own and laughed at the concentration on the small face.

"You'll be a heartbreaker when you get older, won't you, beautiful

Tallulah? My wish for you is that you find your one true love early and enjoy that time like a great hidden treasure you find buried in the sand. And may you be happy, sweet pea, because you deserve no less."

"That's my wish for her as well." Julia stood at the door. She'd gotten up in a panic when she found Tallulah missing, but the feeling had fled just as quickly when she heard the one-sided conversation going on outside. "I'm sorry I dropped off like that and you had to deal with her. I think it's the most sleep I've gotten since the little princess made her appearance."

"Don't worry about it. We were having a wonderful time solving world hunger and good will among men. But it's a good thing you got up. We were about to leave without you, and that would've been tragic since you wouldn't have gotten to share the great lunch I had delivered." Poppy stood up with Tallulah.

"You had lunch delivered and they came inside without me hearing them?" Julia kept her position by the doorframe, curious to see if Poppy would be anxious to give Tallulah back.

"Yes, I did. Thank God you're on a friendly island, Miss Julia. If not, I'd fear for your safety. You sleep like the dead, lady." Poppy looked down at her small charge to make sure she was still happy with her situation before moving past Julia into the house.

Lifting Tallulah against her shoulder, she headed for the kitchen counter where the picnic basket was sitting. With the baby comfortably ensconced in one arm she fished her phone out of her front pocket.

As Poppy talked on the phone with Mickey, Julia slowly took in her clothes, smile, sandals, and ponytail, and found herself attracted to this seemingly self-assured rogue. Poppy's khaki shorts appeared as worn as the navy T-shirt she had on, but to Julia the choice of clothes brought out not only her eye color but also Poppy's laid-back personality.

Poppy issued some instructions, then said, "Add in one of the infant lifejackets if you would, Mickey. I'll bring the *Piper* around, then head back out in the same direction." Her smile disappeared as she listened for a few seconds. "Pay them for the days they've been here and ship them out today. If you want I'll take care of it." The smile returned, and Julia noticed the slight laugh lines around the blue eyes. They really hadn't spent that much time together, but she was sure that she could give anyone a good description of Poppy's face and what about it made it beautiful to her. "Thanks, pal. I owe you one."

"Problems?" asked Julia.

"Employee issues. Some people think they can put whatever they want on an application and get away with it. A couple of them are getting ready to find out they can't."

Julia shivered at the words. The fact was they were there under false pretenses, and she'd hate to be on the receiving end of Poppy's obvious displeasure if she found out. "That's an understandable policy."

"It happens, but don't worry about it. It's an easy problem to fix." Julia's expression hadn't changed, making Poppy think she was having second thoughts about their outing. "You two are still coming with me, aren't you? I promise to have you back at a decent hour so Rayford won't worry."

"You invited us already, so there's no going back on your promise now." Julia moved closer with her smile firmly in place. Teasing Poppy so she'd relax, she said, "Tallulah went on about it after you left this morning, so we wouldn't want to disappoint her." Julia extended her arms. "I'll take her and go get the diaper bag and everything. We'll be right with you."

"You don't need to come back here." Poppy showed no sign of returning Tallulah. "Just wait at your place for the porter. You can hitch a ride, and it'll save you the long walk to the dock."

Julia looked out at the sailboat tethered to a buoy offshore. "How are you going to get the boat?"

"I'm going to swim out to it." The hum of a golf cart cut off any response from Julia. "Ready to go, Tallulah?" Poppy made like she planned to take the baby along on her trek to the boat.

"Hold it," Julia shouted.

Poppy handed the baby over with a lopsided grin, one that made Julia blush. As hard a time as Rayford had given her growing up with his constant teasing, she wasn't used to it from anyone else, and having Poppy do it caused her sudden panic over Tallulah. She put her hand on Poppy's arm once she'd handed Tallulah back to her, in an effort to keep her close. Why Poppy had taken such an interest in her and her daughter wasn't clear still, but she was going to do her best so that they would spend as much time together as possible.

❖

Two hours later, under the tarp she'd set up for shade at the front of the boat, Poppy listened contentedly to the water hitting the sides of the craft. They were anchored off one of the small islands close to Carly's Sound and had eaten lunch a little earlier. She had two large red snapper iced down in one of the boat's coolers for later cleaning, and was just enjoying the stillness of the moment.

She had found in Julia someone who, like herself, enjoyed the quiet of what this part of the world could offer. Here there was only the wind, the water, and the trees that swayed in the distance. Poppy remembered a movie she had seen once where one of the characters had said trees were like the arms of God waving at you, telling you to stop and see the beauty around you.

Poppy rolled onto her stomach and turned her head in the direction of the island. The wind cooled the sweat on her body, and a feeling of lethargy ran through her. Behind her, Julia had taken off her shirt and was feeding Tallulah, who had not cried once since arriving on board the *Pied Piper*.

Absently glancing toward her hostess, Julia marveled that for the first time in her life, she felt as if she wasn't on trial for her actions. She knew there would be no judgment in Poppy's eyes when she looked up and saw that Julia had shed her top. There was nothing sexual in her nudity, and it made a change to be with someone who didn't act as if there were. Poppy had a way of making her feel at ease. Julia felt so good that even the seasickness she'd been plagued with since childhood hadn't ruined her day yet.

"Do you dream?" Poppy asked the question without turning around.

"Yes. I don't always remember them, but I know I do dream. To tell you the truth, it's been so hectic since Tallulah was born I haven't had the opportunity to indulge in much quality sleep, so my dreams seem…remote. Why do you ask?"

"I suppose because I've been dreaming more than usual since I got here, so call it curiosity."

"Well, Carly's Sound has been a gift so far. I've been dreaming and I even remember them." Julia looked at the back of Poppy's head and wished she were sitting closer to her. A question hovered in her mind. She hesitated to voice it, then reasoned that Poppy could always decline to answer. "Can I ask you something?"

"Sure, I'll answer if I can." Poppy turned her head to give Julia her undivided attention, and the look on her face communicated plainly that Julia was still attractive after Tallulah's birth. Faintly startled, Julia was aware of a boost of ego with the knowledge.

For Poppy, the fleeting expression she saw was a reminder of Carly's admonishments about her not having a poker face. Julia was creamy white and amazingly attractive. She still had some fullness Poppy attributed to her recent pregnancy, and the sight of her half-naked had brought Poppy's libido out of hibernation at the worst possible time.

"I'm sorry." She turned her head in the other direction as fast as she could. Her ears felt like they had a severe sunburn.

"It's okay. I didn't mean to make you uncomfortable. The solitude out here got the best of me." Julia wanted to move closer to the embarrassed Poppy and offer support, but Tallulah wasn't finished. "You can turn around, you know. I don't mind."

With some hesitancy Poppy turned once more and concentrated on Julia's face. The warm smile she found there relaxed her again. She enjoyed Julia's company enough that she didn't want to jeopardize it by making the young mother think she was sexually interested in her.

"You wanted to ask me something?" Poppy made a conscious attempt to move beyond the uncomfortable moment.

"Well, it's not any of my business really, but what's your connection with Carly's Sound?"

With a wrinkle in her brow Poppy blinked a few times. "I'm not sure I understand the question."

"What is it you do, exactly?" Julia lost sight of the blue eyes in front of her when Poppy closed them and let a small smile break out on her face.

"I own it."

Poppy waited to see what the reaction would be. Julia had known her only for her good deed in the coffee shop, and for the day they'd spent together so far. Poppy had learned over the years that women and most men were willing to do or say anything to get close to her. It had nothing to do with wanting to be her friend, she was smart enough to figure out, but because of her money.

"Carly's Sound is owned by Valente Resorts, which is owned by Raquel…" Julia lapsed into silence before finishing the name.

She felt like an idiot that she hadn't added two and two. She had talked with Rayford on a few occasions when he was attending his training in New Orleans, and that was the name he'd given her when she asked about the company he was going to work for. Why hadn't she recognized it in New Orleans when Poppy had furnished at least part of it? And why hadn't it occurred to her that if the owner's normally empty bungalow was now occupied, the occupant wasn't just a member of the staff?

Remembering Poppy's conversation with Miguel earlier made her nauseous. The last thing she'd intended was to mess things up for Ray, and Matlin had assured them everything would be all right. But Poppy's comments about false information echoed in her mind.

"Raquel Poppy Valente," Poppy supplied for her. "At least that's what I answer to. I'd hate to think there's more than one of me. My mother would never survive."

"I'm sorry, I should have realized." Julia clutched Tallulah and stared at Poppy like she'd grown fish scales.

Laughing inwardly at her brief worry that her guest would suddenly behave like a sycophant, Poppy asked, "Is that going to be a problem?"

Not knowing what else to say, Julia just rambled on with the first thing that came to her. "No. I just never imagined you'd be so young. You don't compute with the picture I had of you in my head." Shaking her head, she said, "I'm sorry. That didn't come out right, did it?"

"I think most people are surprised." Poppy tried to make it easier for her.

"What I was trying to say is, being around my parents for business functions sometimes, I've met the heads of major corporations. They don't look like you."

"Thanks, I'll take that as a compliment. Just for the record I've met some of those guys too, and I don't ever want to be mistaken for a fat white guy with a farmer's tan. I just did what I loved, Julia, and I got lucky. So what you see is what you get."

"I like what I see," said Julia in a soft voice.

Poppy closed her eyes and allowed the short statement to stay with her, happy that she'd found a new friend and that they had the time to explore the possibilities of what that meant. Eventually, she felt Julia put the baby between them and lie down. It had been a long time since she'd taken a nap with anyone, but Poppy felt happy lying beneath the tarp with mother and baby, all three of them drifting toward sleep.

Her thoughts wandered as they always did, to Carly, and for a moment she almost expected to see her materialize on the deck as if summoned. But there was no mist and no familiar voice. Poppy decided that was a good sign. If she didn't see Carly all of the time, that meant she still had control over her mind.

❖

Julia was tired by the time Poppy pulled alongside the dock at Carly's Sound at sunset. Poppy called for a cart once she'd tied the boat down, and Tallulah went to her without protest, as she'd done all day, enabling Julia to step back on dry land.

As the porter retrieved the diaper bag and carrier from the boat and strapped them to the back of the golf cart, Julia looked to Poppy to ride back with them.

"You aren't coming with us?"

"No. I need to motor the *Piper* around and get her settled for the night. I have to free up the dock for the supply shuttles."

"Okay." Julia felt a twinge of disappointment that she could prolong the day no further.

Poppy kissed Tallulah on the head and handed her back. "Good night, ladies. I'll leave you in the capable hands of Javier, who will escort you home. Thank you for coming with me. I'll make sure to have the cleaned fish delivered to your bungalow."

As the golf cart puttered toward the bungalows, Julia looked back over her shoulder, watching Poppy fold and store her sails, then turn on the engines. Only when the *Piper* was out of sight did she return her gaze ahead. Unseeingly, she took in the tropical gardens. In her mind's eye an image lingered—Poppy asleep on the deck beside her.

The sound of the water had awakened Julia, and she had stared at her hostess for at least five minutes before a movement under her eyelids signaled that Poppy was waking up.

"Did you know you hum in your sleep," Julia had asked.

"No, I didn't know that." Poppy sat up and faced Julia. The way Poppy looked at her made her feel as if she could read what was written in her soul. Instead of being intimidated, she felt almost like a lifeline had been thrown out by someone who really wanted nothing from her but to know exactly who she was.

That level stare stayed with Julia as she showered and tried listlessly to sleep. Finally concluding she must have napped for too long that afternoon, she got out of bed and wandered into the den. Sitting on the sofa, Rayford was watching a Cowboys football game courtesy of the satellite system Poppy had installed.

"Hey, looks like you got some sun today," he said as Julia came in and sat next to him.

"I went fishing." She batted away the hand he put up to feel her forehead.

"You went fishing? Who are you, and what've you done with Julia Johnson?"

"A friend asked, so I went. No biggie. You'd think that after being out there all day with Tallulah I'd be exhausted, but I can't go to sleep."

"Who's this friend?" Ray rubbed her shoulders. He didn't bother to hide his amazement. "You don't even like to fish, Jules. Why the interest now?"

Julia relaxed against him and tried to come up with a good explanation. For the time being, she wanted to leave Poppy out of the conversation. Ray could be a bit of a suck-up, if given the opportunity, and since Poppy was technically his boss, Julia wanted to avoid putting her in a potentially awkward position. It was wrong to keep him out of the information loop, but Ray was a chronic liar and if he knew who Poppy was he might be tempted to add more spin to their deception. Ultimately that could cost him his job as well as costing Julia Poppy's friendship.

Rayford aside, Julia also realized that leaving now, before she really got to know Poppy, was something she couldn't accept. She didn't believe it was mere coincidence that they'd been brought together again. Whatever was meant to be, she wanted to see it through. She would tell Poppy who Rayford really was and why they were pretending to be married, when the time was right.

Dropping a kiss on Rayford's cheek, she said, "Get some sleep. Tomorrow's a big day." She got up and went into the kitchen to get something to drink.

Automatically, she tried to look past the trees to Poppy's bungalow to see if any lights were on yet. She had been keeping watch out of her bedroom windows to make sure Poppy made it home safely. The fact she was not back yet was starting to concern her.

Julia vacillated for a moment, then pulled her robe tight and wandered down the trail, not worried about leaving Tallulah since she was full, asleep, and Ray was home. She walked slowly since there was only a little light coming from the sliver of the new moon and the garden lights dispersed throughout the foliage. From the end of the trail she could hear the sound of water coming from somewhere near the bungalow.

She had moved closer to investigate, when the water stopped and Poppy stepped up to the porch. The sight of the body glistening in the night stopped Julia's forward progress, and she just stared. Viewing Poppy like this, Julia could see the fluidity of her movements usually covered by clothes.

"She look good, don't she?" asked a voice from behind her, and Julia spun around, surprised she hadn't heard footsteps coming up the trail.

Her first reaction was to be embarrassed, having been caught staring. But the woman approaching her had a kind look on her face that told her she had no need to feel bad.

"You were here before," Julia said, remembering the woman in white she'd seen a few days earlier.

"Come with me, child, and help me put your fish away, now you know your captain is home and headed to bed," the woman said without giving her name.

Julia followed her back to the bungalow, where a neat pile of plastic bags full of fish filets waited on the porch in a pan packed with ice.

"Thank you for doing all this. Should I set some bags aside for Poppy?"

The woman didn't answer for the longest time, making Julia think she hadn't understood the question. Julia had to fight the urge to pull back when a callused hand took hold of one of hers. It felt like the woman had a high fever, her hand was so hot, but she looked perfectly healthy, and after the initial shock Julia felt a sense of peace come over her and she felt sleepy.

"Don't worry none about Poppy, child. She gonna be fine. You give her some time and those scales on her eyes, they gonna fall away and she gonna see you and that baby. Ain't no changing your fate, Julia, and there ain't no sense fightin' it. Just go with what's written in the stars and don't run away from your heart. She waiting for you. Just give her the chance to show you that."

When Julia blinked her eyes open, her first thought was that she didn't remember closing them, and why was she so tired? And why, after two meetings, did she still not know the woman's name? She tried to break through the fog in her brain as she stood outside on her porch in her robe and gazed at the pan of fish at her feet. Looking around and seeing no one, she carried it inside and put it in the refrigerator.

When her head hit the pillow a few minutes later she was asleep. It was a deep, dreamless sleep that left her half dazed for most of the next day.

CHAPTER EIGHT

H ow about dinner?" The invitation had come out of her mouth without permission from her brain, and Poppy immediately rambled to get out of it. "I'm sorry. Maybe I should let you get home. I've monopolized all your time for the last couple of days, and I don't want to cause problems for you."

"Why in the world would you think that?" The stars behind Poppy were so vivid Julia blinked her eyes up at her hostess like they were causing a glare. She felt exhilarated and tired at the same time.

Poppy had taken them sailing each afternoon since their first on the *Piper*, not to fish but to introduce Julia to the area she said she'd fallen in love with years before. Sometimes they were alone on a private island with just themselves for company. At other times, sailing, they would see nothing but the vastness of the water with a small island dotting the horizon every so often. The rest of the world seemed miles away.

They returned by nightfall each day, and each morning, Julia couldn't wait to see Poppy again and would hurry from the house soon after the sun came out. Poppy had opened her eyes to the beauty and solitude of the green-blue water, and had opened her heart to the beauty her future could be.

"You and Rayford just got here," Poppy said as she towed them to shore on the small dingy. "I'm sure he'd like to spend time alone with you and Tallulah. I hear the owner of this place is quite the slave driver."

The thought of Julia and the baby leaving made Poppy want to stop talking, but she reasoned with herself that in all probability Julia had agreed to spend time with her because she was her husband's boss. It was time to stop acting like an ass and let the young woman get back to her family. The fact that if Carly were still with her, they would be spending a romantic night alone, was beside the point. The woman whose time she'd been claiming had a husband to think about.

Julia watched Poppy's face as she seemed to be having an internal argument over something. "Trust me, you're not causing problems for me at all. Rayford and I..." Julia paused, trying to think of how to describe her relationship. Having firsthand knowledge of how Poppy felt about liars, she wanted to say something without digging herself any deeper.

"Is everything all right?" Poppy squatted down to be at eye level with Julia. "You can come to me if there's ever anything you want to talk about. You know that, don't you?"

Julia went with the most reasonable response she could come up with. "Would you trust me if I told you I'd rather not talk about it right now? I promise you'll be the first to know when I am. I know that's asking a lot since we just met." She stopped when Poppy gave her an understanding smile.

"You can take all the time you need. I just want to help, not push you." Poppy stood and pulled the dingy in far enough so Julia wouldn't get her feet wet getting out. Poppy had to smile every time she looked at little Tallulah wearing the smallest life vest she had ever seen. Though she was never one to be selfish, Poppy decided to ignore any of her concerns and ask for what she wanted. And what she wanted was Julia sitting across from her for as long as she could make the night last. "How about that dinner?"

"Sure, if you give me a minute to change and feed Tallulah." Julia accepted a hand out of the small boat.

"No need to change. I was thinking we could eat here. Let me fire up the grill and put on some of the fish we caught yesterday. You're free to use whatever room in the bungalow you wish to feed Tallulah."

By way of an answer, Julia just smiled and walked past her and into the house.

Poppy jumped into the outdoor shower so that Julia could have privacy getting cleaned up in the bungalow. When she stepped out, toweling off her hair, she was a little shocked to find her robe hanging over the porch railing. Next to it was a cold beer, her favorite brand.

After she'd finished drying herself, she went indoors and found Julia lying on the sofa in the living room with her daughter. Wrapped in one of Poppy's spare robes, she looked so cozy Poppy couldn't hide her smile.

"I'll dress and be with you in a minute," she said.

Julia yawned. She looked languorous and relaxed, Poppy thought, and somehow even younger. Her fine blond hair was a shade darker and combed back after her shower, but it still appeared soft against the sofa cushion. Even though Poppy had tried to keep them in the shade for most of the day Julia's cheeks were pink, but this made her lips appear redder and fuller. Tallulah was content gnawing on her fist so Julia was free to follow Poppy's movements, her green eyes showing the only signs of energy as she continued her study of her new friend's physical attributes.

Before she made it to the bedroom, Poppy turned one more time to just enjoy the sight of mother and child. As much as she had dreaded coming back here to the memories, having Julia and Tallulah in her home had dulled the severity of that ache. If she was honest, though, she would admit to an odd fear that she might get used to the joy of having the two here, appearing to be so at home. If fate had taught her any lesson at all, it was that the people who worked themselves into your heart had a way of disappearing like smoke from a dying fire, leaving you with only the memory of happiness.

"Who is she?" Julia indicated a photograph of Carly on the wall nearest the sofa.

"That's Carly, the person the island's named for." The picture in the beautiful old wooden frame had been taken on the porch outside the bungalow. Poppy was sitting in the old rocker with Carly on her lap. The final rays of the sun highlighted the wildflower garden, and they were oblivious to the photographer.

Julia allowed her gaze to drift around the walls. There were several other photographs of the same woman, and every single one made her irrationally jealous that it was someone else who had put that look of adoration on Poppy's face. "How long has she been gone?"

"Two and a half very long years." From Poppy's sigh at the end, Julia could tell it was an answer she wasn't used to giving, and despite the time that had passed, she still couldn't discuss Carly without difficulty.

"Why'd she leave? From the pictures, it looks like you were happy together."

"We *were* happy together. She was a fighter until the end, but sometimes not even a strong unwavering desire to cheat fate works out. Carly died of breast cancer." Poppy ran her finger along the frame on the piano she was leaning against, the echo of Carly's laugh running through her head. The picture had been taken on the *Pied Piper*, and an unexpected spray of water had made Carly break out into that carefree laugh that was her signature at the surprise soaking.

"I'm sorry, Poppy. I didn't know." Julia pushed herself up and sat Tallulah on her lap.

"No need to be sorry." Poppy smiled, but this time the crinkles Julia was coming to like didn't appear next to the blue eyes. "As much as losing her still hurts, I try to dwell more on the years we did have together. You can't know what it's like to lose someone who is totally ingrained in your heart. In Carly, I found a beautiful spirit who brought joy into my life."

Julia drew Tallulah closer almost like a shield against the anguish in Poppy's voice. They didn't know each well enough for her to feel that she could offer Poppy comfort. "She was lucky to have had someone like you love her. By now, after a loss, most people would have moved on."

"There are a few things I have to figure out before I can do that."

Not being able to stand the distance between them, Julia held out her hand to Poppy in invitation to come and sit. "What things? If it's something I can help with I'll do my best to try."

When Poppy joined her she handed Tallulah to her and rested a hand on Poppy's shoulder.

Kissing the top of the baby's head, Poppy leaned closer to Julia. "I appreciate the offer, but this is stuff that my head has to eventually convince my heart to accept as fact. I have to stop waking up in the morning and reaching over for her. I need to quit walking into familiar places and stopping to listen for her. I still reach for the phone when I just need to hear the sound of her voice, and that reflex has to end too. My reality is that I'll live out my life missing the piece of me that died along with her."

"Just know that I'm here if you need any help or someone to talk to."

"Thank you, but please don't feel obligated."

She squeezed Poppy's shoulder gently, then covered Poppy's big, tanned hand with her own. "Obligation is not a word I'd use to describe why I'm here."

The declaration didn't need a response, and Poppy didn't give one except to smile. This time Julia claimed a small victory, in that she could tell from Poppy's face, the smile was genuine.

❖

They ate dinner outside under the stars and by candlelight. The fish they had caught the day before was accompanied by a salad and steamed vegetables they had made, working together in the kitchen like a seasoned team.

Julia sat back with her first glass of wine, which was only half full, and indulged in looking at her dining companion. She wondered what her life with Carly had been like. Had the smiling woman in all those pictures felt like she felt now? The gaze being directed at her assured Julia that, despite their beautiful surroundings, she was the center of Poppy's attention. If Carly had experienced just a little bit of this, it was probably why she was smiling.

"What?" Poppy mirrored Julia's relaxed position and arched a dark eyebrow in question.

"Nothing, just enjoying the night air. Hopefully this one glass of wine will relax Tallulah enough to skip one of those late-night feedings," said Julia with a teasing smile.

Poppy clinked her glass against Julia's to complete the toast. "What're your plans for tomorrow?"

"My social calendar has been just hectic since I got here. What did you have in mind?"

"How about a picnic lunch at a place I found around here just recently?"

"You have a date, Ms. Valente."

The answer earned Julia a full smile, one she noticed Poppy didn't use very often. It made Julia blush, which made the smile spread wider.

A long sigh escaped Poppy's lungs. Spending time with Julia and her baby was starting to heal her heart without Poppy knowing it, and the thought of tomorrow, any tomorrow, didn't carry with it a sense of depression. "Let me walk you girls home then, so you'll be well rested enough to enjoy the day."

Reluctantly Julia stood. Every step back to her bungalow would only be a reminder of how many hours it would be before she saw Poppy again.

The baby had left a large drool mark on Poppy's shoulder by the time their slow walk was over. Julia thought she glimpsed Rayford watching from the window of the living room as she and Poppy said their good nights, but he was in bed by the time she made it indoors. No doubt he thought she wouldn't know he'd been spying on her.

She hesitated at his door, wondering if she should say something to explain her constant absences. Rayford had to have noticed that she was spending most days in the company of the tall woman from the neighboring bungalow.

Any explanation would come with a little white lie attached since she wasn't ready to be completely honest about who Poppy was, though, so she continued to her room. They had been born only thirty minutes apart, but the ability to spin tall tales was something her brother had talent in. Considering she wasn't that great a liar, avoidance was her best route for now.

CHAPTER NINE

In New Orleans, Lizzie sat reading in an old chair Carly had given her for her ninth birthday. Her mother had affectionately called her a little bookworm and thought she deserved a comfortable place to enjoy her passion. The chair had been re-covered to match the colors mother and daughter had chosen for the house Poppy had bought years later, but the memories that came whenever she used it never changed.

Most were happy. Some were blended with sorrow. This evening, Lizzie had allowed her thoughts to drift to the day thirteen years earlier when her mother had returned from Aruba and asked for a divorce. She had stood in the doorway listening to her parents speak to one another as if each had only just realized the slow-acting poison they'd consumed was finally exacting its toll.

"I just want to pick up Lizzie, then I'll be leaving," her mother had said. "I think she's old enough for the two of you to work out some sort of schedule of time together without us having to jump through all the legal hoops I'm sure you have planned. I left the number and address by the phone in the foyer if you need to get in touch with me. All I want is for you to pay Lizzie's tuition."

Lizzie had braced herself for a cutting response, but her father had just sat and stared out the window like he was trying to process what he was hearing. She could almost see him reasoning with himself. It couldn't have been the cheating; after all, he had been doing it for years, and it had never bothered her. Why would it now? He tapped his index finger on the arm of his leather desk chair and pushed the tips of his toes into the ground to make it rock, pausing like he did in court to gather his thoughts so he could deliver his defense.

"Why?" He wouldn't look at Carly. Lizzie recognized the ploy; he used it to unnerve her, too.

"This is no time to start to play the ignorant one," Carly said. "I want nothing from you, other than my freedom."

Thomas gripped the edge of the desk and swiveled his chair around to face her, his stare glacial. "I'll never let you take my daughter. You want out, then get out, but Lizzie stays here. Be careful what you ask for. You might just get it and then some. Once you see how it is in the real world, you'll be back. Only you might find that I've changed the locks on your cushy lifestyle."

"Daddy, I'm not staying here with you." Lizzie walked up behind her mother. "I'm going with Mom, so don't make this harder on yourself."

That morning she had packed the last of her things and was anxious to leave. Her mother seemed like a different person away from the house. While they had been decorating the new place, Carly had looked like one of Lizzie's teenage friends, especially when the phone rang and it was Poppy on the other end.

The youngest child, Lizzie had been the one her mother spent the most time with, and she'd figured out, long before that day, what the cause of her mother's unhappiness was. Her father didn't hide the truth of his extra women very well. Lizzie didn't hate him. She just didn't respect him, and he had waited a month after they left before he called. That was hard for her to forgive.

Lizzie could still see him standing in front of the little house in the August heat, a bouquet of roses in his hand. He was not a man who liked change of any kind, and this past month had obviously rocked him, especially being served divorce papers. She had answered the door, and seeing the seersucker suit and the flowers in his hand, for a moment she'd felt sorry for him. Behind her, sitting on one of the side tables, was a huge arrangement of wildflowers that had been a gift from Poppy. Lizzie didn't know where she got them, but they were replaced every week with a new bunch, after her mother had mentioned they were her favorite flowers.

"Daddy? What're you doing here?" she asked, hurt that he hadn't called her in over a month.

"It's nice to see you too," he said sarcastically. "Is your mother here?"

He pushed past her without waiting for a reply, but before he could intrude any farther, Carly emerged from the living room. "Thomas, is there something I can do for you?"

He took in her white T-shirt and blue shorts with an expression approaching incredulity. Lizzie wondered how long it had been since he saw his wife without makeup and with her hair loose and unstyled. She looked ten years younger.

He held out the roses. "I came to see when you two were coming home."

"Didn't you get the papers my attorney sent two weeks ago?" Carly took the flowers and walked to the kitchen to put them in water.

He stalked after her. "I think your little lesson has sunk in. If Rita was the problem, don't worry. She's gone. Things can go back to normal, and I won't hold this little foray against you."

Carly looked at him like he was either mentally ill or there was a tumor pressing on the logical, thinking part of his brain. "Was that supposed to be your attempt at humor?"

"What do you mean? We both know you can be inventive when it comes to these little games of revenge. You wanted to get my attention and teach me a lesson, and you've succeeded, so it's time to come home."

"Unbelievable is the only thing I can think to say to you. This isn't me teaching you a lesson, Thomas. This is me getting on with my life and being happy. Thank you for the flowers, and I wish I could stay and chat, but Lizzie and I are heading out for the day."

Lizzie didn't wait to hear any more but ran past them and out the front door, as she caught the familiar sound of Poppy's Jeep. She had come to enjoy the company of her mother's new friend, and had warmed up to the revelation that her mother was gay. She was vaguely aware that her father had followed her, but could not understand his frozen demeanor.

Thinking back now, she realized that somewhere deep inside his mind her father had known in that moment that he'd lost. Standing there in the yard stood his replacement, and he had envied her from that moment on.

Lizzie knew the love she'd developed for Poppy had cost her any affection she might have had from Thomas, but in all honesty she couldn't believe she'd missed out on much. Knowing that hurt on some level, but only because it was hard to accept that a parent's love could be conditional.

It had never been the case with her mother. Or with Poppy.

Lizzie started when the phone next to her rang.

"If you fall asleep in that chair again your neck will eventually just freeze from the crick you're going to get."

"Poppy."

"Hey, kiddo, how's it going?"

"Sometimes one day blends into the other, but that's not necessarily a bad thing. The ones that change dramatically usually mean we've had a kitchen fire or something. I miss you, though."

"I miss you too, but I keep marking the days on my calendar until you get here."

"Pop, you've never kept a calendar in your life."

"True, not on paper, but I've got a good head for stuff like that."

The book in Lizzie's lap dropped to the floor as she shifted to get more comfortable. "Tell me you aren't just moping around down there."

Poppy yawned. "No on that note too. I've been out on the *Piper* for the last couple of days."

"Isn't that dangerous alone?" Any lassitude in Lizzie's body drained at the sudden worry of something happening to Poppy. "Mom didn't like you going out alone."

"Ah, I wasn't alone."

"Good. But you shouldn't drag Mickey away for hours. He has so much to do before the opening."

Knowing Lizzie was only warming up, Poppy cut in before she worked up to a lecture. "It wasn't Mickey, so rest assured he's working hard. Remember Julia, the girl with the cute baby?"

"From the hotel coffee shop?"

"That's her. We've been exploring together to stay out of everyone's way. She seemed a little freaked to find out who I am, but aside from that, we're becoming friends."

Lizzie's mind generated a picture of the pretty blonde and her equally cute baby, and she wondered if the woman had any hidden motivations for wanting to get close to Poppy. What better way to advance your husband up the company ladder than to befriend the owner. "That's good."

Lizzie enjoyed the deep laugh that came over the line. "Quite the ringing endorsement," Poppy said. "Trust me on this one, she's really nice. You'd like her."

"I'll have to have lunch with her when I get there."

"I'll let her know. She most probably will be ready for someone new to talk to by then."

Lizzie held the mouthpiece away from her face and surveyed the ceiling of her bedroom. "Oh, I seriously doubt that, blue eyes. In two months she'll be lucky to notice there're other people on the island, much less have lunch with one."

A sharp "Lizzie" pulled her away from her mutterings.

"Have fun and don't worry about anything," she told Poppy. "We have everything under control."

"Thanks, I'll call again soon. I love you."

"I love you too."

"Are you sure you didn't adopt that one?" Poppy asked after she'd hung up.

Carly had popped in and sat on her lap while she was on the phone.

"Nope, Lizzie's mine. She's just hard to explain. When they put her in my arms after her birth she looked at me with what I can only describe as a curious stare. That questioning part of her personality doesn't ever change, and you only made it worse, always wanting to know the why of everything." Carly ran her finger along the curve of Poppy's ear. "Lizzie taught me how to have fun. Then you came along and completed my education."

"My only issue with you is you left before school was out. And if I can't make love to you, stop messing with my ears." Poppy turned her head and gave Carly a mock frown.

"Let's go for a walk if you're not going to let me have any fun." Carly held out her hand, and when they reached the water's edge, she said, "Strip, Valente, and let's get wet.

"You must be real," said Poppy in her most serious voice.

"What makes you say so?"

Poppy stripped off her shorts and T-shirt and tossed them in a pile where the waves wouldn't soak them. "There's no way in hell my head would make you up, only to torture myself with. If you're a figment of my twisted little brain, getting wet with you would have nothing to do with salt water." She laughed when Carly blushed. "I'm not up on paranormal experiences, but do ghosts usually have the ability to blush?"

"Being one, you'd think I'd know. Come on, raunchy talker, let's go swimming." When they were deep enough, Carly swam up and put her legs around Poppy's waist and leaned back to look at the stars.

"Are the stories the nuns told me true? Are those really the heavens?" Poppy looked up too, trying her best not to think about the position they were in, and where it had usually led them when Carly was alive. Sex or any other intimate matter hadn't been something she'd dwelled on, even before Carly had died. Her lover had been so sick Poppy had been happy just to hold her and spend those last days telling her how she felt about her.

"Do you ask because you fear death?"

"The standard answer is usually yes, but I don't. Not any more."

Carly pressed her palm against Poppy's chest, over her heart. "Why not?"

"Before you died my reason would have been because I enjoyed every one of my days so much. I lived, I loved, and I was a good person."

"But now?"

"Now I look at you and see that living life that way brings the ultimate of rewards."

The kiss this answer prompted made Poppy glad she was able to still touch bottom. Had the water been any deeper she would have drowned them both. Well, technically, only her. "I thought you said we couldn't do this."

"I figured kissing's allowed if the moment calls for it." Carly kissed her again, only this time, her lips landed on Poppy's forehead. "You've got nothing to fear from death, my love, but you've got years before you have to concern yourself with it."

"I don't know if I can last that long. In a way I resent life now because you're not here to share it with me."

"Let me teach you something now, grasshopper. When we met, you were my confirmation that I hadn't squandered my life. Children are a part of the legacy you leave on the earth, but they're only one small part. They don't choose to be born or what family they get to be a part of. Not like your mate. That person has to look beyond your flaws and idiosyncrasies and find something to love."

"I did love you with all that I had. I still do."

"I know you did, honey. I think that's why, even after my life ended, what came has been so full. We taught each other what love could be. To deprive it of the chance to be part of your life again upsets the balance of that lesson."

Poppy sighed. "But I've already met and lost my soul mate. If there was anyone after you she wouldn't get all of me. It doesn't seem fair."

The water was barely able to get between them when Carly pulled closer and put her arms around Poppy's neck. "My darling, had I lived another twenty years you'd know what I always did. The cancer spared me the pain of that particular truth."

"I would never have left you. Age, and the difference in ours, was never an issue for me. Only for you."

"I know, love. And I adored you because of your nobility. Fate cheated us, but not you."

Poppy shook her head. She didn't want to hear any more. Carly was giving her permission to let go and move on, free from guilt. Was that what she wanted for herself? She stared into Carly's eyes, aware of a deep uncertainty, almost a sense of rejection if that was indeed what Carly wanted. For her to let go.

"No one else could take your place," she said.

Carly held her gaze without blinking. "When a soul is special enough, it has room for more than one mate. Letting her in when you find her doesn't taint my memory. It only gives it more meaning. It tells the world I left behind a gentle person, capable of great things, but above all else, capable of loving without restraint. That, lover, is better than any tombstone with my name and some trite description of who I was."

"You were mine."

"Yes, I was. I hope the next Mrs. Valente understands and appreciates my ultimate sacrifice."

❖

With the sun shining against a backdrop of a cloudless sky, the *Pied Piper* left the dock with Poppy, Julia, and Tallulah on board. Julia sat on the padded bench behind Poppy with her eyes closed, not caring where they were headed. The wind that filled the sails combed her hair back, and she was fighting a battle to stay awake.

Standing behind the wheel, Poppy looked down at the sleeping child by her feet securely strapped into her carrier, in awe of the fact that such a small being, who couldn't even hold her head up really well, could bring such joy to those around her. In the few days they had spent together, Tallulah would look at her with big green eyes, as Poppy would sing all the lullabies and goofy songs she could think of. The stare was so intent at times that Poppy halfway expected Tallulah to put words to whatever she was thinking.

"Grows on you, doesn't she?" It was the first time Carly had made an appearance when she was spending time with mother and child.

Poppy nodded, then glanced over her shoulder to see if Julia was sleeping. Carrying on a conversation others could hear only half of was not the way to impress anyone with her mental lucidity.

"She's sleeping, honey, don't sweat it."

"I missed you this morning," said Poppy.

"Sorry, I'm not ignoring you. I just wanted to give you time to get reacquainted with your new friends. The reason I'm here is to ask you a favor."

"Anything you want, my love."

The rapid affirmative answer made Carly's face light up from the size of her smile.

"I want you to show your two new friends around the islands."

"That's what I'm doing."

"Everything, love. Show them why you fell in love with this beautiful area. Teach them to love it as much as you do."

"Why?"

"Because I asked you to." She vanished from sight before she finished the comment, leaving Poppy behind wanting more. *"Because it'll remind you as well, my sweet. I need you to open your eyes before I can get you to open your heart."* With that, Carly was truly gone for the day.

The splash of the anchor woke Julia from her nap. She opened her eyes in time to watch Poppy strip down to her bathing suit and dive off the *Piper*. She barely made a splash, and as she cut through the water with graceful ease, Julia had a hard time conjuring up a picture of her living any other way. Poppy was a wild adventure waiting to be explored, like the island behind them, an adventure Julia was willing to bet would take more than one lifetime to get to know.

"Good morning. I hope I didn't get the two of you up too early this morning?" The question surprised Julia, who looked down to find Poppy treading water about ten feet from the stern.

"I blame it on the wind, a full daughter, and a very good captain."

"How would the Johnson girls like to go for a swim?"

Julia hesitated at the thought of putting Tallulah in the water. It wasn't about the sun; Poppy had slathered Tallulah down with a sunscreen with such a high SPF number it was like a liquid umbrella. It was a matter of trust. Did she trust Poppy to keep them both safe out here where it was just the three of them? And if she did, what did that signify for other parts of her and Tallulah's life?

Pulling herself out of the water, Poppy stood dripping before Julia, ready to take back her offer. The dingy could be just as effective in getting them to shore. "Give me a second and we can use the boat."

"No, a swim sounds great."

With that they came to an unspoken understanding. Nothing would happen to them in any situation, with Poppy.

An hour later, Tallulah didn't appreciate her personal lifeguard taking her out of the warm clear water. Julia had watched as Poppy played with the infant, getting more than one squeal out of her. At this rate her daughter would be swimming before she was six months old.

"She's either hungry, or she's ready to get out of this rig." Poppy held the baby as she moved to the shade of the trees, picking one that didn't have any large coconuts growing in it. She unbuckled the life jacket and stripped the floppy hat off Tallulah as soon as they reached the blanket Julia had spread out for them.

Julia handed her another swim-proof diaper and a wipe. "I think she's just getting spoiled."

"That's what you're supposed to do with beautiful babies."

Tallulah kicked her legs and cooed when Poppy tickled the bottom of her feet.

Watching the two enjoying one another, Julia felt herself slithering into emotional terrain she preferred to avoid. She wondered if there had ever been a time when her parents played with her. As far back as she could remember they had been little more than a shadowy presence in her life, unable even to make it for birthdays.

"Where'd you go off to?" Poppy's hand on her cheek chased away her morose feelings.

"Nowhere as nice as this."

"Let me show you something even nicer." With Tallulah in her arms, Poppy led Julia to the waterfall she'd found on her trip down to Carly's Sound. Maybe Carly was right and she needed to show Julia more of what was out here, if for no other reason than to watch her drink it in.

Eyes closed, Julia took a deep breath, as if to capture the scent of the salt water. Looking at her peaceful expression, and enjoying the weight of the baby in her arms, Poppy felt some of the anger she had held onto from losing Carly slip away.

Poppy sang them a song as Julia lowered one of the straps of her bathing suit to feed Tallulah. As soon as the baby finished they could attack the lunch Poppy had gone back to the boat for.

"Thank you for all of this," Julia said.

"You don't have to thank me. I'm having fun."

"We are too. You're spoiling us both." The skin around Julia's green eyes crinkled a little when she smiled, and Poppy found she was getting addicted to the face before her.

"Would you allow me to spoil the two of you a little more?"

"What did you have in mind?" Julia moved Tallulah to her shoulder to burp her.

"How about I show you another island and take you out to dinner? I wouldn't want to make you suffer through another night of my cooking. If you'd like, why don't you invite Rayford?"

"We'd love to go, but I don't know about Rayford. I'll ask, though. He surprises me every so often."

They packed up everything they had brought on shore, and Poppy towed Julia and Tallulah back to the *Piper* on the dingy so they didn't have to sail back to the resort wet. With no shuttles headed to the island, Poppy left the boat at the dock and drove the cart back to the bungalows. She carried Tallulah inside for Julia, taking her time to look around the Johnsons' place and assess her crew's decorating talents.

Poppy's interest in the completion of the resort had waned considerably after Carly's death, so Lizzie, Matlin, and Sabrina had done most of the interiors. The room she was in resembled her own main room, aside from the mementos that made it a home, and Poppy made a mental note to send her team something for their efforts.

"Make sure you all pack an overnight bag. We're going to enjoy the Valente Company's hospitality tonight."

"I'm enjoying that now," said Julia, smiling up at her.

"Wouldn't you rather do it some place that's already up and running?"

"I'd have to leave the island for that."

"Yes, you would. I'll be back at six to pick you up."

Julia watched her go from the front door. Rayford walked up the path from the direction of the guest area as soon as the cart disappeared around the back of Poppy's bungalow.

"If it isn't the cute mariner and her sidekick?" he teased as he picked up the baby.

"How goes it in the world of upper management?" Julia asked, recalling that he'd spent the day arranging a party for the staff that night as a reward for all the extra hours they had been putting in.

"Brutal. Listen, I'll be out late tonight for this thing. I didn't think you and the munchkin would want to come, but you can." The tone he used let her know her staying home would not be met with resistance.

"Relax, I won't even be here." He stopped bouncing Tallulah and looked at Julia, waiting for her to go on. "I got a dinner invitation. Don't look so shocked."

"I'm not. I'm glad you're making new friends. You deserve that."

❖

"You look beautiful" was all Poppy could think to say when Julia stepped outside holding Tallulah. Both blondes had on sundresses with sandals, but the ones Tallulah was wearing gave new meaning to the word adorable.

"Aren't you going to give me a hint as to where we're going?"

"Dinner. Rayford decided to stay for the party?"

"Rayford's missed few parties in his lifetime, so you're stuck with just us."

Poppy helped her up the steps into the helicopter, holding Tallulah until Julia strapped herself in, then taking the seat next to hers. They watched the sunset from the air during the brief flight to Curaçao. The plane that was waiting for them was a ten-passenger Lear jet with the Valente logo painted on the tail.

Poppy's pilot, Bob Wallis, was a slim, energetic man who had flown combat missions in "Nam," as he referred to it, and there were times when Poppy was sure he thought Charlie was still on his ass. As his employer, she had paid more fines for buzzing towers around the globe with the old guy than she cared to count. But Carly had found and hired him, so until he either crashed and killed them all, or was too old to fly, Bob was a fixture.

For all of his strange behavior, he was also a superb pilot. The military had been his home and family for so long he seemed to feel more comfortable conducting his life as if he were still enlisted. Immaculately pressed as always, he greeted her with a formal, "Good evening, Commander."

"Evening, Bob, how's it going?" She flexed her fingers in preparation for the flight, knowing there was a good chance she'd have to clutch the armrest before they landed.

"A-OK, sir."

Feeling a little guilty for not calling to check on him, Poppy took a few minutes to catch up. "The folks at our place treating you well?"

"Yes, sir. They're feeding me so much I've had to add a couple of extra miles on the treadmill every morning." He relaxed his stance a little, plainly happy that Poppy wanted to go somewhere that required his services.

"You'd better add another mile to that run. Your favorite chef is on Carly's Sound, and I want you there for the opening. Elizabeth says you're not to even think about missing it. You're part of our family, so if it takes a direct order to get you there, consider it issued." Poppy smiled to take any sting out of her request.

"Thank you, sir. If you're ready, we've been cleared."

Bob's voice conveyed little of his emotions, but Poppy sensed he was touched. She was well aware that Valente Resorts gave him a sense of identity and belonging she sometimes suspected were a reason to live. She introduced Julia and Tallulah, and they followed Bob onto the plane.

Julia tried to act like being taken to dinner in a private jet was a normal occurrence in her and her daughter's life, but it was hard to hide her awe. The second Poppy's seatbelt clicked closed, Julia turned to her and asked, "Commander?"

"Let's just say I have a don't-ask-don't-tell policy."

"Your pilot's being gay bothers you?" The idea sounded so weird Julia had to know the answer.

"Gay?" Poppy laughed. "No, not gay—crazy. I have a gut feeling he is. I just don't want to know about it."

Julia was just starting to relax in the leather chair when Bob informed them they would be on the ground in less than five minutes. Out the window, she could see the outline of Curaçao from the lights that seemed to be more clustered along the shoreline. She turned to Poppy with a huge smile when Bob put down a smooth landing and taxied to a stop. A cab pulled up as soon as the plane's engines cut.

"Thanks, Bob. We'll meet you back here after dinner. Say in about three hours?" Poppy and the pilot had visited the island before, and she knew he liked walking around Willemstad to people watch. The city's center was a gathering place for locals and tourists after dark, and anyone could spend a pleasant evening sitting on one of the park benches viewing the activity and street performers.

"I'll be here waiting, Commander."

"Don't just sit here. Go into town and have dinner. My treat." Poppy pulled out a wad of local currency and pointed Bob to the second taxi pulling up.

"You're a nice person," said Julia when Poppy got into the cab.

Poppy's laugh came from deep in her chest. "Some people might not agree with you."

"Their loss. Now I insist you tell me where we're going."

"A place with a nice view I thought you might find acceptable." The drive took thirty minutes up the steady incline until it leveled off at the top of a large hill that overlooked the harbor. The building where they stopped looked like a fort.

"Is someone planning an invasion during the appetizers?" asked Julia.

Poppy shook her head as she unbuckled the carrier from the back seat. "Welcome to the Fort Nassau Restaurant. It was a fort until the 1950s, when it was opened as a restaurant. Even if the food was bad, which it's not, I'll show you why I thought you might like it."

Julia grabbed the diaper bag and followed her tour guide and

Tallulah up the stone walkway. When Poppy stepped aside, Julia was treated to a spectacular view of the capital Willemstad and the beach beyond it. The sun had set, but the lights coming from the downtown area and from the quarter moon were more than enough to let her make out the palm trees and marina, the boats bobbing gently in the breeze.

"I was kidding about the attack," she said.

"I know. Let's go have dinner. Then we'll head back out here."

They walked through a thick stone entryway into a cozy room with vaulted ceilings and very small windows. The host's reaction to Tallulah softened when Poppy pressed a tip into his hand.

A short while later, their waiter headed to the kitchen with their order, and Poppy spent some time telling Julia about the island they were on. Poppy's depth of knowledge surprised her, since most people who traveled to places like the Dutch Antilles came for the beaches and the sun, not for the rich, sometimes dark, past of these island paradises.

Poppy explained how at one time Curaçao was the center of the slave trade, and while she did, Julia also took in Poppy herself, especially the way she talked with her hands and how she seemed to watch for Julia's reaction to things as if wanting her to enjoy their time together and not be bored. Julia could tell that Poppy had put as much thought into their night as she had into her choice of the perfect outfit— pressed tan pants and a dark blue cotton shirt. As much as she liked the relaxed Poppy who took her sailing, Julia decided this polished look was something her companion pulled off just as well.

After dinner, the waiter poured a cup of decaf for Julia and one small glass of the blue liquor named for the island it was made on for Poppy. To Julia's amusement, Poppy was able to juggle her mango and papaya strudel dessert, her drink, and Tallulah.

"Are we in a hurry, or do I have time to feed her?"

"We always have time for that," Poppy said.

They sat outside on the low stone wall that ran for part of the perimeter and enjoyed the view.

❖

The flight back went as smoothly as the first, and this time a car from the Esmeralda Verde Resort was waiting for them when they landed. The thought that they were lost crossed Julia's mind when they turned into a drive with a thick canopy of foliage. It was a fleeting feeling when the car cleared the cover of the trees and the resort came into view.

Unlike Carly's Sound, this was a huge building curved like someone had built a circle and cut half of it away. The lobby entrance was tiled with clear green, small, odd-shaped mosaics that were one of the only things left untouched when the resort was refurbished. The front of the main floor was the only part with a solid wall because the back was a series of columns and open spaces. The steps all along the back led down to more gardens, a café, and a very large pool. Hidden through the grounds were enough lights to make walking easy, but they were sufficiently muted to provide a romantic atmosphere.

The manager greeted Poppy as she walked to the desk, and the two fell into conversation, giving Julia the opportunity to look around the lobby and grounds. The picture hanging on one of the wide columns would have clued her in as to who the establishment's proprietor was if she hadn't already known. Sitting in the rocker Julia had been using for the past few mornings to feed Tallulah, only her feet and hand visible, Poppy looked out over the gardens and pool area Julia was admiring now.

"Escort you to your room?" Poppy held the card key up.

"I'm guessing you must know the way."

"I think I can find it."

They entered the elevator with Tallulah and got off on the top floor. The windows in the hallway looked out toward the road and the gardens they had driven through. Julia was surprised not to find another set of doors for guest rooms. She was used to staying in places where the rooms either looked out to whatever was in the front of the hotel or the back. The Esmeralda Verde had only one view, and that was of the back.

"The whole place's only one room deep, which means everyone gets a waterfront view," Poppy said. "No one wants to come to Aruba to look at the main road. We were lucky to get rooms in the high season."

Julia walked through the door Poppy had just unlocked. "Imagine that. You must just be lucky that way."

The comment made Poppy laugh and shrug her shoulders. Julia put the diaper bag down and walked around looking at the suite they'd entered. The amenities were spectacular, one of the reasons Valente Resorts were so successful.

When Julia tried to hide a yawn, Poppy discreetly looked at her watch and was amazed to see it was past midnight. "You'll find your bags along with Tallulah's things in the bedroom. If you need anything else call the desk and ask for Jorge. Thank you for coming with me tonight."

"It was our pleasure, but I should be thanking you. Tonight was a unique experience."

"A good unique experience, I hope?"

"The best."

"I'll be next door if you need anything. Good night."

When the door clicked shut behind Poppy, Julia stood frozen in the middle of the room.

"The only thing missing was the good-night kiss," she whispered down to her sleeping daughter. She had come to this foreign place to run away from her parents and her life, and found the last thing she was looking for. "Tallulah, I think Mommy's falling for the innkeeper. What in the world am I going to do?"

❖

Poppy opened the door to her room and suddenly had no desire to be in there alone.

"Here's an idea. How about a few songs on the piano to while away the time?" Carly stood at the center of the room wearing a beautiful pair of silk lounging pants with matching shirt.

Poppy leaned against the door and enjoyed how good Carly looked. "I don't know about that."

"I do. Come on."

The lobby was mostly empty due to the hour, and the staff left Poppy alone as she made her way to the bar. This was one of her favorite places, since for one whole summer she had played here to an audience of mainly four. Carly, Lizzie, Matlin, Sabrina, and the occasional construction worker had enjoyed trying to stump her, requesting songs they thought she might not be able to play.

"I'm sure it's like riding a bike, sweetheart. Go on, give it a try." The encouraging words from Carly got Poppy to step closer to the stage.

"How about a beer, boss?" The bartender spoke just loud enough for her to hear him.

Poppy tried to remember his name without having to cheat and look at the tag on his shirt. "A beer, Eddie. Whatever you have on tap."

It was the beard and the slightly long hair that made her remember. Eddie, the New Yorker who had run away from a high-paying job and the high levels of stress that went with it. He made a mean margarita and had an endless supply of jokes. Just one more of her mutts, who made up the menagerie of Valente Resorts and whose personalities made each guest's stay that much more memorable.

The piano bench creaked when she sat down, but the cover over the keys opened silently. There was no audience, except for Carly and Eddie, so Poppy started playing without the worry of missed notes or forgotten bridges. If such mistakes happened they would turn a deaf ear and be glad she had even ventured to try, but Carly was right. A person didn't spend years of a lifetime enjoying something so much only to forget because of a temporary abandonment. Her practiced fingers found the right keys and the tempo was right, but there was a difference.

The tune Poppy picked to play wasn't too technically difficult, but sounded richer when played by someone who had known suffering. In New Orleans, some of the old players said it was what separated the good payers from the great ones. Jazz and her sister the blues were better played by those who knew sacrifice.

The tune had been one of Carly's last requests, about a week before her death, and, as always, Poppy gave what was asked of her. She had never heard her voice crack so much in the span of one song.

"You want anything else, boss?" asked Eddie.

"Nah, go home. I'm just having trouble sleeping. No sense in both of us being up. I know where the tap is, and I know the owner personally."

"It's been awhile since I heard you play here."

She hit the keys after taking a long swallow of beer and started another song. "Yeah, but then it's been awhile since I've played anywhere."

"Carly, she loved when you played that. A couple of summers ago she invited me to sit and listen with her on a slow night, and you started playing that song you just finished."

Poppy kept playing with a small smile. "Did she like it?"

"She talked a little during the intro, but she never took her eyes off you. It was a look you wish someone shoots your way some time in your life, you know?" Eddie leaned against the piano and moved her glass closer when she reached for it.

"I know."

"She said, 'Eddie, that's my favorite song.' I didn't think she was going to say anything else, but she said you played it every so often, but not so often to make it lose its appeal. She said you'd asked someone what her favorite was so you could play it for her. Because you did, she told me she was the luckiest woman alive. I asked why and she said, 'Just look at her.'"

"Thanks for telling me that story. Carly didn't always know the depth of her impact on people, did she?"

He blushed when the little crush he'd carried seeped into his telling. "No, probably not. Everyone you know has most likely told you it'll be okay."

Poppy's glass now sat empty and Eddie refilled it. Poppy took a sip. "But you have something else to say, right?"

"It's okay to miss her, and it's better if you remember nights like that when she was looking at you and you didn't know it."

"I'll let you in on a secret, Eddie. If you'd been looking at me, you'd know I noticed." She laughed, which stopped any apology he thought of offering. "It's okay, and thanks again for telling me and reminding me. Stuff like that does help."

They were alone again when Eddie said his good nights, and Poppy pointed to the closest table and started Carly's song again. Only this time she added her voice, and like she had on the night Eddie had mentioned, her eyes never left Carly's.

"Did you like it?" she asked when she lifted her hands up after the last note died away.

"It was as beautiful as the first time, and I know this is the last."

"A beautiful song for a beautiful woman. It's like you're a special part of me I don't care to share."

"Thank you, love, and don't forget in the days ahead to keep asking."

Poppy bunched her brows together, not understanding. "Asking what?"

"The questions that set you apart and make you such a great catch."

Poppy made it back to her room with Carly's laughter ringing in her head. If what happened was a lesson, she'd learned there was one more thing she could still do, and do well without Carly. She could sing. If she was meant to study and ponder on Carly's parting words for some other meaning, she was too tired to contemplate the possibilities.

CHAPTER TEN

The next morning Julia stepped out onto the balcony to look out across the fantasy world Poppy had created by the pristine waters of the Caribbean. It was only a little past six, and the grounds crew was already cutting, pruning, and watering the gardens around the property. They were working at a rapid pace, no doubt trying to get done before most of the guests went down for the day. Yet, incredibly, not one worker was using a gas- or electric-powered tool.

"It's not meant to be cruel."

Julia glanced sideways and saw Poppy sitting on her own balcony sipping from a cup of coffee. "I didn't see you sitting there, I'm sorry. What's not meant to be cruel?"

Poppy pointed to the employees working below them. "The hand tools. I saw you looking."

"They'd finish faster if you got them at least a blower."

"True, but consider this. A floor below us, Tucker and Anita Bloom of Seattle, Washington are in room 421. Tucker sells cars and Anita stays home with their three children. Tucker saves all year, every year, so he and Anita can fly to Aruba for a week to celebrate their anniversary."

Absorbing the story Poppy was spinning for her, Julia asked, "How do you know all this stuff?"

"This is like the story I told you about how I got the name Poppy."

"What do Tucker and Anita have to do with how you got your name?"

"Only that the more you interrupt me, the longer it'll take me to get to the end of the story."

Poppy's smile and the lilt in her voice let Julia know she was kidding so she took a shot of her own. "Who's a smart-ass now?"

"You have no idea. Back to our guests in 421. This is their fifteenth anniversary and their seventh trip to the Esmeralda Verde. For one week every year they forget the Seattle rain, the kids, the bills, and their everyday routine to come here. They'll eat lobster, snorkel, dance, and take long walks along the moon-drenched beach, but you know what Tucker and Anita love most about this place?"

"What?"

Poppy studied the woman asking the question and decided she carried off the just-out-of-bed, rumpled look adorably. "That after the drinks, sunbathing, dancing, dining, and beach walking, some dumb ass with a blower won't wake them up at six in the morning."

"You could've just said that from the beginning."

"But then you wouldn't have understood my theory about paradise." Poppy put her cup down and unlocked the divider so Julia could join her.

"Enlighten me."

"In paradise, there are no blowers, weed eaters, or mowers."

Julia fell back into the chair next to Poppy's and laughed. "You're making this up as you go along, aren't you?

"When it comes to paradise, but more importantly, making other people happy, I never make anything up. It's something I feel strongly about." The way she gazed into Julia's eyes made her believe it.

❖

Breakfast down in the restaurant by the pool was a humorous outing for Julia. At one point Poppy had to take the coffee carafe from their waiter to stop him refilling the cups after each sip.

"He must have recognized your feet from the picture in the lobby," said Julia.

Poppy rolled her eyes and tried to tame her embarrassment.

A couple holding hands strolled into the restaurant and spotted Poppy as they were waiting for a table. They were both wearing floral print shirts that clashed with their sunburns, but the fashion mistake didn't seem to diminish the fun they were having. They walked toward Poppy and Julia, the manager chasing them through the restaurant.

"Hi, Poppy, we didn't realize you were here." The volume of the man's voice made Julia and everyone else in the restaurant turn toward them.

"Tucker, Anita, how's the vacation coming?" Poppy waved the restaurant manager away, not wanting to embarrass the friendly couple.

"Just like every year," Tucker replied. "This place just keeps getting better. We wanted to come over and thank you for the champagne and the basket of goodies in our room. You never forget."

"You're very welcome." Poppy made quick introductions.

"Are you and your baby here on vacation, too?" Anita asked Julia.

"No, we're at Carly's Sound. Poppy was nice enough to take us to dinner in Curaçao last night, and we stayed over."

"We sure have missed you, Poppy, the last couple of times we were here. Did Carly not make the trip down with you?" Anita continued her probing.

"Carly passed away some time ago, Anita."

From the tension lines in Poppy's face, Julia could tell the intrusive question had sliced through her tall friend's heart. The hand sitting flat on the table looked so stiff that Julia covered as much of it as she could with her own. Wanting to get Poppy away from the stress of the interaction, she did the only thing she could think of and stood, pulling Poppy up with her.

"Why don't you two take the table and enjoy breakfast," she invited Tucker and Anita. "We're done, and I need to go up and change Tallulah."

"I'm sorry, Poppy, I didn't know," said Anita.

"Don't worry about it. Enjoy your stay and maybe we'll see you next year." Poppy resituated Tallulah on her shoulder and followed Julia without protest.

Heading toward the beach, they walked down the steps at the back of the hotel and into a tunnel of blooming bougainvillea plants. At the end of the trail they kicked off their sandals and headed toward the water's edge.

"You didn't tell me the part of the story about Tucker and Anita being jerks with a taste for loud, tacky clothing," said Julia.

"I was saving that for when you met them." Observing that Julia didn't seem amused, Poppy said, "I'm kidding. Seeing you and the baby must have given her the impression I'd moved on to new territory."

"Like your life is any business of hers."

"No harm done, but thanks for getting me out of there." With the sleeping baby breathing on her neck and Julia's hand in hers, Poppy found it easy to move beyond the awkward moment and focus on the here and now. In an attempt to lighten the mood, she said, "The shirts I have no explanation for, although my father would have a few thoughts."

"What's his theory?" The warm, clear water felt as wonderful to Julia as the hand holding hers.

"Papi says people who dress like that are points of reference."

"I don't get it."

"If you were in the restaurant just now and wanted to know where the bathroom was, I could have told you, 'See the guy over there with the really loud shirt? It's to the left of him.' Like my father said, point of reference."

"He sounds like a funny guy, your father."

"Raphael's my idea of a perfect parent. Both he and my mother gave me the freedom to be myself even when it didn't fit with what they had planned for me."

Julia gazed up at her companion and noticed again how comfortable Poppy seemed holding Tallulah. Considering she didn't have any children, she was amazingly at ease with them. Julia had discovered, in just a few months of being a parent, that people couldn't fake that.

"They didn't care for your relationship with Carly?"

"It didn't exactly thrill them at first, no. There was the fact she was a woman, and the age difference didn't help. And did I mention she was a woman?" The way Poppy asked the question made Julia giggle. "Isabelle thought I was going through a phase, but when the reality sank in, she loved me no less. Carly was my partner, and that's how my parents accepted her."

The fact they were still holding hands gave Julia the courage to find out if there was a chance to get closer to Poppy. "Will you tell me about her? You don't have to. But I'd like to get a sense of her." Julia called to mind the woman who smiled from all those pictures in Poppy's bungalow, the woman she had built all these beautiful places with.

"Why do you want to know?" Poppy wasn't reluctant to talk about Carly. But she was curious as to why Julia was asking.

"Because she was important to you."

The simple answer brought what had happened the night before slamming into the front of her brain. *Don't forget to keep asking.* Isn't that what Carly had said? Poppy weighed up what she could say that wouldn't reduce her to a big crying mess. "I met Carly when I was twenty and about to graduate from college. She was married at the time, which should have sent me packing, but there was something about her that made me want to know her and made me want to come back for more. You know what I mean?"

Her tone seemed almost devoid of emotion, which surprised Julia. One glance at the misty blue eyes and she knew detachment was the only way Poppy could insulate herself from the residual pain of her loss.

Julia reached up with her other hand and squeezed Poppy's bicep. "I'm getting familiar with the concept."

A nervous laugh passed Poppy's lips before she continued her story. "I kept coming back and she was always there for me, and I fell in love with her. The way she used to tell it, I gave her the courage to leave a bad situation, and she gave me the courage to build on what I wanted."

"What do you mean?"

"She got a divorce, and I gambled the first place I got to buy another resort. I didn't set out to be Valente Resorts at first."

Julia glanced up toward the sun. It was getting to be late morning, and she and Tallulah weren't born with the same tanning genes Poppy possessed.

"Need some shade?"

"Yes." Julia stood, slightly disconcerted that her companion seemed so attuned to her body language. "You're very observant."

Poppy shrugged. "It's my business." She didn't pass Tallulah back, instead shifting the baby a little higher onto her shoulder.

Julia considered her comment as they walked away from the beach and toward the trees. Obviously Poppy was talking about being in the hospitality industry, where paying attention to detail was part of the job.

Poppy chose a palm and they sat down to lean against it.

"You didn't want all of this?" Julia asked.

"I'm glad I have the resorts. All this and the others like them helped build the one place I did have in mind."

"Carly's Sound?"

"Yes. All the rest started out as someone else's vision, but Carly's Sound is all mine. I let other people continue with the work, when it became unimportant in the scheme of things."

Again Julia detected a growing detachment in Poppy. "Wouldn't it be her wish for you to finish what you started?" Aiming to lighten the mood, she added with a gentle smile, "You wouldn't want her to start haunting you."

Poppy seemed taken aback, then she laughed. "No, we wouldn't want that. Feel like going down to the market?"

"Sounds good, but we really do have to go and change the princess before she messes up that great-looking shirt."

Playfully, Poppy handed Tallulah back in a hurry before jumping to her feet and looking down at her chest. She helped Julia up, and they walked back hand in hand. Julia was vaguely aware of a few staff members stealing second glances at their linked hands, but Poppy's grip remained firm.

❖

The tourist market in Aruba was surprisingly a fairly large enterprise, considering the overall size of the island. During their leisurely stroll through the area, Julia spotted a large number of the mandatory T-shirt shops, but mixed in among them were a variety of other stores. More than one shopkeeper recognized Poppy and stopped to admire the baby she was holding as Julia browsed through the merchandise.

"Poppy, look." Julia held up a small carved boat, complete with rower carrying his purchases back home, she guessed. The little man in the back, his stem of bananas, mess of fish, and pile of oranges were all carved out of the same piece of wood with an amazing amount of minute detail.

"Are you telling me it's time to feed you again?"

"You're so funny." Julia stuck her tongue out as she held her find higher for Poppy to see. "Isn't this cute?"

"You should get it and put it somewhere in your bungalow." They hadn't known each other long enough to discuss future plans, and Poppy found a part of her brain freezing up at the thought of Julia's not staying.

The price was reasonable for the amount of workmanship that had gone into the piece, but in true old Southern fashion, Julia was living off the kindness of others. To add whimsical purchases to such generosity would be rude. "It's cute, but I'll pass."

The way Julia caressed the piece one more time and her long look at the price tag made Poppy think she really wanted the carving. But she didn't buy it and that puzzled Poppy. Every couple sometimes fought over money, and no one knew what went on in anyone's life, but Poppy knew precisely how much Rayford was making. The knickknack was nothing. It wasn't like Julia would be coming home and informing her husband she'd bought a car.

When Carly asked her to look at some new purchase, it was usually at home being pulled out of a shopping bag. Carly's decision to buy something was not up for discussion, and Poppy had wanted it that way. Anyone who used money to lord it over someone they purportedly cared about didn't deserve a person as wonderful as Carly. Or Julia. The more she pondered it, the lower Rayford's stock fell in her mind.

"Well, if you aren't going to buy anything, let me introduce you to Oscar." Poppy waved toward the door, making a silent promise to call Matlin and ask some questions. She wanted to know what type of man Julia had gotten involved with.

"Oscar?"

"A guy with a little place on the beach. His specialty is fish and bananas, but if you make sweet eyes at him I'm sure he can come up with an orange or two."

As Julia laughed, the store owner picked up the carving before a potential sale walked out the door. "We wrap this up for you, Mrs?"

Julia looked at the piece one last time and shook her head. "It's beautiful, but no." Feeling like her bladder had suddenly shrunk to the size of a small walnut, she asked Poppy, "Will you and the baby be all right for a second?"

"Sure. We'll wait right here for you." Poppy lifted the happy, gurgling baby higher in her arms and waved Tallulah's hand at her mother. When Julia looked back before turning the corner, Poppy's smile grew at not having to come up with an excuse to double back to the store.

Julia took her time walking back from the restrooms, so she could watch Poppy with Tallulah. They were standing near a wind chime display, Poppy pointing and talking away to the attentive baby. It was rare to meet someone who had so much patience with a small person whose day revolved around eating, sleeping, and getting cleaned up from the effects of the first two.

"Hey, what are you thinking so hard about over there?"

Julia refocused and started moving again. "Just window shopping, but now I'm hungry."

The little restaurant was everything Poppy promised, and after two orders of fried fish and chips, Julia was ready for a nap. They drove back to the Esmeralda Verde, where the staff had prepared the most secluded spot on the beach for them. Within minutes, Julia found herself under a canopy of palm trees on a comfortable chaise with a playpen for Tallulah set up next to it. Beside her, Poppy had her eyes closed and her breathing was starting to even out.

"Poppy?"

Julia's voice seemed far away, but Poppy shook herself into a mumbled reply. "Yes?"

"Could I bother you to put some of this on me?" Julia held up a bottle of sunscreen.

Nodding, Poppy started to get up when Julia beat her to it.

"Stay, I'll come to you."

Poppy was sure she detected some extra roll in Julia's hips. She certainly used the short distance between them to best advantage, each step languidly self-aware. The lethargy Poppy was experiencing from lunch disappeared in the time it took Julia to sit down and drop the straps of her bathing suit. The large dollop of white lotion mixed in with the slightly tanned shoulders, and Poppy found herself enjoying the feel of Julia's skin. She ran her hand slowly, going as far down Julia's back as the one-piece would allow. When her job was done, she felt slightly disappointed.

"There you go." She flipped the cap closed and was about to give the bottle back when Julia turned around.

"I want you to do the front." Her voice sounded husky, like she too had enjoyed the effect of Poppy's fingers on her skin. "If you don't mind, that is?"

Poppy forgot to breathe. *Jesus Christ, why does she have to be so beautiful?* It was the massive amount of cream gushing over her hand that brought her musings to an end. She'd squeezed hard enough to pop the cap off the bottle.

Staring down at the sunscreen oozing between her fingers, she waited for her brain to restart the fire of basic intelligence. Weakly, she said, "No problem."

"Are you sure?" Julia asked in a tone Poppy hadn't heard her use before. It was an equal mix of desire and amusement. "'Cause that's an awful lot of lotion you have there. We'll have to find somewhere to put it."

"Let's start with your arms," suggested Poppy.

Julia peeled her bathing suit down a little more. "Maybe I should work on evening out my tan."

The conservative one-piece was slowly becoming something much more sensual the lower Julia moved it. Poppy gave up all pretense of looking at Julia's face. Her eyes were riveted to the full breasts now uncovered. The more she stared, the harder the pink nipples got. Slowly, Julia dragged Poppy's hands up her abdomen to cup her breasts. She lifted them as if offering them to Poppy as a gift.

"How about we start here?"

"Julia, I don't think…" Poppy started speaking, but she was mesmerized by the chest she was studying. It wasn't as if she hadn't seen it before; Julia nursed the baby all the time. But seeing her now, with the black suit just below her breasts, Poppy saw more than just a mother.

Without too much effort Julia pushed Poppy back into a reclining position on the chair so she could straddle her legs. "Don't think. Feel me and touch me like I've wanted you to do for days now." With a glob of sunscreen in one hand and the bottle in the other, Poppy sat back, unsure of what to do next.

Julia threw the bottle in the sand and grabbed both of Poppy's wrists. "I've thought of us like this from the first day I saw you. Your hands are at the center of so many of my fantasies. I've wanted to know for days what they would feel like on my skin. What they would feel like stroking my most sensitive spots. Would they get me as wet as they do in my dreams?"

She pressed Poppy's hands together to cover both of them in cream, then placed them on her chest. When the slick palms moved up a little, Julia threw her head back and moaned.

Slowly and sensuously, Poppy caressed the contours of Julia's body, wanting to memorize every rise and hollow. She looked amazingly sexy, with her head thrown back and her swimsuit slung down to her hips.

"You feel so good," Poppy murmured.

Julia responded by pressing her lips to Poppy's. The kiss felt like Julia had attached a string to the part of Poppy's body that defined desire and was pulling hard. Julia buried her fingers in the hair at each side of Poppy's head and slid her tongue into Poppy's mouth, but just as quickly retreated to let Poppy take control. It was a lack of air that finally drove them apart.

"Please, baby," Julia begged.

"What?" Poppy asked. Having Julia panting in her ear was driving her mad.

"Touch me, I need you to." Julia was so wet and so turned on. "Take what's yours." She grabbed hold of Poppy's right wrist and encouraged her to do just that.

"But, what about Tallulah?" Julia's lips silenced the protest, but Poppy's addled mind insisted that there were so many reasons not to be doing this. The baby. Their location. The number of staff she knew for a fact were walking around. And the rest of the tourists that were not that far away.

"Tallulah is fine," Julia said. "Do what you feel. It's just you and me here now."

Poppy didn't need any more encouragement. The hands in her hair and the seductive voice spilling into her ear had formed a tide she couldn't fight. The need to put her hands on this woman poised so wantonly above her consumed Poppy in a way she'd thought she would never experience again.

Julia moved up on her knees a little and moved her legs farther apart. Her body was ready to be touched, and Poppy did what she asked. Her soul felt like it had come home again when her fingers slid into Julia's most intimate place.

"Julia." She was still for a moment, reveling in the wet heat surrounding her fingers. As much as she wanted to move forward and make Julia feel good, it was the knowledge that she had brought her to this level of arousal that she was enjoying. This intimacy wasn't something that her head had sought out, but her heart welcomed the act only because it was Julia in her arms.

A baby's cry broke through the fog of desire, and Poppy drew a sharp, startled breath and woke up.

CHAPTER ELEVEN

*I*know why I sent that boat adrift. Part of me didn't want to; I never had anyone who truly wanted to share my life until Poppy, and letting go of her wasn't easy. The price for having her had been steep. There were times when my decisions, and Thomas's hatred, weighed on me, and I doubted myself. Perhaps the hardest of those came with the approach of our first Christmas holidays.

I'd always loved the last-minute shopping with Lizzie in other years, but this time I just couldn't get into it. I remember sitting in the Canal Place Mall in downtown New Orleans, staring at those large wreaths and beautiful poinsettias, and each one made me think about the fractured mess my family had become. We would be spending Christmas apart for the first time—Tommy and Jo were going with their father, and Lizzie was staying with me. I had wanted her to go and enjoy the holiday with her father and siblings, but she wasn't about to leave me alone.

I sat there on a bench by the fountain, people-watching while I waited for Lizzie to finish. It felt like a small oasis in the madness around me, and I so seldom had the chance to think about the changes I'd made that I started dwelling on the what-ifs, and you know how that goes. Self-doubt creeps in and you start thinking about what you would have been doing if everything had just stayed the same.

Was a lifetime of pretending better? If I'd answered yes and turned away from what I really wanted, I would have been at the grocery picking up the last-minute things in preparation for another Stevens family traditional Christmas dinner.

I didn't realize I was crying until the woman next to me on the bench handed me a tissue. Then I heard it. There had been a grand piano in the main corridor of the mall ever since they built it, and when someone played, you could hear it on all the floors. Around me, people were slowing down to listen, and I laughed when the player started singing, and some of them began snapping their fingers. They probably had the song's name on the fringes of their brains, but it was elusive since it wasn't one of the now-stale Christmas tunes they'd heard hundreds of times over the past weeks.

I recognized the long introduction because it was my favorite song, but I had no idea how Poppy knew this. Not that it mattered. Listening to her rendition in a place where the acoustics were so good made it sound so wonderful, I forgot about everything but her.

I found a place to stand near the piano, and, after the applause, Poppy came over with a bouquet of wildflowers and wished me Merry Christmas. She always chose the flowers I loved best—Louisiana purple irises, daisies, and zinnias.

I asked her how she knew about the song and she said, "I asked."

That was something she did. She asked other people all sorts of things about me, things you wouldn't think were important. She took the time to find out what I liked, and said making me happy made her happy in return.

That day, she said, "Call it a gift, freely given from me to you. Along with it comes my blessing if you want to go home because this is too hard for you. Christmas isn't a time for sadness, and it certainly isn't a time for tears."

I asked her if she wanted me to go back, and she looked like she was praying for strength.

She said, "I want you to do what's best for you. I can't force you to be happy with me, or to forget the pain that being with me is costing you. What I'm telling you is, I'll understand if you can't. I won't hold you to promises you'll be miserable trying to keep."

"I can't lose you too," I said.

Of course, she had a wise way of looking at everything. I used to wonder sometimes if she'd been born that way; she seemed too young to know what she knew.

She said, "Carly, there'll be things in your life that'll always be beyond your control, like the balance of our days. That's Fate's way of keeping us guessing. What you can count on is, I'll try to always respect your wishes. I'll try to help you through the bad times and be the best partner in all aspects of our relationship. My plan is to keep asking until

I know your favorite color is the color blue the sky is on bright summer days, that you prefer wildflowers to any others, and what your favorite song is. It's the best I know how to do, but it won't always be enough."

Then she told me she loved me and walked away. I needed to cry some more, and I had to meet Lizzie, so I went back to the bench I'd been sitting on earlier. I had no idea I was being followed until an older, attractive woman with short, perfectly coiffed silver hair, and wearing a navy wool pantsuit and Donald Pliner boots, sat down next to me and announced herself with one of her worldly wise declarations.

"If one lives long enough one gets to experience all sorts of things."

Emily St. Claire. Could my day get any more stressful? Emily was a grand dame of New Orleans society, and an old friend.

I was never all that wrapped up in the party scene, but separating from Thomas meant my name was dropped from more than one guest list. Old friends showed new colors over those months, choosing to believe the venom Thomas had an endless supply of. I wondered if Emily was about to join their ranks. She must have seen me with Poppy, and I still had the flowers in my hand.

She always got right to the point, and this was no exception. She said, "I've been meaning to call you since I heard about all this nonsense with Thomas, so I apologize for not following through. I couldn't help but overhear what that young woman said to you by the piano. I'm greatly disturbed."

I was immediately angry, anticipating condemnation. To get in first, I said, "I don't live my life for other people, so I don't give a crap what you find disturbing. I love her, and if, because I do, I never get invited to another function crowded with opinionated, full-of-shit airheads, them's the breaks."

Emily gave me a patient look and said my argument was excellent but unnecessary. She explained herself this way. "What I meant by experiencing things with age is that I just saw a noble soul with her heart in her throat because you've caused her to doubt what she means to you. She loves you enough to let you go—how often do you see that? I'm disturbed because I know you better. You don't need anyone's blessing to choose happiness."

I had to stop and think about that for a moment, partly because I had not expected to find support in this quarter and felt ashamed that

I had misjudged my friend, and partly because they were the words I badly needed to hear. Emily went on to tell me she thought Poppy seemed like a lovely girl, and I owed her an introduction.

I told her she was just the kick in the ass I needed; then Lizzie came up, and I couldn't wait to get to the car because I was afraid my bout of insecurity might have cost me something in Poppy's eyes.

The Valentes had invited us to dinner, their way of acknowledging I was not just an infatuation of their daughter's. Gifts weren't a part of the Cuban Christmas tradition, though many families adopted the American way of doing things. The Valentes usually celebrated Christmas Eve over a traditional meal of roasted pig, black beans, and yucca. After the meal that first year, Lizzie and I stood around the piano with Poppy's parents and the friends they'd invited, helping Poppy sing old Cuban torch songs.

Eventually, most of the guests went to midnight mass, and Lizzie and I were left alone with Poppy. I asked whether she could keep up if we sang something, and she laughed until we started singing her favorite song, one of the first she'd learned to play well.

She took my hand, and Lizzie's, and asked me how I knew. I was tearing up already, but I told her, "I care enough to want to know, so I asked your mother." Then it all came pouring out. I said, "I'm sorry I got scared, but it was all about me. The thought of being with you is uncharted territory for me so I get a little nervous. But the thought of being without you devastates the part of me I need if I'm going to survive."

I told her she was my family now and that I loved her. I released my guilt and gave myself permission to accept all of what Poppy offered. I never forgot that Poppy had been willing to let go of me because she loved me and would've borne the pain of my loss for just that reason. That blessing remained with me all the rest of my life, and it was now time to return the favor.

That's why I had to set the boat free.

That same nobility was holding Poppy back now. She wouldn't let go and start over because she was stuck. She'd convinced herself that it would somehow taint what we'd had. That day in the mall an old friend had untied me from a past that was dragging me down, and now I had to do the same for Poppy. More than anything, I wanted to give her the chance she was denying herself, and if it took the same kick in the ass

Emily gave me, then I would keep thinking of ways to show her what I meant—that happiness is her right.

It's strange to feel this, to know I am ready to do this. I am setting Poppy adrift, but not without destination. She'll find her way home, only this time the woman waiting there will be alive, vibrant, and very much in love with her. Once that happens, I'll be free to raise my own sails and set a new course.

❖

For what seemed like an eternity, Poppy couldn't figure out where she was and why she felt like she was on fire. Then the dream rushed back into focus, and she jerked upright in her chaise lounge, staring first at her hand, then at Julia.

"Sorry, I couldn't wait anymore. She needs a diaper change." Julia offered the apology as she rummaged around in the bag at the foot of her chair. Lifting a delicate hand, she pushed her hair back, revealing a slight smile on her lips and some very visible pinking across her cheeks.

As relieved as Poppy was that their encounter was only a dream, she was a little disappointed as well. Julia was still in her own chair, and she was fully dressed.

"No problem." Poppy cleared her throat. The dream had left her sounding like someone had sandpapered her tonsils. "If you don't need any help I'm going for a short swim."

Julia smiled. "Go ahead. Let me finish this and we'll join you." She watched Poppy jog slowly to the water before taking care of Tallulah. The way Poppy had moaned her name in her sleep had sent chills through her body and instantly hardened her nipples, both of which had nothing to do with being cold.

"I wonder what that was about, baby girl?" Julia said as she put a new swim diaper and pink bathing suit on Tallulah. "If it's what I think, it's a start, a start that'll make us both happy."

The clear water felt like ice against Poppy's skin, but that didn't stop her from diving in headfirst as soon as she was deep enough. Dreams weren't usually so vivid or so palpable, at least not in her experience. She had felt Julia's essence as it coated her fingers just as surely as she had felt the woman's nipples get rock hard against her palms.

Good God, Valente, you're becoming lascivious with age. The thought occurred to Poppy right before her head cleared the water as she came up for air. People in their thirties should be well past the wet-dream stage, in her opinion.

"A lascivious thought or two never hurt anyone, darling." Carly was floating next to her on a sky blue inflatable raft.

Facing her now was too much, so Poppy opted for sinking. She didn't get very far before Carly grabbed the top her head and pulled her up like a cork.

"Don't be embarrassed, sweetie. Stuff like this just means you're getting better." Carly cupped Poppy's cheek. "Not that it's not flattering when you dream about me like that, but it's, as they say, an exercise in futility. I can't give you satisfaction, but she can."

"Carly, she's taken. There are wonderful people in the world, but most times it's not just me who notices. I mean, who wouldn't want to be with someone wonderful?" The cloudless sky came into view when Poppy flipped over to float on her back.

"And sometimes people settle for what they think is the best life has to offer when it's not. Which is the greater sin, to suffer through commitment for the sake of commitment, or to take a chance on being happy?"

"I'm sure, knowing you, you've met the Almighty, so why don't you answer the question?" With a quick dip of her head, Poppy sent a stream of water toward Carly. "With your infinite wisdom and experience, you're better qualified to give an opinion is my guess. The fact I couldn't stop you if that's your intention is my other guess."

"See, you're never too old to learn," Carly teased as she dipped her fingertips into the water. "As for the Almighty, She's very nice, but neither She nor I are here to do your thinking for you."

"Then I'm really in trouble." Poppy made a show of sliding back beneath the surface like a drowning woman.

Carly hauled her up, sputtering. "Quit fooling around and listen. Listen to what the free-spirited part of your heart and mind are telling you."

"It was just a dream. I'd never act on something like that just because it would feel good."

"Sure you have, lover. Plenty of times and you're damn good at it." Carly wiggled her eyebrows to emphasize her point, making Poppy blush. "Honey, nothing's ever exactly as it seems. I should be proof enough of that for you. What I'm telling you is, take things slow. You have plenty of time to see what life will gift you with next. Enjoy the afternoon, then take her out to the marina."

"Why?"

Carly rolled her eyes. "Because I asked you to. Because I'll pop into your head and start singing the beer song if you don't." She paused and smiled sweetly before adding, "Extremely off key."

Poppy groaned. It wasn't an idle threat, if she knew Carly at all, which she did. "Okay, now I get it. The real reason ghosts hang around is to torment the people who love them."

With a long-suffering smile, Carly said, "Just remember, honey, *I* died. Not your libido or your ability to love."

"Hey, you're too deep for us," called Julia.

Her ghostly advisor had disappeared after delivering her last bit of advice, so Poppy dove to the bottom and kicked off toward Julia. A few seconds later, she popped up close enough to take the baby.

"You okay?" Julia could have sworn she had heard Poppy talking to herself as she and Tallulah entered the water.

"I'm great. Why, you two ready to head home?" Poppy spun Tallulah through the water in a circle, getting the infant to laugh.

"Trust me, we're not so easy to get rid of." Julia closed the distance between them and reached toward her.

Poppy stopped spinning, waiting breathlessly to see where Julia's small hand was going to land and with what intent. Julia's body pressed lightly into hers as she trailed her fingers down Poppy's back. Almost immediately she withdrew and held up a long strand of vegetation.

"Look. Seaweed."

"On this beach. We'll have to complain to the management."

Poppy's low rumbly voice gave Julia goose bumps. The vocalizations had a way of making her feel like she was being caressed.

She laughed and moved back just a little. "How about we let it go this one time. Just see it doesn't happen again."

They both turned as a male voice interrupted. Jorge, the resort manager, stood at the shoreline in bare feet with his pants cuffed to keep them out of the water. "*Perdóneme*, Poppy. A moment, *por favor.*"

Julia grabbed Poppy's arm before she could move. "If you're

trying to ditch your lifeguarding duties, that might go down as number two on my list. The seaweed was bad enough."

The mock threat, and the teasing awareness in Julia's gaze, seemed downright flirtatious. Certain she was not imagining the heat that suddenly flickered between them, Poppy handed Tallulah over. "Try your best to stay afloat and I'll be right back."

Julia tried to interpret what she was seeing as Poppy spoke to her manager. If Poppy's body language was any indication, something was wrong. Her face wore a disgusted expression as she headed back into the water, but she concealed this as she drew closer.

"Do you have to go back to work?" Julia asked.

"Not exactly, but you and Tallulah will have to fly back to the island without me." Poppy held out her arms, and Julia gave her squirming daughter back to her favorite swimming partner.

"I see, so you're trying to get rid of us." Julia poked Poppy's shoulder with her finger and tried to sound menacing. The effect was comical enough to make Poppy laugh.

"You know better than that. Something happened to the *Piper*. It came loose from the buoy sometime last night, and a fisherman towed her in this afternoon. She won't do me any good picking up new barnacles here, so I need to sail her back, which means you get to fly home."

"We could come along and keep you company."

Moving into deeper water, Poppy dipped Tallulah in up to her shoulders to keep her cool. "You might not handle the distance too well. Have you found a cure for your seasickness or something?"

Julia smiled at her walking Dramamine pill. "Something like that." Sailing with Poppy was so enjoyable, she mostly forgot the bobbing the boat was doing. Especially when she concentrated on studying the tall rogue behind the wheel.

"We'll head over later and make sure nothing happened on her solo cruise over here. If I find out who untied her there might be a death." Poppy was teasing, but the boat couldn't have escaped without some help. She didn't have to strain her brain to figure out who was responsible. Carly was taking her matchmaker role to new heights.

"How long a sail is it?" asked Julia.

"About three hours if the wind holds up, and it always does. Why, changing your mind?"

"Do you want me to?" There was a trace of challenge in Julia's stare, as if she were trying to provoke Poppy somehow.

"I'm fine about going alone if you think it's too much for the baby."

"Too much for the baby? Are you kidding me? I'm beginning to think you two are attached at the hip."

Poppy conceded that with a wry smile. "We'll have to spend another night here. Is that all right?"

"I'm sure I'll find some way to tough it out. This place is so primitive and all. One more piece of Belgium chocolate on my pillow might send me over the edge." Again, Julia's eyes flashed provocatively, and when she grabbed her chest in mock horror and staggered back a bit, Poppy laughed.

"You'll have to find a way to muddle through since I'm quite fond of the little bugger, and her mother's not bad either."

The blush that ran up Julia's face was extremely cute and only darkened when Poppy made a point of studying her face.

"Stop," Julia protested.

"Stop what?" Poppy was all innocence. "Come on. We'll go check out the boat, and I'll introduce you to Huey."

"Huey? Do you know everyone on the island?"

"That's why I picked this area. It's so small, there weren't that many names to memorize."

"Again with the less-than-funny commentary from you," Julia teased as they gathered their stuff together.

Jorge had a Jeep waiting for them, and as they headed away from the resort, Poppy at the wheel, it struck Julia that Poppy had accomplished something truly amazing—more than most people managed in a lifetime. Aside from the beauty of the resorts, the large number of people she employed genuinely seemed to enjoy their work. Even when they were not on duty, the staff Julia had seen looked happy.

"Do you ever sit back and just gloat over all this?" she asked.

"Gloat? Do I come across as an egomaniac to you?"

"Sorry, maybe gloat is too strong a word. How about awe-inspired?"

"I don't need the properties to prove anything to myself, but I never fail to smile a little bit brighter when I drive up to a place like the Esmeralda Verde. Maybe you'd consider coming with me to New Orleans to see my definition of awe-inspiring." Poppy was enjoying her time in the islands, but one of the things she was looking forward to was a more extensive exploration of the Piquant after the small taste she'd gotten right before she left.

At the idea of Poppy going home, Julia felt like someone had punched her in the stomach. She sagged against the Jeep door for support; if she'd been standing, she'd have slid to the ground, her knees felt so weak. "You're…you're leaving?"

"Not right away, but in a couple of months I'm going to pick up my girl and bring her to the opening. You okay?"

"You have a girl?" Julia could feel herself getting paler.

"If you're talking romantic involvement, then no, I don't have a girl. I was talking about Carly's daughter, Elizabeth." Poppy slowed the Jeep a little and cocked her head to the side. "Are you sure you're all right?"

"Just admiring the view and enjoying the company. This really is a beautiful drive." It sounded lame even to her, but it was the best Julia could do.

"I'm glad you think so even if you don't always get my sense of humor."

Julia gave Poppy's knee a gentle slap. "Maybe a joke book for Christmas might help you out, but I think you're too far gone." She couldn't help but laugh when Poppy pouted and acted deeply wounded.

"If I can't make you laugh I'll have to settle for showing you beautiful things."

The Jeep headed away from the populated side of the island, toward the interior where, with every yard they traveled, the landscape became sparser. A colorful home dotted the roadside every so often, each with a two-foot-high fence around it painted in a matching pastel color. Poppy explained that these were intended to keep goats out, and Julia thought she was joking until a large herd crossed their path. The ridiculously low fences made sense after seeing the wild creatures trying to get over the stones with no luck.

Julia could hear their final destination before Poppy stopped the Jeep. The waves were huge and brutalized the coast with a constant barrage of attacks. In places, the water had won the battle and left fascinating cuts along the shoreline.

"Welcome to the natural bridge of Aruba." Poppy pointed to a formation close to the shore. After centuries of pounding, the waves had cut a circle out of the middle of one of the massive stones littering the coastline. What was left looked like a bridge over the water, a tenuous last stand against total defeat by the waves.

Leaving a napping Tallulah in the back of the Jeep, they both got out and sat on the hood to enjoy the solitude of the area. The surf was so loud it was hard to talk over it so they, like the few other people present, sat in silence, letting Mother Nature have center stage. It was an afternoon Julia knew she would always remember, no matter what was destined to happen. Next to her, with her head slightly tilted back with her eyes closed, Poppy looked completely happy. Julia allowed herself a moment to take in the long loose limbs and the serenity of Poppy's face and began to understand her companion better. Poppy had money; the way they had traveled to dinner the night before and the resorts she owned were ample evidence of that. Yet Julia sensed it wasn't material things that made Poppy happy. She was one of those rare individuals who could live in the moment and who knew what was really important in life. Poppy was not about appearances. She had too much personal integrity to pretend anything.

Acknowledging that fact made Julia's heart race. Poppy truly liked her, maybe even more. Julia called to mind the attraction she'd seen in those Caribbean blue eyes more than once. It mirrored her own feelings, and that was exciting and unnerving all at once. What did it mean if there was something happening between them? Could a relationship that started on half-truths be one that could survive?

Tallulah napped all the way to the marina and was ready to be fed when they neared the *Piper*. Huey was already on board taking inventory to make sure everything was accounted for and functional.

"Don't tell me we need to have another lesson in the tying of knots, young lady?" he asked as he caught the diaper bag Poppy threw at his head.

"See, he's funny," teased Julia.

"Are you interested in being dragged behind the boat all the way back to Carly's Sound?"

"That would be no." Julia smiled up at Poppy and tried to look contrite.

"One more crack like that and it'll be your only option." Poppy gave her a growl before introducing her old friend.

The talk turned to the condition of the boat and the *Piper*'s readiness to sail as Julia opened her blouse to accommodate Tallulah. It made her smile to see Poppy standing in front of her as a shield, even thinking to dig out a light blanket to drape over Julia's shoulder as the baby nursed.

"I don't get what could have happened," said Poppy, moving to the front of the boat to do her own check.

"Maybe those two pretty blondes back there got you tied in enough knots you forgot to do the same to the boat," Huey suggested.

"You really are a comedian, aren't you?"

When she finished looking over the boat, Poppy sat down next to Julia and enjoyed catching up with Huey. Neither Julia nor Huey made a comment when Poppy put her arm around Julia and reached down for Tallulah's foot. Huey leaned against the wheel, looking slightly uncomfortable at the intimate scene.

"What are you two doing for dinner tonight?" he asked.

"I was thinking the resort restaurant unless Julia's in the mood for something else. Why?" Poppy felt a small shift in Julia's posture as she took advantage of their position to lean against Poppy.

"Nino and the boys just got the *Aruba Sun* out of dry dock and are taking her out for a trial run before they start their season. He invited Loren and me, but I'm sure he'd love to see you and meet Julia." In a nervous habit Huey took off his hat and twisted it up in his hands.

"How about it, Julia? Want to go on a dinner cruise with some people nuttier than I am?"

"I've just met you and I find that hard to believe, but yes, I'd love to." Julia tried to keep the growing feelings she had for Poppy out of her expression.

Small creases next to Poppy's eyes appeared as she smiled. The reflex to simply be happy was returning, and it made her take a deep breath to reflect on the feeling. Carly's death had caused her pain she could never have imagined until she felt her lover's life force slip away. Since then, she'd thought the agony would never end.

Growing up with loving parents and living a life she thoroughly enjoyed had provided Poppy with no point of reference by which to measure or understand her anguish. The best she could do was get through each day. She'd found a way to compartmentalize her grief so that she could function, but she'd never expected the numbness would change, let alone that someone would sweep it aside.

It was tempting to give in to what Julia seemed to be offering, but Poppy wouldn't delude herself. Julia was not in a position to freely give Poppy what she wanted. That reality made her sad, but pain was no stranger to her; it was such a constant companion she had become an expert at trying to keep it at bay. These days she measured her disappointments with a different ruler, making the small ones easier to accept. Only Julia wasn't a small disappointment.

Poppy stared past her companions across the water and allowed herself to feel the full weight of her emotions. She cared for Julia and wanted more from her than pleasant, passing companionship. But circumstances gave her no choice but to accept that they would only ever be friends.

CHAPTER TWELVE

The *Aruba Sun* looked like an old pirate's ship moored alongside the stately yachts in the marina. With Tallulah in one arm, Julia used the other for balance as she walked along the pier. She trusted that Poppy would not to let her fall in, but was relieved when she felt her free hand engulfed by one of Poppy's big paws.

"We're going swimming tonight, but I didn't want you to start now, daydreamer." Poppy adjusted the empty baby carrier in her other hand to keep from smashing it into a piling.

"And my grandmother thinks chivalry is dead."

Poppy laughed as they came even with the gangplank. "You'll have to tell me more about the wise Tallulah, but in this case chivalry doesn't have a thing to do with it. I just figure I'll have to sit next to you, and I don't think it'd be a very pleasant sensation if you were all wet."

The statement was an innocent tease, but Julia couldn't help herself. With an arched eyebrow much like Poppy often used, she asked, "Really? I thought you'd be used to such things."

Poppy's tan was no match for the severity of her blush. She tried to think of a comeback but could come up with nothing that wouldn't get her into deeper water. "After a comment like that I might just not save you from Nino's flirtatious clutches, Ms. Johnson."

"Oh, no, Ms. Valente. I'm from Texas and we have a saying."

"Shoot first and be the last one standing?" Poppy teased, oblivious to the crew standing at the boat's railing watching the exchange.

"You've got to dance with the one who brung you, wise ass."

"Wise ass is part of the saying?"

"Only when it's said in reference to you."

Poppy laughed again and brought her face even with Julia's. "Just for that you'll be sorry about the dancing part later."

I bet not, thought Julia before someone screaming welcome interrupted them. "Ahoy, mates," Nino yelled from the top of the plank.

"Nino, cut the crap or no tip for you later." Poppy handed over the baby stuff and dive bag to one of the crew, making Julia's smile bigger when the one thing she didn't let go of was her hand.

"One more snide comment out of you and I'll make you sing for your supper." The Venezuelan boat captain, an older man with salt-and-pepper hair and a slight paunch that pulled his T-shirt across his stomach, took his fists off his hips and shook a stern finger at Poppy. "Stop your own flirting and get up here."

Poppy took Tallulah, and Julia accepted Nino's hand to get on the boat. A rustic exterior gave way to comfortable-looking padded benches on two levels with a bar close to the front. A crew of six walked up to welcome Poppy and meet her guests, taking drink orders before heading back to their posts. Once Huey and his striking auburn-haired wife, Loren, arrived to join the small group Nino had invited, they were ready to sail. It was an hour until sunset, and they headed toward the sunken freighter off one of Aruba's beaches for a short snorkel trip before dinner.

"What a gorgeous baby." Loren reached over and took hold of a chubby hand Tallulah was waving from Poppy's lap.

"Thank you so much. I've been blessed. The only time she's been cranky has been a case of colic, but we've found a cure for that." When Loren tilted her head slightly in question, Julia explained, "Poppy sings to her and she's out for the count."

"Who wouldn't want to sing to this cutie?" Loren put her hands out to see if Tallulah would come to her. Once she'd settled the baby in her lap, she said, "Why don't you and Poppy go for a swim and let me fantasize about being a grandmother for a little while? Huey and I promise to keep an eye on Tallulah."

"Don't you want to go snorkeling?"

"I think I've counted every rivet on that old wreck, so it's not worth messing up my hair over tonight. I'd much rather hold this cutie and walk her around a bit. You two go on and have a good time. Don't worry. If she gets fussy you're only a shout away." Loren didn't flinch when Tallulah was lucky enough to grab onto her sunglasses and throw them overboard.

Julia couldn't believe the baby had launched such a coordinated attack to fling the woman's glasses into the water. She had no idea Tallulah was capable of that. Mortified, she started to say she was sorry, but Loren gently reprimanded her.

"Don't you dare apologize. I live on an island. Sunglasses are something I have plenty of."

"I insist on replacing them when we get back. The resort has some similar frames in one of the gift shops, so I'll give them to Huey in the morning before we leave."

"It's not necessary, but leave the new pair with my old salt if it'll make you feel better." Loren kissed the chubby hand that had carried out the deed and nodded in an attempt to make Julia feel better.

"Grab your gear, guys, if you want to go see some fish," yelled Nino, and the crew dropped the sails and the anchor well away from the wreck.

There was a little over thirty minutes of sunlight left; then the area around the boat would come alive under the strong spotlights the *Aruba Sun* had mounted along her hull. Poppy had wanted Julia to see the emergence of a different variety of sea life and hoped she would agree to stay in the water. Not everyone enjoyed swimming when the water turned to what some referred to as black ink.

"Come on, Julia. Grab your stuff and hit the water." Huey held up a mask with a snorkel and a pair of fins.

Not that she minded Huey helping her, but Julia was more than a little disappointed Poppy hadn't waited for her. According to Huey, she'd jumped overboard while Julia was distracted by the sunglasses incident. Now he pointed to a figure in the water a couple of hundred yards away.

"Don't look so dejected, sweetheart. She's been swimming like the dickens to try and catch up."

He and Loren played with the baby while Julia watched Poppy approach. It didn't take long for the experienced swimmer to close the gap.

"Did you get hot or something?" Julia asked.

"Or something." Poppy looked up at the face she had known would be there. "Wait for me and I'll help you get your diving gear on right."

The crew had moved a section of railing aside to lower a dive ladder and platform, and Julia studied Poppy's dripping body as she mounted the steps. She was wearing a navy one-piece suit that had only a small logo above her right breast for adornment. To Julia she was a little too muscular to be described as having a swimmer's body, but Poppy was well proportioned. Yet what came to mind wasn't how attractive Poppy was, but how much Julia wanted the comfort level between them to grow to the point that she could just walk up to her and touch her. The way her chest was heaving from the exertion and the water was rolling down her smooth contours made Julia want to help towel her off and keep her arms around her.

"Here, this might get your good mood back." Poppy unfastened a small bag tied to her wrist and handed it to Julia.

The bag didn't weigh very much, and its contents weren't really visible through the tight mesh. "It won't bite, will it?" The look Poppy gave her was balanced between humor and hurt. With a small groan, Julia said, "Don't look at me like that. You have to be familiar with Rayford's sense of humor."

As soon as Julia uttered the name, Poppy's eyes turned a little sad. Had theirs been just a casual acquaintance, she might have missed the expression Poppy tried to hide, but they were beyond that now. Regretting her thoughtlessness, she opened the bag and reached inside. Her fingers folded around Loren's lost glasses.

"That was sweet, thank you."

Poppy shrugged. "You just looked so upset."

"I figure until she's an adult and capable of making her own choices, I'll feel responsible for her actions."

"That's what I thought. I didn't want you to worry about that when you could be enjoying tonight. Nino and his gang really are a lot of fun, so why don't you return those to their owner and we'll get to it."

Julia wanted desperately for the light to come back into Poppy's eyes and her smile. She had killed her friend's good humor, and Julia recognized a little of what Poppy felt. Guilt was something that sucked the pleasure out of most things people in their position found enjoyable. But tonight wasn't the time for it, and Julia needed to find a way to let Poppy know that.

"Could I ask you to sit with me for a second before I get ready?"

"Julia, I love talking with you, but I really want you to see the wreck before the sun goes down." Poppy moved a step closer. "Wait, you aren't sick, are you?"

"No, I'm fine. Let's go. We'll talk later." Julia returned the glasses to Loren, then went down to the small platform to get ready. Poppy adjusted her gear before they took off, and with each nicety Julia's urge to cry grew.

"You ready?"

With her shoulders slumped, Julia nodded. She didn't trust her voice, and crying now would only embarrass her and further ruin Poppy's night. What she really wanted was not going to be attained on a dinner cruise, so she tried to push the sudden surge of emotions back, even if it took the proverbial plunger to do it. One day soon she would have to work up the courage to discuss the truth with Poppy. Until then, she would just have to act as if all she wanted from Poppy was friendship. Any dreams about a future together would have to be kept behind the door that fear kept locked.

Poppy didn't know what was wrong with Julia, but she was fairly certain you couldn't enjoy a snorkeling trip when your eyes were about to spill over with tears. Trying to convince herself Julia and Rayford's relationship wasn't any of her business wasn't working. Neither was trying to find reasons why Julia hardly spent time at home. If she could have one question answered, it would have to be: was Julia using her as an excuse to escape a bad situation?

She enjoyed Julia's company, but that didn't make her I.Q. drop dramatically. The woman had a story, but knowing all Julia's secrets might bring an end to their time together much sooner than Poppy wanted. If guilt kept a person from taking the path of regret, denial was the antidote that could keep it at bay for another day.

"How about we do something different?" Poppy took Julia's mask back before reaching down and removing their fins. When she stood up to hand the gear to one of the crew members, she caught Julia tilting her head back and blinking to clear her eyes.

"I'm sorry, Poppy. God, you must think I'm a total nutcase." The self-deprecating statement came out as a whisper as more tears fell. "Why don't you go without me?"

A crewman handed Poppy a life vest. She slipped it on but didn't snap it closed. Not expecting her offer to be refused, she slid into the water and held a hand up for Julia. When they were far away enough for privacy, she faced them toward the setting sun and enjoyed just holding Julia and floating with the help of the jacket.

"Honey, I don't know what's wrong," she said eventually. "If you think this is inappropriate, we'll head back to the boat and join the others."

Julia put her hands over Poppy's arms where they held her at the waist and squeezed so hard she thought she'd leave bruises. "No, I want to stay here with you."

"Relax, I'm not going to leave you." Poppy pulled her closer and tired to comfort her the only way she had available. "You don't have to tell me what's wrong unless you want to, but I want to help. Sometimes life seems unmanageable when you don't have someone you can talk to. I'm your friend, and I'll do whatever you need if you give me the chance."

"I can't, not yet."

"What I mean is if all you need is a shoulder to cry on, I'm here. Sometimes that's enough."

Julia turned around and buried her face in Poppy's neck. She cried past the sunset, and Poppy just held her and kept her afloat. She wasn't completely comfortable with how the evening was turning out and the position they were in, but she didn't have the fortitude to turn her back on the woman in her arms. The problem was, not having the guts to do it would later bring that much more heartache when she finally had to let go.

"Feel better?" asked Poppy. She felt Julia nod slightly as a few more sniffles escaped. "I'm glad you were comfortable enough to let me do this for you." Julia's head bowed so low her nose almost went under the water when Poppy pulled back enough to look at her. Despite the red swollen eyes she still looked beautiful under the full moon. "Don't be embarrassed. A good cry always helps. Take it from an expert on the subject."

"I wanted you to have fun with your friends tonight."

"I did have fun. I got to hold you and watch the sun go down from this great spot. I drove out to one of my favorite places earlier and shared that with you. That's a perfect day, if you ask me."

The joking tone of Poppy's voice made Julia smile, and she moved her arms from around Poppy's neck to around her waist. "I'll bet you can't wait to get rid of us, huh?"

"I could have sworn I said I wasn't going anywhere. You want to get something to eat? Nino's crew makes a mean grilled fish."

Julia squeezed Poppy before letting go. "I'm sure Tallulah's ready for me to get back, but I must look pretty scary."

"You look beautiful. A few tears can't change that."

"Thank you. That's a really sweet thing to say, even if it's not true." Julia decided it was no wonder the only way Carly left Poppy was by dying. Her bleak feeling faded a little more when Poppy took hold of her hand and started swimming toward the boat.

❖

"Here you go." Poppy put two plates down next to Julia, glad to see the depressed look gone from the pretty face. "Nino's famous fish special."

"Is it as good as yours?" asked Julia.

"Could be, I'll let you judge."

The spot Poppy had moved them to on the upper deck was deserted except for the three of them, thankfully. Water gently slapped the side of the boat as Nino sailed close enough to the shore for his passengers to be able to distinguish the outline of the resorts they were passing. Poppy relaxed back into her seat and started eating, not pushing Julia into any deep conversation.

When they were finished and one of the crew members had retrieved their plates, Julia leaned back and silently gazed in the opposite direction. In the distance were the lights off the Venezuelan coastline that had fueled her imagination since her arrival as she made up stories about individual homes. Would anyone ever look into the distance and see her home's lights, and wish their life were as idyllic?

At their feet, Tallulah sucked on her hand to entertain herself. From the main deck Nino had turned on the sound system, and light romantic music filtered through the strategically placed speakers all over the boat. He had remarked earlier that nights like this with just his friends on board were different from the usual cruises. People wanted to travel to places like Aruba to have a good time and be entertained, so on a typical trip his crew would have had the passengers doing the limbo by now.

Julia was happy to have missed out on the tourist experience. Although she'd been deep in thought since their meal, she was very aware of the warm body sitting close beside her. In the water it had been a dream to be held so lovingly by Poppy. Even through her small breakdown, she had tried to memorize the feeling of Poppy's skin. Julia sighed softly. The moment was gone, and there was no reason for Poppy to hold her again.

"Making wishes?" Poppy asked, her voice as mellow as Nino's music selection.

"Just trying to survive this embarrassing night, actually."

The big hand resting on Julia's shoulder came close to making her shiver. "If I cried over something that was bothering me, you would think less of me?"

Julia shook her head. "I'm just sorry all that came spilling out and we didn't get to go snorkeling. It wasn't my intention to ruin your time with your friends. They haven't seen you in a couple of years, have they?"

"Carly and I lived here for just over a year when I bought the Esmeralda, and people like Huey and Loren made us feel like part of the community. Most of these places are chain owned." Poppy pointed to the resorts they were sailing past. "People aren't used to having an actual owner here every day, making sure the knobs on the bathroom cabinets are straight. When Carly died I didn't want to be comforted by anyone so I stayed away from people."

Julia rested her hand over the one on her shoulder, offering what Poppy had just admitted she didn't want. "But why?"

"I really don't know how to answer that. She died, and I felt like it was my job to bring her home to New Orleans. Once I did, that's where I stayed. So in a long rambling answer, I haven't seen them in a while. The thing is, they're good people willing to wait for me to make up for my rude behavior. What I'm trying to say, Julia, is pain comes from blind corners sometimes and hits you so hard recovery seems like an unachievable notion. I lost the one woman I wanted to share my life with, and you…" Poppy lowered their hands and turned Julia to face her. "I can tell you carry your own share of hurt."

"It's just—" Maybe Julia could have found the words to follow that opening, but two callused fingers pressed against her lips, preventing her from going on. Poppy clearly intended that they enjoy each other's company longer.

"Let me finish, then you're free to either tell me whatever you want, or you can wait until you're more ready. As strong and victorious as pain seems, there is a cure or, should I say, a solution. Pick what you want, the one thing that'll bring you joy, and don't quit until it's sitting in the palm of your hand."

Julia looked down to their linked hands and felt a bolt of lightning run up her arm when Poppy's eyes dropped to the same sight. "What happens if I do that?"

"You find an ally to keep the wolves at bay. The darkness pain plummets your life into is no match for your heart when you find something to be happy about."

Strands of blond hair obscured Julia's face. "Thank you for telling me that and for being so patient."

A livelier song queued up, and Poppy decided to try and get Julia comfortable enough to join the others. "Would you say I was the one who brought you here tonight?"

When Julia looked up, her breathing hitched as long fingers brushed her hair back. "As sorry as you probably are over that fact, yes, you did."

"Oh, I'm not sorry. Actually I was thinking about your home state and the rules you told me about."

"Rules?"

"I brought you, Miss Julia, so that means you have to dance with me." Poppy tilted her head toward the dimly lit deck beside them. She figured a couple of twirls around the impromptu dance floor to the old rock song would bring Julia's smile back.

"I'd love to."

No sooner had Poppy helped Julia up, than Nino changed the mood again with a love song. If Julia had any second thoughts, Poppy couldn't tell as she walked her away from the bench and took her in her arms.

The blond head tucked under her chin smelled both citrusy and salty. The body pressed closely to hers felt like something she was having trouble finding words to describe, it was so good. Having Julia so close answered so many questions Poppy hadn't realized her heart was asking. Julia's hair was that soft, and the skin along her shoulder was just as pleasing to the touch.

Once again, Poppy recalled the dream she'd had earlier, and a new list of questions blossomed in her head, making her wonder if the next stage of her grief over Carly would be insanity. *Stop thinking about this girl's body and start thinking about her husband, the guy who's your employee. Remember him?* The reality was, Carly was gone and Julia belonged to someone else. Infidelity was not something Poppy wanted to be known for.

For Julia, she was willing to give Nino a thousand dollars if he played the song they were dancing to at least four more times. Poppy felt so good, and the big hands on her hips made her think about how she would react if they took to wandering. There was no time for any further fantasies when she heard the last moments of the song finally come.

As Poppy went to pull away, the hands on her shoulders tightened. "One more," Julia requested with her head tilted up, her eyes looking like summer grass in the moonlight.

Poppy looked at her date, because it was exactly what the night had turned into, and nodded. Agreeing meant she had blown the chance to stop what was happening between them, but how could she deny the small part of her heart that enjoyed the way those green eyes took her in. "Sure. It's not often I find such a great dance partner."

"You're in luck then, I'm a debutant," joked Julia, keeping her head tilted up so she could keep looking at Poppy.

"There were a lot of occasions in the Texas social season you got to dance with big gangly women, huh?"

"Nope, but that's my loss. Usually it was eager young men in tuxedos more interested in getting me out of my dress than in avoiding stepping on my feet. You're already leagues ahead by keeping those big hooves to yourself."

Feeling reckless Poppy leaned Julia over and dipped her. "If those were happier times for you I'll see what I can do."

"Trust me, you're doing great."

Nino brought them into the dock around midnight and extracted a promise from Poppy and Julia to come back so Poppy could sing to him. One of the crew carried their bags to the Jeep, leaving Poppy with the baby carrier in one hand and Julia's hand in the other.

"You had fun tonight?" asked Poppy.

"Despite my waterworks, I had a wonderful time."

"Good. We have time to come back here before the resort gets crazy with the opening, if you're interested, that is."

"I'll come back as often as you'd like." Feeling like she could now, Julia reached over and dragged Poppy's hand into her lap once they were in the Jeep.

Poppy smiled at the answer and the gesture before looking up to the full moon. *I hope this isn't a mistake.* She wished Carly did have some insight into the future.

CHAPTER THIRTEEN

As long as she'd been sailing, Poppy never got tired of hearing the snapping sound the sheets made when they caught the wind.

Near her, Julia stood at the wheel trying to remember all of Poppy's instructions as they cleared Aruba's coastline and headed into open water. The best part of her new duties was watching the muscles in Poppy's arms and back as she worked the mechanisms that lifted the sails. Another bonus was that she would be spending the next three hours with Poppy on a sea that looked like cool green glass.

"How's it going, Captain?" she asked.

Poppy dropped onto the bench behind Julia and twisted open a bottle of orange juice she'd fished out of the cooler. "Okay, now. The lifting is the hardest part so it's clear sailing from here on out." She offered the bottle to Julia. "Use that small strap to tie off, then you can sit if you want."

The bench Poppy was sitting on ran the length of the back curve of the *Piper's* stern, but Julia chose the cushion next to her. As she took her first sip of juice, Poppy's cell phone rang.

For a moment Poppy considered not answering, but it was Matlin, and they hadn't spoken in a while. By now, Poppy figured she and Sabrina had probably finished breakfast and were waiting for Lizzie to arrive so they could head to the airport. Poppy had surprised them with the gift of a vacation for their hard work on the Piquant project. They were leaving today.

Teasingly, she said, "Couldn't stand it anymore, could you?"

"We could be calling you to thank you for the very generous gift, you shit," answered Matlin.

"Is that any way to talk to your boss, I ask you?"

"You could've called to tell us how you're doing. We've been worried to death. Maybe that's why I called you a shit."

"Lizzie tells a different tale, Ms. Moore. You and Sabrina are too busy boozing it up on my liquor to be worried about me."

Julia heard the name Moore and started to move along the bench, away from Poppy. She was unsure how Matlin would react if she knew how much time they'd been spending together. Worse still, she had Matlin to thank for arranging that she could come to Carly's Sound in the first place. All she needed now was for her to tell Poppy the whole story.

Julia hadn't found the right time to explain everything herself, and she knew she had to stop putting it off. Her stomach bunched with tension, and she shifted again, but a familiar hand stopped her from moving any farther away.

Poppy drew Julia to her side as Matlin said, "Your note left explicit directions for us to booze it up so be quiet and tell me how you're doing before the enforcer gets out of the bathroom."

Poppy laughed and stretched her legs out. "I'm fine, don't worry. I have my sails full of wind and nowhere I have to be. How much better can life get?"

"It would be better if you weren't alone."

"Then mark your day complete. I'm not alone. I found some great sailing partners, and I'm introducing them to the concept of island hopping."

The bottle of juice was too small to hide behind so Julia guiltily opted for almost burying herself in Poppy's side.

Enjoying the feel of their bodies in close contact, Poppy draped an arm over her shoulders, lightly enough to let her escape if that's what she wanted.

"I'm glad you've decided to start talking to people again," Matlin said. "Or is it something to do with the girl I keep hearing about?"

"A little of both, so quit worrying and start thinking about what you're going to buy me for being so nice."

A flutter in the sails caught Poppy's attention, but instead of hanging up she asked Julia, "Do you know the rambunctious Matlin Moore?" Julia's face seemed to freeze for a split second, then she gave a nod. "Talk to her for a minute while I set us right. If not, you might find yourself stuck in Mexico with me when we wander off course."

"And that's a threat because…?" Julia laughed, confident her muttering had been swallowed by the wind. "Hey, Miss Matlin," she greeted the woman in New Orleans.

"Julia, you doing okay, sweetheart?" asked Matlin.

"I'm fine, but—" Julia started, only to be interrupted by Sabrina. Over the years Sabrina had accompanied Matlin to various events in Texas, and Julia had come to know them both as friends of the family. She had no idea if Matlin had told Sabrina about her supposed marriage to Rayford; she just hoped she wouldn't let anything slip to Poppy.

"No buts, darling. Just have fun and drag the brooder to as many spots as she'll take you. She only *looks* like a big idiot, but in reality Poppy's very astute to the needs of those she cares about. Everything will be fine."

"I sure want it to be."

"It will be, sweetie. And if she gives you any shit, we'll be there for the grand opening to knock her into shape."

Julia laughed. "I'll try and remember that." She heard Matlin's muffled voice telling Sabrina their ride had arrived so she got up and said, "Thanks, Sabrina. I'll hand you back to the skipper before you have to go."

Poppy took the phone, pleased to see Julia smiling. She had the impression her guest had been reticent about talking to Matlin at first.

"Double-teaming me, huh?" she asked Sabrina.

"You know us—the three musketeers here to bug you until the sun goes down." She hesitated. "Well, two of them, anyway. It's not the same without Carly…our lead troublemaker. You okay?"

"I'm great. Call me from Paris and we'll go over my wish list."

"You don't mind us calling you?"

"No. I love talking to you guys. So get to a phone somewhere between the wine and chasing men," teased Poppy.

"Forget about the men, honey. Do you think I could find one just like you in Europe? Maybe with a French accent. If I did, my chasing days would be over."

"You could try, but my mother swears she broke the mold after her first try at perfection."

"And women find you attractive with this ego?"

"Extremely," purred Poppy, raising the hair on Julia's neck. "Go have fun and don't forget to call. Every so often I worry about the two of you, as well."

"We love you," Matlin and Sabrina replied in unison.

"I love you too, and stay out of trouble. I don't want to be watching CNN and see you involved in some sort of international incident."

After their laughing good-bye, Poppy disconnected the call and scanned the horizon for a possible lunch site. The closest land was about an hour away, and she was in no hurry to get back. She was about to ask Julia if she had any time constraints when the baby monitor emitted a whine, sending Julia below to see what Tallulah needed.

"Is she all right?" Poppy called down after a few minutes.

Julia's head appeared at the entrance to the galley. "She's just hungry. Big surprise. It's kind of sunny, so I guess I'll feed her down here."

Reacting to the disappointment in her voice, Poppy offered a solution. "Want me to set up the tarp in the front?"

"Can you do that with the sails up?"

"They were coming down at lunch anyway, so what's a couple of hours. We can drift for a while, then eat on the boat. Sound good?"

"Sounds great since I'll have your company."

Julia returned to the sleeping compartment and lifted Tallulah out of the small padded playpen Poppy had gotten for the boat. Rocking her to quiet her, she felt the *Piper* bleed off speed when her sails dropped and could hear Poppy humming as she worked. She was about to head back up to the deck when she noticed a picture on the wall.

The shot was taken from the front tip of the boat, so parts of the sails were visible, as was the water the *Piper* was cutting through. If her wake was any indication, she was at full speed. That alone would have made a wonderful subject, but the photographer had only used it as a backdrop for the woman behind the wheel. Poppy's head was turned to the wind and her eyes were closed, but her expression spoke volumes. She was obviously indulging in the moment and the freedom she felt on the water.

"Changed your mind?" Poppy dropped down into the galley and seemed to fill up the room.

"Just admiring Carly's handiwork with a camera. This is a nice shot of you."

To have a picture of yourself hanging in your boat had always struck Poppy as egotistical, but Julia was only half right. Carly had mounted the photograph, but she hadn't taken it. To her own amazement she blushed.

"Actually, Elizabeth took it, not Carly. I should take the thing down. I forgot it was in here."

"No, leave it. She has a good eye. Of course it's hard to mess up when you're aiming at such a perfect subject."

"Maybe you've had too much sun if you believe that," said Poppy, trying not to let Julia's smile affect her too much. "I'm far from perfect, but I always give it my best shot."

Taking Tallulah from Julia, she headed up top, and with a final glance at the photo, Julia followed. She was finding the live subject infinitely more pleasurable to look at.

They settled on the cushions Poppy had put down at the helm beneath the sturdy tarp, and Poppy let the *Piper* drift, knowing there wasn't much to worry about in the way of reefs until they were close to land. She stretched out on her back and listened as Tallulah suckled.

"Tell us a story." Julia requested, reminded of the first time Poppy had taken them sailing, what seemed like years before.

"How about a song instead? I don't know that many stories." Poppy chose a Spanish song her mother had taught her, and unlike their first trip together, this time she watched as Julia fed the baby. There was something so beautiful about the way Julia cradled Tallulah and the way the baby opened and closed her hand.

For the first time since the Johnsons had come into Poppy's life, she felt bad for the young couple. Why wouldn't Rayford want to share fully in this part of his child's life, and did Julia regret she wasn't with a partner who wanted just that? Time, Poppy reflected, was a cruel, unforgiving bitch. It never gave second chances, so if you failed to act on something, the moment was lost forever. If Rayford continued to squander these times with his family, he was going to look up one day to find a teenager where his baby had been.

❖

"Hey. How are my two girls doing?" Rayford stood waiting on the pier as one of the porters tied off the *Piper*. "I missed you."

Surprised he'd even noticed they were gone, Julia said, "Hey.

What are you doing here?" She was standing close to Poppy at the back of the boat. As soon as the crew finished securing the lines, she handed Tallulah over to Poppy, then accepted Poppy's hand to assist her off the boat.

"I'm the welcoming committee. I thought I'd claim you and the kid for dinner before your social calendar gets any busier." He directed a quick glare at Poppy, then smirked. "The cooks are making a fish special in the restaurant tonight, and I thought you might be up for it."

"Chefs," Poppy corrected.

Rayford shrugged. "Whatever. If they cook they're called cooks where I come from, just like people who manage are called managers."

"At Valente Resorts, the staff members are called by their proper titles," Poppy shot back, trying not to sound as irritated as she felt.

Sensing Ray was about to dig himself into a hole, Julia gave him a warning look and spoke across the beginnings of his reply. "Dinner sounds good. Why don't you join us, Poppy?"

"No. I've taken up more than enough of your time, and I'm sure you and Rayford have a lot of catching up to do. Have fun."

It wasn't exactly a dismissal, but it came close. Dismayed, Julia feigned a casual smile and said, "Well, thanks again for taking us out. Tallulah always sleeps so well on the *Pied Piper*. Actually, I do too. It's so serene, being out there on the ocean with you."

Catching a puzzled look from her brother, she fell silent, realizing that she was only talking to delay the unavoidable parting.

"You're welcome aboard any time," Poppy replied. "I enjoy the… distraction."

The irony in her tone even made Rayford blink. Not knowing what else to say, Julia waved and forced herself to turn away and begin walking toward the golf cart Rayford had brought with him. It felt like a physical wrench.

As the cart was being loaded, she said, "Ray, your mouth is going to get you in trouble. You know that, don't you?"

"Who in the hell calls them chefs? Come on, Julia, that was just a put-down. I don't care if she is some kind of relative of the Valente family. I'm in charge around here, and I can't have underlings challenging my authority."

Julia rolled her eyes and held on tighter to Tallulah. "Is that what you learned in training?"

"Give me some credit, babe. I don't know what's up with that woman, but she seems to think there are special rules for her just because she's allowed to stay in the owner's bungalow."

Julia bit back a comment. Poppy had been very clear about wanting to keep a low profile around the people who didn't know her, Rayford included. How he could fail to guess her position amazed Julia, but he had always been determined to be right, and having decided Poppy was some kind of family hanger-on, he would be blind to anything that could contradict his theory.

"No one else here gets to spend every waking moment sailing around," he continued darkly. "I don't know what her responsibilities are meant to be, but I plan to find out."

With a sigh, Julia climbed aboard the cart. "Let it go, Ray. I'm sure you have more important things to do."

They had barely started moving when the Piper's engines started up and the porter threw the lines back on the deck. A part of Julia's heart wanted to plead for Poppy to stay just so she wouldn't be sailing away alone. Julia wasn't conceited enough to think she was Poppy's salvation, but she knew the time they spent together helped her forget her pain.

❖

Poppy spun the wheel once she'd cleared the mouth of the marina entrance and headed north. The wind made for a rougher ride, but was more suited for the *Piper's* ability. Though the fifty-foot yacht was big and comfortable, she was also built for speed. Poppy hadn't indulged in this kind of sailing since her arrival because of Julia's land legs and because it would be too much for Tallulah.

Carly had always loved fast sailing. She would stand right behind Poppy, who needed to watch the sails and their direction. She missed that weight pressed up against her back. She missed their adventures together. She missed having someone to share her life with. When Carly died she didn't just lose a lover, but a steadfast companion who was always ready for what came next. Not one time did Poppy ever remember suggesting something and having Carly turn her down.

Loneliness wasn't life threatening by any stretch, but it sapped motivation. Other people couldn't fill the black hole Carly had left behind, and Poppy hadn't felt like seeking human company anyway. Until Julia, it had been all she could do to allow someone into her personal space for short periods. She couldn't imagine wanting to spend entire days with anyone. As for picturing a future with another person—she hadn't wanted to. It had seemed inconceivable.

But not any more. Julia had dusted off more than Poppy's libido. Somehow she had infiltrated her imagination, making her daydream about the next tomorrow instead of dreading it. Poppy wasn't sure how she felt about that. Guilty and hopeful at the same time. Carly had urged her to live again and be happy. She was only thirty-three. Did she really want to be lonely for the rest of her life?

For a second, she almost turned the *Piper* around, picturing herself stalking to the Johnsons' bungalow, shoving Rayford out of her way, and leaving with his wife and daughter. She had a feeling there wouldn't be any protests from Julia. With a groan, she kept the yacht firmly headed north. If Julia wanted to end her marriage, that was a decision she had to make for herself. Poppy was not going to force the issue. She'd been there, done that, once already, and she had seen what it cost Carly to miss out on the life she should have had with all three of her children.

It had never been her intent to break up Carly's marriage, but after falling in love with her there was no way in hell she was going to just walk away and try to forget her. Falling in love had happened so fast, yet months had passed before Poppy figured out that's what she'd done. She didn't know if other people could pick a particular moment in time and say, "That's when I knew," a moment when you slapped your forehead and thought what an idiot you'd been for not figuring it out before—you were in love. For her, one night she looked at Carly and just knew.

She thought about Rayford, an aggravation she normally avoided. How could Julia be in love with a person like him, assuming she was? As far as Poppy could see, there was no chemistry and very little affection between them. Had they married because Julia was pregnant? Was it one of those unfortunate responses to a personal crisis, the kind with long-term consequences people don't think through properly? She'd wanted to ask Julia more about her situation, but every time she touched on it she got a prickly response. In the end, it was as if they'd reached an unspoken agreement to give the subject a wide berth and just enjoy the time they could steal away from their respective troubles.

Carly often used to tell her she overcomplicated life and got herself tangled in her own mixed emotions. Poppy had never been one to follow sets of directions, claiming they were for people with no common sense or imagination. She'd always been confident that she could work things out for herself, despite the occasional disaster like when she assembled sets of shelves, certain she knew what she was doing, and ended up with expensive firewood. Now, suddenly, she was not so certain any more. Losing Carly had sapped her confidence in some crucial way. She supposed feeling totally powerless to save the person she most loved had something to do with it.

She'd felt powerless in a different way watching Julia on the pier with her husband and their baby, powerless to escape her own anger and hurt. She was jealous. And frustrated that she had so little control over the things that really mattered. She had tried to be a friend to Julia, knowing it was futile to hope for more, but part of her had resisted. If Poppy were honest with herself, she knew Julia was an all-or-nothing proposition. Poppy didn't want a brief affair with a married woman, and she wondered if that was exactly what Julia was offering.

Bothered, she wiped salt spray from her face and wondered if she should leave before she did something she would regret. This place, more than any, made her ache for what she couldn't have. Perhaps that was why she found comfort in Julia and Tallulah. She craved touch and she missed being needed. They'd put an end to her two-year stupor, awakening feelings she thought were dead. For that she would always be thankful. And for that she owed Julia the space to make the right choices for herself and her baby.

She would stay long enough to open Carly's Sound because she'd promised Carly she would, but there was no reason for her to come back after that. She was ready to run her business again. There were people who depended on her, and Lizzie, Matlin, and Sabrina had carried her long enough.

Poppy gazed up at the white sails with the palm tree embroidered in the center, waiting for the change in wind currents when she rounded the western side of Carly's Sound. The ropes creaked from the sudden gust that propelled her forward, making the *Piper* seem like she was plowing through the water, her wake was so evident.

Her eyes were firmly planted on the horizon on the lookout for any dangers lurking in the water. The one thought she had as the wind blew hard enough to sting her face was that's how she would live the rest of her life. If you only looked ahead and took everything at neck-breaking speed, then maybe it would be easier to miss the things and people standing right next to you. Especially if it was something or someone you could never have.

❖

"Okay, who is she? I mean she walks around like she owns the place, but Miguel won't give me a straight answer. Every time I mention her stupid name, he just keeps telling me to leave it alone." Rayford picked up his third vodka tonic and took a healthy sip.

"You've been introduced. I don't know what else I can tell you. "

"I want to know who she is and what she's doing here, and I have a feeling you can tell me."

"She's taking it easy, I guess." Julia stayed vague, trying to respect Poppy's wishes.

"Does she answer to Matlin and Sabrina?"

"How would I know? We don't discuss work." Wanting to put an end to this line of questioning, Julia said, "Ray, don't make waves. You'll only draw attention to us, and we'll have a lot of explaining to do if people find out I'm not your wife. I don't think Valente Resorts offers to pay for sisters and nieces to tag along with their employees, do they?"

"Yeah, okay. But just because she's a Valente doesn't mean she's entitled to different treatment." Ray took a moment to pick anything remotely green from his appetizer. He was a steak-and-fries man. "She's on the payroll like everyone else."

Julia maintained a patient silence as he repeated himself some more, but the grumbling was only half-hearted. Rayford didn't want their deception out in the open; if anything, he cared more than Julia did about keeping up their facade. Both their father and Matlin had sold him on the idea that being a married man with a baby made him more employable to Valente Resorts because it suggested maturity and stability. Rayford seemed to like that idea, and he'd recently boasted to Julia about getting more respect because he was a family man.

Weary of him, and dismayed about Poppy's angry departure from the marina, Julia pushed her meal aside and said, "I'm tired, Ray, and I need to put Tallulah to bed."

"I'll walk you back." He glanced around, obviously disappointed to be leaving when the crowd was just getting more interesting. Several young women had entered the restaurant, and one waved flirtatiously at him.

"No, stay," Julia said. "I'll be fine."

"You don't mind?"

"It's an island. I don't think I'm in danger of getting lost on the way home." Julia lifted Tallulah out of the high chair the staff had provided.

She always enjoyed the slow walk to the far end of the island. It was like knowing a great gift was waiting at the end of the hall on Christmas day and lying in bed as long as possible to savor the anticipation. She took her time, enjoying the tropical foliage swaying in the breeze and trying to remember the names of the various plants and trees. When she reached her bungalow, she paused, Tallulah sound asleep on her shoulder. Common sense told her she should go inside and forget her idle fantasies. Even if Poppy knew Julia was not a married woman and forgave her for the deception, what difference would it make? Julia could tell she was still so raw from her loss, there was no room for anything more than the uncomplicated contact they had.

Her feet carried her along the familiar route to the last bungalow, stopping only when she turned the corner to stand in front of the porch. The house was dark and quiet. A soft breeze ruffled the wildflowers, but the rocker on the porch stood still. Julia looked out to sea. The *Piper* was tied to its buoy, so Poppy had to be home. Had she retreated inside to sulk? She didn't seem like the type. Something moved at the water's edge, and, in the moonlight, Julia saw Poppy sitting on the sand close to the water. She had released her ponytail, and her hair was blowing as gently as the flowers.

Julia climbed the steps to the porch and, confident Poppy wouldn't mind, let herself into the bungalow so she could put Tallulah to bed. When she returned to the porch, she hesitated for a few seconds, wondering if she should wait for Poppy or join her on the beach.

Hoping things between them would not be chilly and awkward, she strolled down through the trees and found Poppy spreading out a towel on the sand.

"Expecting me?" Julia teased.

"Can't blame a girl for hoping." Poppy sat down on the damp sand next to the towel and held up her hand to help Julia down.

"You don't want to share?" Julia invited quickly.

"My pants are already wet, so let's make sure the same doesn't happen to that great dress."

Smiling at the compliment, Julia got comfortable on the towel, leaning back with her hands resting in the sand, enjoying the breeze and Poppy's profile. "There's something I need to explain." She summoned the courage to be honest. About everything. "Rayford and I—"

"There's no need to explain." Poppy pressed two fingers to Julia's lips. She had no intention of becoming the confidante of a married woman with relationship issues. "Listen, Julia, I could weave some elaborate story here, but I'm going to be completely honest. After I dropped you off earlier, I tried not to think about you and Tallulah, but I missed you. I tried to imagine being here and not seeing you, but that wasn't very appealing."

"I would hate that," Julia said, her mouth still tingling even as Poppy's fingers fell away.

"But I can't keep taking up your days. You have your own life to lead."

The breeze picked up a little, and Julia sat up so she could push her hair out of her eyes with both hands. "Do I have any say in this, or do you get to decide for both of us?"

"I can see you're a woman who doesn't like to be argued with."

"I'm not arguing." Julia broke out in laughter, aware her voice had risen. "I guess it sounds that way, doesn't it?"

"How about you and I make a deal, Miss Julia?"

"As long as it doesn't involve asking me to go."

Poppy gave her a long look. "I'll be here every day. I have no expectations, so if you want to spend your time doing something else, you can."

"And if it's you I want to spend my time with?"

"All you have to do is turn that corner," Poppy gestured toward the bungalow, "and knock on my door."

Julia extended her hand. "Then we have a deal."

Poppy took the hand and held it. Not going with her gut would make it that much harder to walk away. But as long as Julia kept coming, she would never turn her down. "Maybe some time soon we can renegotiate the terms."

"You might find I drive a hard bargain when it's something I really want."

"Then you might find I'm a real pushover when it's something I want as well." Poppy turned her head to the water again, but Julia's hand stayed firmly in hers.

CHAPTER FOURTEEN

There's a big industry in books about the afterlife. I read some when I was dying. They tell you what to expect—the dark tunnel and the bright light, which sounds more like birth to me. A sense of well-being. Loved ones waiting. Impressive spiritual beings like angels.

Most of the books said love continues, but none of them said anything about anguish. I suppose I thought the sorrows and regrets of a lifetime would just drop magically away, leaving only the joys. I thought all my physical pain would vanish and I would float off on a cloud of bliss. It wasn't exactly like that. I remember leaving my body, but I took with me the incredible pain felt by those I left behind. It was so strong that peace has been an elusive reward for me.

Can we experience love without knowing pain? Probably not, but pain is never too high a price to pay for the rewards love brings. I hope my daughter figures that out one day.

Elizabeth was always a serious child, determined to achieve her goals. No small feat since she set her personal bar so high. Her reaction to my death was no different, and I watched as she spent hours at the Piquant trying to bury her grief under a crushing workload. The pain she was in made me ache for the little girl who would run to me so often during the day to show me some new wonder she'd discovered, like a four-leaf clover found after hours of searching in the yard.

My darling girl was never full of mischief, instead content to lose herself in a good tale. When I changed my life by following Poppy, it was the best thing that I could have done for the child who stole my heart. Poppy helped Lizzie lift her head up out of her books and showed her, as she showed me, what extraordinary women we are.

Now I watch Lizzie, and I want her to find once more that adventurous spirit Poppy brought alive in both of us. Sometimes I speak to her just before she falls asleep; I so badly want her to hear me. I want her to know that joy and love can still grow in the barren landscape of anguish she feels over losing me. That choosing happiness will bring her the courage to face whatever sorrow, strife, and hatred is thrown into her path.

Of all the times I have comforted my child and guided her, it's now she most needs me, and I can't bear for her to think I'm not here. I need to tell her, I'm here watching over her. And I'll be here when she finds the one who'll completely heal her heart. Just as I'm here for Poppy.

❖

Lizzie stared around her dark living room, feeling better that she'd talked herself into finally calling Poppy, and worse because there was no way to dress up bad news so it was easier to hear.

"Let me guess. Your father sued us and took all the assets?"

Lizzie laughed just enough to unclench her jaw. "It's not that bad, but still a big pain in the ass."

"I think I need a beer."

"Poppy, not everything in the world is cured with a beer. I'm trying to be serious here. We've got problems. The strike rumblings in Florida are getting louder. It's the high season and we just refurbished the golf course. We can't afford this right now."

Two muffled thumps from Poppy's end announced that she was on her way to the icebox. When she returned, she said, "Take off those toe killers you call shoes, go grab a cold one, and join me. The doctor is in."

Muttering beneath her breath, Lizzie carried the phone with her out to the refrigerator and selected a bottle of Abita Amber. "It's too many people to replace if they walk," she said, walking through the living room and out onto the patio. "Service is going to take a major hit. My only out will be to close off some of the rooms and amenities at the resort, and I don't want to do that."

"Lizzie, have you ever seen the Grand Canyon?"

"Is this story going to have anything to do with our problems?"

"None whatsoever. It's just a question."

"If I did, I was too young to remember it."

"Pull out that book you carry around all the time and pencil me in. I'm taking you."

"Are we opening a place there?"

"Lizzie, you know I love you, right?"

"Yes."

"Then I say this with love. You're becoming one of those people who gets avoided at parties. Relax, sweetheart. Not everything revolves around business. I want you to see it because it's so beautiful it'll make you cry. It will also show you that slow and methodical can pay off in a big way."

"What in the hell does that mean?" Lizzie set about pulling the label off the bottle. Just listening to Poppy's deep voice, she was already forgetting why she'd had such a bad day.

"The Colorado has flowed through there since forever, and it worked slowly away until it made something so beautiful countless painters and writers have tried to capture the beauty and spirit of the place ever since. I mean, way back when the cavemen called it the Dinky, only the river knew what it was capable of."

Lizzie choked on a mouthful of beer. "The Dinky?"

"Yeah. It was only a ditch back then. Carried maybe a couple of pebbles a day downstream."

"You're very disturbed—you know this, right?"

Not missing a beat, Poppy kept going. "So this is what we're going to do, Dinky. You're going to delegate this issue and allow a month for these people to discover how to be reasonable. In the end I'll step back like I always do and marvel at the beauty you create."

"It did have a moral after all. I should've learned by now."

"Remind me the next time I see you—I owe you a whack for doubting me."

"How's the vacation coming?"

The response intrigued Lizzie. Poppy rambled on for at least ten minutes. She hadn't been this talkative since Carly was diagnosed. By the time she trailed off, Lizzie could hardly wait to meet the Julia she'd now heard about from several parties. The woman had apparently worked a miracle. Her mind working overtime, she tuned back into the conversation and realized Poppy must be waiting for her to say something.

"Sounds wonderful," she said, thinking that would cover pretty much anything.

Poppy was silent for a few seconds, then she asked, "You going to be okay, honey?"

"I'll send someone, but if it doesn't work you have to come back and deal with it. They'll listen to you. They have no choice since you scream louder than any of us."

"Finish your beer, smart-ass, and I'll check in with you in a couple of days."

Lizzie tapped the phone against her chin and lifted her gaze to the moon. She felt better after talking to Poppy, but days like the one she'd just had made her aware of a niggling loneliness, of coming home to an empty house and having no one to share this view of the waning disk with.

"Mama, do you see the moon from where you are?" she asked aloud. She'd started doing that a few weeks after Carly died. "If you can hear me, I miss you. I went shoe shopping the other day, and the salesclerk thought I was having a meltdown when I started crying. But I just hated that there was sixty percent off and you were missing it. I bought a pair in your honor and gave them to a maid at the Piquant who wears your size." Lizzie took a deep breath, then finished her beer and stood up. "She wanted me to thank you. I love you, Mama."

She got as far as her back door when something in the wind stopped her. There was no movement, nobody there, but she had an overwhelming feeling that she was not alone. "Hello. Do you hear me?" she asked, her heart thumping loudly in her ears.

"I've heard you from the day the doctor told me you were coming. Death doesn't change that."

The answer came softly from somewhere, not exactly behind her or in front, but not inside her head either. The bottle dropped from Lizzie's hand and shattered into pieces on the old brick floor. Lizzie swung around. "Are you there, Mama?"

"I'm always here, Lizzie," the familiar voice continued. "You can't begin to know how sorry I am for leaving you, but I see you. You're my child—I won't ever leave you completely. I miss you too, Lizzie. Death may bring heaven, but there isn't anything like you there. I love you."

For once, the stillness of the night was broken by a breeze and the first drops of a cold rain, but Lizzie found herself unable to move. Dark wet spots started to appear on her business suit and before long she was drenched, but she didn't feel the cold. There were no trumpets and no angels to announce what had just happened and to prove what she knew.

"Thank you, Mama," she said, and the downpour stopped suddenly.

With it went Carly.

❖

Two strange things made Poppy wake up. The smell of bacon was wafting out of her kitchen, and her hand was resting on naked skin.

Soft blond fuzz tickled her chin and her throat, which Tallulah was using as a pillow. For some reason the baby was dressed only in a diaper, and Poppy felt a wet spot on her chest where a towel clung damply.

"Thank God you live on a friendly island, Valente," Julia said from the side of the bed. "Tallulah and I were having breakfast in here, and she lost hers on your chest. I did my best to clean you up."

"Somebody threw up on me and I slept through it?"

"Evidently. How about an omelet to make up for it?"

The soft baby skin under her palm was almost too nice to give up, but food sounded good. "Think she's asleep enough for bed?"

"You don't mind me letting her sleep here, do you?" Julia asked.

Showing a proficiency that belied the childless status of her life, Poppy sat up without disturbing Tallulah from her spot. "Eventually one of us has to answer some of these questions. I'll go first. I'd love an omelet, especially with bacon, and I don't mind this precious kid being near me or in my arms one bit. She smells better than I do, though, so do I have time for a shower?"

"Sure. I'm still crumbling bacon for the eggs."

Julia was humming as she mixed the ingredients for a western omelet, when there was a knock at the front door and Julia opened it to find one of the porters holding a large, colorfully wrapped box under his arm. Julia asked him to wait for Poppy, but he insisted she take the gift and left before she could find money for a tip.

"You don't have to wait for me." Poppy padded into the room, wrapped in a thick robe, her big smile topped off by a wet head.

"Why would I be getting a gift?"

"Because Valente Resorts missed your birthday last year, and we want to make up for it."

"Poppy, you didn't know me last year." Julia knew her scolding tone and the hands she planted on her hips would be more convincing if she could drag her eyes off the box.

"How about we consider it a down payment on this year's?"

"You didn't have to, but thank you."

Julia went on a tearing binge. When she was done even the bow was in tatters, and she was left with a plain brown box. No store name, no insignia or markings to give any clue as to what was inside. She slowed down to savor the surprise.

"What is it?"

"Open it and I'll tell you," teased Poppy. "Go on. I promise it won't bite."

Julia slowly slid a finger under the edge of the box and popped the tape that held it closed. Poppy couldn't help but notice her diamond ring and wedding band, and was reminded of the day she was given her own. From the moment Carly slipped it past her knuckle, Poppy had seldom removed it.

One of the most painful things she'd lived through was having Carly's rings handed to her before the funeral director began preparing the body for cremation. Poppy had never come so close to physically striking someone for simply doing his job. The rings he seemed so casually to drop in her hand symbolized something too precious to be checked off as inventory delivered to the bereaved.

After that, Poppy had never felt the same about the plain band Carly had given her. Somehow it represented the sense of belonging lost to her forever.

"Should I read the card first?" Julia extracted a plain white envelope from the tissue paper that concealed the contents of the box.

"The suspense isn't killing you?"

Julia's only response was a delighted giggle. Resting the box on her lap, she pulled the card out. The handwriting was a good reflection of its owner, the pen strokes not exactly neat but readable: *To help you feel like you're home. Poppy.*

Julia lifted the tissue away and emitted a small gasp as she saw the carving she'd fallen in love with. Tears made her lower her head.

"You like it, right?" Poppy asked, trying to catch her eye.

Julia nodded but her focus stayed on the gift. "You shouldn't have."

"Just call it bribery. I thought if you liked it enough, you might want to stay."

"I want to stay even without this, but thank you." Julia moved to Poppy's side and decided she loved it there and that leaving was not an option.

❖

For the next two months, Poppy showed Julia all the sights that made this part of the globe so popular, and without realizing it at first, she also showed Julia parts of her heart. The days melted one into the other and the small intimacies between them grew, but neither woman acted on them. Poppy stuck to her plan to let Julia make her own decisions in her own time, but Julia didn't seem ready to make them.

Sometimes Poppy was confused by the mixed messages she picked up on. Julia seemed to relish physical affection and Poppy sensed an invitation to go further, yet Julia said nothing about changing her living situation and avoided talking about the future. Poppy took that to mean she wasn't included in it.

She rationalized that she could deal with that. She had plenty else to think about. Almost without her realizing it, Lizzie had eased her into taking over the reins of Valente Resorts once more. On one of their last evenings together before the management team was due to arrive on Carly's Sound, they cooked dinner, then sat on the beach to watch the spectacular sunset.

"Well, it's back to the real world soon," Poppy said. "I hope you don't forget about me once you have more people to talk to. I've really enjoyed spending my time-out with you."

"I have been where I've most wanted to be," said Julia softly.

They watched in silence as the sun made its final plunge into the water and the night sky illuminated with a billion stars. The moonlight had turned Julia's hair almost golden, and Poppy had a sudden urge to run her fingers through it to see if it was as soft as it looked right at that moment.

Julia placed her palm on Poppy's cheek. "Promise me you'll set aside some time to spend with us after all the commotion starts?"

"I promise." Poppy leaned into the touch. "We only have a short time before the first guests arrive for the opening, but I promise things between us won't change."

The phone beside her rang again, foretelling the million little problems that every opening seemed to stir up, and Poppy sighed before answering. Julia turned her attention to Tallulah as she started to fuss, wanting her evening meal.

With Poppy so focused on her phone conversation, Julia whispered her dilemma to the only audience available to her, "Yeah, Tallulah, Mommy's in deep and doesn't have a clue what to do next."

CHAPTER FIFTEEN

Poppy laughed when Lizzie stepped out of their private jet in a pair of old shorts and a T-shirt. "That can't be the big kahuna of Valente Resorts, can it? I thought the Armani business suit was part of your physical makeup."

"Shut up and hug me, you big goon." Lizzie almost skipped to Poppy and threw herself into the welcoming arms. "I missed you so much."

"Me too, squirt." Poppy released her and greeted Susanna, then helped Bob load the two women's bags into the jeep that would take them to the *Piper*.

Neither was a stranger to the yacht, having sailed with Poppy and Carly. Once the sails were up and their course was set, they talked about business, if only to get it out of the way. The Florida situation seemed to have reached a stalemate over the past weeks, and Poppy feared it was about to rob her of the options she wanted to keep open just as death had robbed her of Carly. She wasn't ready to leave Carly's Sound yet; she was afraid she would never see Julia again if she did.

Lately, she'd realized Julia was trying to find the courage to talk with her about something. She'd made a couple of false starts, then changed the subject. Poppy had been keeping a close eye on the Johnsons and had observed a distance between them that made it clear their marriage was on paper only. They didn't sleep together. She knew that much from the housekeeping staff, who gossiped about these incomprehensible domestic arrangements. And Rayford blatantly flirted with any pretty young woman who crossed his path.

Poppy wasn't sure what Julia was waiting for and wondered if she felt stuck because she was financially dependent and had a child. Poppy had been tempted to come right out and tell her money was the last thing she needed to worry about. But offering an escape route was a form of interference, so she remained silent, keeping faith with her pledge to keep out of the situation. If Julia was going to end her marriage, the decision had to be hers alone. Over the past two months, Poppy had had plenty of time to think about what she wanted, and one thing was certain: she did not want to be the default choice of a woman who felt stuck and just wanted to run away from her problems.

Julia could stay on Carly's Sound indefinitely as far as Poppy was concerned, regardless of what happened, or didn't, between them. But she had the impression that Julia would never ask that of her. If Julia decided to change her life, Poppy suspected she would return to her grandmother to lick her wounds.

The thought of saying good-bye to her and Tallulah made her queasy. It was getting more difficult by the day to spend time with Julia who, no matter where they were or what they were doing, somehow ended up practically on top of her. Lots of personal space had never been an issue for Poppy, and obviously it wasn't for Julia either. Poppy never turned down her affection; in fact, she was starting to expect it. Their physical closeness had come as quite a revelation, making it clear to her that, given the right woman, her life could be full once more. Just months before, she could not have imagined this, but now she could easily see herself waking up with Julia for the rest of her days and building a family with her.

Hiding how much she'd started to want that was becoming exceedingly difficult. Poppy had always looked beyond the superficial and found beauty in all people. Julia was no exception. Poppy had been attracted by the kind of person she was, more than what she looked like. Yet there was no denying her increasing preoccupation with Julia's body.

With her eyes closed, Poppy could describe her figure, her face, the exact shade of blond her hair was, and just how green her eyes were. She knew Julia's smell, the texture of her skin, the feel of her firm curves. Her unconscious sensuality teased Poppy constantly, awakening yearnings that had slept for two years.

That's what didn't compute with Rayford. He had in his bungalow one of the most desirable women Poppy had ever laid eyes on, yet he saw everyone but her. Poppy had no qualms about admitting it would be quite the opposite if Julia was in *her* bed; the rest of the world would be invisible.

Poppy forced her attention back to the knotty subject of the crew in Florida. "So, you're saying they turned down the offer?"

"I think we should close the place for the rest of the season," Lizzie said flatly. "I don't want to give them the satisfaction of seeing us lose money, but they're working my last nerve with their demands."

"It must be bad, if you're ready to give up. That's not like you, Lizzie."

"Yeah, well, I'm all for fair employee compensation, but these people basically want to stay home and watch television, all for a really nice salary." She accepted a beer from Susanna and patted the cushion next to her so the assistant would take a seat. "It's been a rough couple of weeks. I was past ready to lock my office door and come out here. Speaking of arriving, have Matlin and Sabrina turned up yet?"

"They'll be checking in now, I think." Poppy glanced at her wristwatch. "Miguel called just before you two arrived. He was hoping to talk them into shopping in Aruba for a while, then taking one of the moonlight shuttles to Carly's Sound, but I don't think much of his chances."

"I'll have to tell him to relax. They had a great time in Paris and have been busy in Cancun with the CarMaSa's spa renovations for the last month. I'm sure that means they've been in there every day making sure the massages are given with just the right amount of firmness."

"No amount of massaging is going to mellow those two out enough to not give Mickey a hard time." She turned the wheel a little to keep them on course before tying off and sitting farther down from them. "I think he's still suffering from post-traumatic shock from the opening of that place."

After their first three resorts had started to turn a profit, Poppy had returned to Cancun and purchased a more upscale resort farther down the beach. The CarMaSa was a tribute to the three women who had been such an influence in her life.

"Mom was the only one who could keep them on a short leash, so make sure you don't let them mess with him too much. Speaking of, is he ready for the first wave of guests?" Lizzie asked. "When I told him we'd printed the wrong date on one batch of the invitations, he thought I was kidding."

"Don't sweat it. He was ready a month ago. How'd that happen, by the way? I know you two better than to let stuff like that slip past you."

Lizzie tapped Susanna on the shoulder, and both women stood as the outline of the island came into sight. "No one's 'fessing up," she told Poppy. "But I reviewed the stuff that went to print. It's like the machine reset itself."

"Let's hope that's the only thing that goes wrong." Poppy regretted the words as soon as they left her lips. Saying stuff like that only painted a target on your forehead for fate to take potshots at you.

❖

By six that evening the pool area was full, and the staff was doing an admirable job of keeping up with requests. Poppy was always slightly on edge when a new Valente resort opened; so much could go wrong. But even Rayford seemed to have a sense of the occasion and had lifted his game, staying at the front desk most of the day and ensuring all the guests were well situated. He almost seemed to be enjoying himself. If Poppy didn't know better, she might have thought he was growing into his role. He had escorted Julia and Tallulah to one of the poolside tables, to sit with Sabrina and Matlin, who were sampling cocktails for their inevitable critique of the bartender's skills. They'd been joined by Lizzie and Susanna, and Poppy gave all five women a big smile as she sat down on the stool Miguel had readied for her.

"Good evening, ladies and gentleman, and welcome to Carly's Sound," she said, and took a moment to get comfortable.

As she had all the other times she'd stood in front of a live audience, she let the first song that popped into her head flow out through her fingers. Once she got started, audience requests would dictate her selections, but this was a song she hadn't played in years. It seemed appropriate, since it was dedicated to Sabrina and Matlin, and to Carly. The lyrics spoke of friendship, love, and the passing of time, and Poppy could see the women knew she was strumming the tune for them.

After the opening, she looked toward their table once more and felt happy to see them again and to see they were making Julia welcome. She headed into the next verse and felt a familiar weight settle against her back, as Carly took the place she'd taken so many times before when Poppy was singing her a love song. With a small, private grin, Poppy recalled how often she'd skipped notes over the years, when Carly stood there and let loose her wandering hands.

She closed her eyes and enjoyed a trip back to the past, to other openings that had made for great celebrations with friends and family. Most were already on Carly's Sound, thanks to Lizzie's problem with the dates on the invitations. The only people missing would be present, Poppy was sure, for the official grand opening the following week. But for now, she was enjoying sharing the moment with the woman she had built this for. It made no difference whether Carly was attending in the flesh or not.

She finished playing to strong applause, then launched into some livelier songs. Two hours later, her voice was a little raspier, and the people listening were a lot drunker. Some of them knew who had been entertaining them and slapped Poppy on the back as she made her way to Julia's table.

"Hotter than a Rolex in a pawn shop, ain't she?" Matlin leaned over and whispered in the young woman's ear.

Julia's adoring looks as Poppy sang hadn't escaped Matlin, who exchanged another look with Lizzie as Julia blushed over the comment.

Poppy stopped behind the only empty chair and bowed deeply at the waist. "Good to see you back from your travels. No calls for bail money, no serious hits to foreign relations…congratulations."

Sabrina laughed. "We're so good at foreign relations, the government should hire us, baby. But never mind about that now. You must've done something remarkable in your last life, girl, to get all this wonderful karma. No one gets to be this good-looking, talented, and charming unless they were burned at the stake or something. Come over here and give us both a hug."

As Poppy obliged, aware all the time of Julia's soft, intent gaze, Matlin asked Lizzie, "Where've you been hiding Poppy all day?"

"She's been screaming at the head of yard maintenance in Florida. I'm sure telling him where she was going to put his rake didn't help contract negotiations, but it made me feel better."

"On that subject, I have a conference call in twenty minutes, so you can tell me later how Europe was," Poppy said. "We're making progress with the Fort Lauderdale location, so I have to run." She cut off any impending complaints by hugging and kissing Sabrina and Matlin again.

As she was about to leave, Rayford walked up and put his hands possessively on Julia's shoulders. "How are my girls doing?"

Before Julia could reply, he swept a glance around the other women seated at the table and asked Poppy, "Don't you have something to do? As you can see by the arrival of guests, playtime is over. Get back to work."

Poppy caught the beginnings of a response from Matlin, but silenced her with a look. Coldly, she said, "Sorry, Mr. Johnson. How careless of me to be goofing off on the company clock."

She knew the thinly veiled hostility between them was obvious and hadn't missed the amused looks her friends exchanged. But she didn't want to make Julia feel any more uncomfortable than she already looked, so she refrained from putting Rayford in his place. With a wave, she made her way around the table and stalked off toward the employees' quarters.

Dismayed, Julia got to her feet. She felt like slapping her brother. "Ray, I keep warning you about that mouth of yours." Taking hold of Tallulah's stroller, she excused herself and followed the path Poppy had taken.

Lizzie was also out of her chair, about to go after Poppy, when Susanna held her back. "Not this time, Lizzie."

"But," Lizzie looked down to the hand on her wrist but didn't attempt to break the hold, "Poppy might need—"

"She knows what she needs. She's a big girl. I know you love her, but sometimes it's best to let her fight her own battles."

❖

When Julia got to the last bungalow there was no sign of Poppy anywhere outside, but the door was open, and when her soft knock went unanswered, she entered, carrying Tallulah. The sound of Poppy's voice led her to the office, where Poppy was sitting back in her chair with her eyes closed and her feet propped up on the desk, talking on the phone. The fingers holding the receiver were white with tension, and she looked beyond aggravated.

Hearing someone come in, Poppy said, "Hold it, Rory." She put her hand over the receiver and looked over at her visitors. "What can I do for you, ladies?"

She hadn't been able to inject any humor into her tone, and the hurt look on Julia's face stopped her from making any more stupid comments. She hated the way Rayford had handled Julia, but that was no reason to take it out on her.

"I'll come back later. I'm interrupting." Julia started to back out.

"Wait," Poppy said quickly. "I'm sorry. I didn't mean to snap. Why don't you go and rock the half-pint, and I'll be out in a minute. I've still got labor problems in Florida, and I want to see if I can solve them over the phone and not have to fly there to knock heads."

"Okay." Julia returned to the porch and rocked Tallulah until she fell asleep, then went indoors and put her down on the blanket Poppy now kept on the floor.

She watched her daughter for a moment, marveling at the changes in her. Tallulah would be eight months old soon. Her pale blond hair had filled in some, but not by much. Poppy had bought her an assortment of hats for when they were outside, and Tallulah now liked to take them off and throw them on the floor. No matter how many times she did this, Poppy was always there to pick up after her. Lately they'd had to be careful about leaving her on Poppy's floor for her naps, as she was rolling and trying to crawl.

The thing Julia was going to miss most, with the rapid changes in Tallulah, was breast-feeding. But Poppy was making that transition easier without even knowing it. She loved to participate in Tallulah's meal experiments, coaxing her to try the new baby foods Julia had started her on. Poppy's deep belly laugh usually meant she'd discovered something Tallulah refused to eat and was now wearing it on her shirt and in her hair.

Poppy might not have been there for Tallulah's birth, but she had taken such an active role in caring for her since they'd met that Julia no longer felt alone as a parent. She had no idea how she would do without her if their friendship ended.

With a sigh, she walked back outdoors. She felt sick with anticipation but also deeply content, knowing that Poppy was just a few feet away and would soon be with her. The day had been torturous until she saw Poppy walk out to the pool deck and smile at her. As the official opening event drew closer, Poppy had been increasingly preoccupied with work and with the problems in Florida. Julia tried to stay away, to give her some space, but a large part of her heart craved being in Poppy's presence, and she found it almost impossible to spend a whole day apart from her.

It had nothing to do with their talks or Poppy's generosity, but with the intimacy they seemed to share without words or touch. Julia thought about the woman in white, who had delivered the fish all those weeks ago. Her words hadn't made sense then, but they did now.

Ain't no changing your fate…ain't no sense fightin' it. Just go with what's written in the stars and don't run away from your heart.

Julia had tried to see Poppy that morning, wanting to talk with her. There was so much to say. It was time to tell Poppy she was not married and to talk about the future. But the bungalow had been empty, and there was no sign of her at any of the other times Julia had come looking.

❖

Behind her, the screen door started to open and Julia turned around. Acting on the advice of someone whose name she didn't even know, she walked into the bungalow and into Poppy's arms. She leaned against the tall, strong form and allowed herself the bliss of feeling completely safe and knowing this was where she belonged. She wanted to be held by this woman, to feel their bodies molded together. She had dreamed about it since the night Poppy had held her in the water off the coast of Aruba.

As if Poppy knew exactly what she needed she tightened her arms, and Julia felt her heart speed up. The feeling was so right, she didn't understand the tears that suddenly streamed down her face. Before she could stop herself, she was crying hysterically, clinging to Poppy, feeling as if she would die if Poppy let her go or sent her away.

Poppy didn't let go of Julia, but a war was going on in her head. She wondered how she could be so happy to finally get Julia this close again, but so angry at the same time. Julia belonged to someone else, and whatever was going on between them, he still acted like he owned her. Poppy put her jealousy aside and just held the crying woman and provided the only comfort she could. For the first time in two years, she wasn't thinking about Carly, the pain, or anything beyond the moment.

She soothed the woman who had two fists full of her shirt and rubbed Julia's back in a soothing motion.

As her tears ebbed, Julia allowed her hands to slide up Poppy's back, linking them lightly behind her neck. She pulled down gently, trying to get Poppy to bend a little so her lips were within reach.

Poppy stiffened at the action. She knew if she gave in she'd be lost, and it could only end badly. Either she would have an affair with a married woman that would end in heartbreak, or Julia was just experimenting and would get cold feet. Or perhaps Julia really was in the process of discovering herself as a lesbian. If something happened between them, she might rush into making decisions she'd been avoiding. Did Poppy really want to cause a messy marriage breakup right in the middle of the opening celebrations for the resort?

Teary green eyes looked up at her and a gentle hand caressed her neck. Julia asked, "Please?"

Taking Julia's face between her hands, Poppy stared into her eyes, and her mind flashed to the only other times she'd felt such emotion tug at her. A warm night under an oak in New Orleans, the first time she'd kissed Carly. The day she'd signed the contract to buy her first resort. She knew the universe briefly presented opportunities and that success or failure depended on making the right life-changing decisions.

This time the decision seemed to make itself, and she knew it was right at the first touch of Julia's soft, yielding lips. Poppy meant the kiss to be brief, a short kiss between friends who were perhaps something a little more. But her heart betrayed her. She slid her hand to Julia's hips and drew her closer. The way her body felt, her caressing hands, the plea in her eyes stirred Poppy's passionate inner self to life. Everything about her and what they were sharing seemed so right.

Yet Poppy's doubts lingered. Julia was still married and probably straight. It just wasn't realistic to imagine a future with this woman, and Poppy felt almost cheated at having been shown a glimpse to begin with. *You can live your whole life happier not knowing some things. Ignorance is truly bliss*, she thought as she eased back slightly and leaned her forehead against Julia's.

"What's wrong? Didn't you like this?" The neck under Julia's hands felt tight with tension, but at least Poppy wasn't moving away from her.

"Yes, I like it very much, and I like you very much, but we can't do this. It's wrong. Don't you see that? I won't go through this kind of thing again." Poppy's statement sounded so final.

"But…" It was the pictures that sucked the air from her lungs. There in every frame was the perfect woman who had given Poppy the perfect life and the perfect love. She couldn't possibly compete with that. She had been crazy to imagine she could.

"Of course, I'm sorry. I didn't think." Her lip trembled, and she felt like she was trying to keep her head above the hopelessness about to swamp her. Blinded by tears, she broke away from Poppy and walked indoors.

"Julia, please wait." Poppy followed her and stood a few feet away as Julia struggled to pick up Tallulah. "I don't want you to go. I want you to understand why this is wrong."

Julia shook her head. "No, don't say anything. I just thought…" She tried to find the right words. "Never mind. It doesn't matter. I just have to go."

The pain of watching the two of them leave was so bad Poppy had to lean against the doorjamb to stay upright. She knew they needed to talk about what had just happened between them, but her feet stayed glued to the floor. Julia looked back at her one last time, and there was a finality to the lost, hurt look on her face that made Poppy feel sick. As she heard the screen door close, her knees gave way, and she slid down and struggled to draw air into her lungs. Then she was sobbing.

She had no idea how long she sat there before she felt Carly's hands on her shoulders.

"Honey, you have to get up and go after her." The grip tightened. "If you want a chance at life I'm begging you to get up and find her."

"But she left."

"Because she's as confused as you are. But she wants a life with you. I know she does."

"No." For the first time since Carly had come back, Poppy turned away from her. "I won't go through that again."

"What are you talking about?"

"It doesn't matter what I want. She's gone and it's for the best. If I give in to what I want, it'll only prove him right."

"Make who right?"

"Thomas." The name came out with every bit of venom Poppy felt for him. "He said I make a habit of running off with things that don't belong to me. Julia doesn't belong to me. You belonged to me and you left me. I ended up with what? Money and a pile of real estate. Who cares?"

"How can I finally put it to make you understand?" Carly struck a familiar pose with one hand on her hip and the other pointing at Poppy. "When I was really young, I met a man who seemed to genuinely care about me and seemed to want to share a life with me. All that ended the minute we said 'I do.'"

"It's done, Carly, and because of what I did, we all got punished for it."

"Poppy, I love you, but I swear you're an idiot at times."

In spite of how she felt, Poppy laughed. "Thanks."

"Well, you are." Carly looked at the pictures along the piano top. "If, after we had gotten together, I treated you like shit and didn't give you another thought, would you have stayed with me?"

"But you didn't."

Carly grabbed the sides of her head like she was trying to prevent a scream from bursting out. "Work with me here, Valente, before you waste too much time. Would you have stayed?"

"No."

"Then why make me feel guilty for following my heart? That's what I did when I chose you over what I'd had before. You never pushed or pressured, and you even offered to let me go—remember our first Christmas together?" Carly's voice softened as she dropped to her knees to face Poppy. "The heavens didn't punish you by giving me cancer. That was my fate and mine alone. If I'd been able, I would've changed it, but some things are beyond control. You gave me eleven wonderful years. Not one day felt squandered." She cupped Poppy's face in her hands. "I felt like the most cherished woman alive, and I never once doubted how you felt about me."

"I love you so much."

"I love you too, enough to want to give you more than you ever gave me." Carly pressed her lips to Poppy's. "Julia took a huge chance when she kissed you, and I saw how you responded."

Poppy dropped her gaze, guiltily conscious that Carly's kiss didn't make her lips tingle the way Julia's had. "I just can't."

Carly made a frustrated noise that was loud enough to be heard by anyone within a mile's radius. "You can and you will, even if I have to carry you over there and move your lips for you to get you to talk to her."

"I'm scared, Carly. There, are you satisfied?"

"The young woman I fell in love with and shared my life with wouldn't hide behind fear. Even if you do, will it change what you feel for her? Do you think it'll change how she feels for you? Like I said, I've been on the receiving end of your kisses, and you were kissing her like you meant it. Look me in the eye and tell me I'm wrong."

"Just because I feel something, doesn't make it right."

"Sweetheart, the night in the park when we first kissed, did you put a lot of thought into it, or did you just go with your heart?"

"I thought about it for weeks, but when you looked up at me, I stopped thinking and just kissed you."

Carly pressed her hand over Poppy's heart. "Trust me, honey, stop thinking and start acting. It's been the secret of your success, and this is no time to start messing with a proven formula."

Poppy allowed the words to sink in for a moment, then brought up an uncertainty she'd tried to bury. "I'm not sure what she sees in me. She doesn't seem the materialistic type…"

Carly heaved a long-suffering sigh. "She sees exactly what I saw from the beginning, and it isn't the trappings of your wealth. The money and the places you own don't define you—they never did. It's who you are inside that keeps that beautiful young woman coming back every day."

Poppy wanted to believe it was that simple, but Julia really was beautiful, the kind of woman who could have anyone. Poppy was a thirty-three-year-old with issues. Hardly a catch. She let her eyes rest on Carly's face, studying every line and angle. It had always been, for her, the definition of beauty, and no matter what happened in her future, Carly's image would be etched into her heart forever. Neither time nor new love would erase it.

Her silence seemed to spur Carly on. "What I mean is, your business success didn't change you. You are still humble and sincere. I always found that so attractive about you. Of all the memories of you I carry with me, one I really treasure is that you never seemed embarrassed to show your pleasure in something. Do you know what a gift that is?"

"You make me sound like the village idiot."

"Quite the opposite, my love." Carly studied her tenderly. "You want her, don't you?"

Placed on the spot by the woman she would always love, and would trust with her life, Poppy could only answer with complete honesty. "Yes."

"Then tell her how you feel." Carly pointed to the door. "Go on, tell her."

❖

Poppy took Carly's advice and went in search of Julia. The Johnson bungalow was in darkness when she reached it, and she thumped on the door. "Julia, we need to talk. Are you there?"

Silence greeted her, but she hesitated to knock again in case Tallulah was asleep. Instead she walked around the house, trying to see in the windows. It looked like no one was home, but she couldn't make out much in the darkness.

As she started toward the front again, she heard the sound of keys rattling and quickly darted into some dense foliage. From her vantage point, she saw Rayford stroll to the front door; his hair was untidy and his clothing rumpled. Picturing him dancing with some cutie, humiliating Julia behind her back, Poppy had to grip a tree branch to prevent herself striding out there and sacking him on the spot.

She couldn't do that to Julia. No amount of wishing was going to make Rayford disappear. Carly could say all she liked about what Julia truly wanted, but the woman had not left her husband and wasn't even talking about doing so. What did that say about who was most important to her?

When they'd kissed, Julia could have said something. If she thought she was a lesbian and planned to leave her husband, surely that was the time to say so. It just didn't add up. There had to be something about him Julia loved—why else would she remain with him? Was she deluding herself that she could ride it out through a bad patch and make it work? Was Poppy a convenient distraction—someone she could get emotional goodies from, making it easier to endure a lousy marriage?

As far as Poppy was concerned, Rayford was an idiot for alienating a woman like Julia, but she could not in good conscience go behind his back. Neither would she run after a woman who didn't want her enough to make the kind of choice Carly had made, of her own volition.

Poppy turned away from the bungalow and strode in the other direction. If Julia wanted her the way Carly claimed she did, Poppy would need to see some proof before she put her heart on the line. She was too raw to expose herself to any more pain.

CHAPTER SIXTEEN

Matlin ran her finger along the bottom of a small foot, making Tallulah beam with a big smile that was a carbon copy of Julia's. "She looks so much like you."

"Thank you. I've loved sharing her with Poppy. We'll really miss her."

Sabrina reached over and hugged Julia, trying to stop the flood of emotions before Julia started crying again. She and Matlin had been on their way to Poppy's bungalow when they saw Julia rush out the front door, crying just as much as the baby in her arms.

"What do you suppose Poppy did to her?" Sabrina had asked.

"Don't go jumping to conclusions there, Madame Butterfly. This could just be a case of hormones," said Matlin.

Naturally, they'd hurried after the young woman and insisted she come back to their bungalow. They were now on cushions on the living room floor, with Tallulah on a blanket between them, gradually extracting from Julia a story Sabrina thought would have worked for a *Days of Our Lives* episode.

"But you don't have to stop sharing her," Matlin said.

"I'm afraid I've messed things up. I'm going to have to leave."

Sabrina snapped her fingers at Julia, a serious set to her mouth. "First off, no one's going anywhere, so put that thought right out of your head, young lady. It sounds like our rock-headed friend down the way needs some further education on relationships, and you're the woman for the job."

"I think we're well past that," Julia said mournfully. "She didn't seem too thrilled with the fact I kissed her, and there were things I should have said to her a long time ago, not just about Rayford."

"It's not too late. Listen to me, sweetheart, when two people meet and fall in love it changes their lives, usually for the better. But it doesn't always make for the smoothest of rides."

Matlin nodded. "Remember Poppy and Carly and the Mardi Gras ball?"

"That's a story." Sabrina laughed. "Why don't I fix us all a drink, and Matlin and I can tell you all about it."

"She doesn't want to hear about Carly," Matlin said.

Julia wiped her eyes. "Yes, I do." There was so much she didn't know about Poppy, and she had a feeling Poppy seldom spoke about her past because it was painful—Carly was so much a part of it. She wanted to know more, if only to make sense of the present.

Sabrina and Matlin exchanged a glance, then Matlin said, "Smart girl. The quickest and easiest way to get where you want to go is to learn all the roads to your destination. The more you learn about Poppy, the better you'll understand how she ticks, and Carly holds the answer to a lot of your questions." She leaned over and gave Julia a reassuring hug. "Poppy was so young when they met. What they shared changed her, and I'm sure those changes will echo in any other relationships she has in the future. But that's not a bad thing."

"She lost a great deal when she lost Carly, didn't she?" Julia asked.

"She did, and she didn't," said Matlin. "Poppy learned things from Carly. Things that'll make her next mate very happy." When Sabrina and Julia burst out laughing, she huffed, "Not that, you two heathens. What I mean is, Poppy's been properly trained in how to conduct and participate in a healthy relationship."

"If only I could find one like that," Sabrina teased, getting to her feet to make drinks. "Carly always joked that when she was done training Poppy, some young thing would come and swoop her away. Before she died, she made us promise we'd do our level best to see that would happen. Poppy's still got a lot of living to do before she punches her ticket, and Carly wanted her to take advantage of that."

"I'm sure she will when she's ready," Julia said. "Carly wasn't... jealous?"

"She said they could work out the logistics of time-sharing once they all got to the afterlife. What we're trying to say is we don't think Poppy rejected you because she isn't attracted to you."

Matlin nodded vehemently. "No, she's definitely attracted. Moonstruck, I'd call it."

"She's attracted to you but it's scaring her," Sabrina pronounced. "Poppy had all of Carly—her love, her family, and the problems that encompassed. Carly's ex-husband didn't go quietly, and if Poppy believes you're married there's no way in hell she's going to come anywhere near you, even if she thinks you might know the location of the Holy Grail."

Matlin sighed. "Thomas is a jerk. The ball really showed him in his true colors."

Julia rearranged her cushions and settled back, taking the glass of wine Sabrina passed her. "Tell me all about it. Goodness knows, I don't have anything else to do."

The story Sabrina and Matlin told her happened not long after Poppy and Carly began living together. The ball was attended by the inner sanctum of New Orleans society. Invitations were delivered to the door by a butler carrying a silver tray, on which rested a linen envelope, addressed by hand, and a bloodred rose.

Attendees wore masks until midnight. There were no exceptions. The ladies wore gowns and their escorts tails.

What had surprised Poppy the most, beside the fact that an older, distinguished-looking gentleman had shown up at their door with a silver tray in his hand, was that the invitation had come addressed to her, not Carly. Her wife had explained that Poppy was considered the head of their family, and Carly's name change to Valente had signaled the hostess as to who should get the invitation. Evidently tradition could move with the times when warranted.

Matlin and Sabrina had obviously recounted this story a few times. Each picked up the tale seamlessly from the other, pausing every now and then to debate a small point—which milliner had supplied the matching black plumed masks they wore, the number of people the social columns said were present. Carly could have been poured into the black sheath gown she wore and looked devastatingly sexy. She had chosen Poppy's tuxedo, with tails as expected, but she'd outfitted it with an old-fashioned shirt, the high-collar type, and a tie that was wider and softer than the customary black everyone else wore.

Julia could picture Poppy's short ponytail secured with black silk ribbon and her piercing blue eyes behind the mask. Little wonder the conversation had come to a conspicuous halt when she and Carly walked out onto the dance floor.

Poppy had taken her by surprise, making a special request of the band leader, and when she heard the passionate guitar opening, she threw her head back and laughed, thinking her friend, Emily St. Claire, would probably remove them from the guest list after this.

Poppy stood behind her, put her hands on Carly's hips, and pulled her close. When the rest of the band joined the lone guitar in playing the tango, Poppy turned her abruptly around, and the world fell away as they danced. They moved as if they were making love on the dance floor. They both wanted to enjoy every moment and paid no attention to the stares they were getting or the possible consequences. On the last note, Carly's chest was heaving—not only from exertion, but also from the soft words of love Poppy had whispered in her ear as they moved together.

Emily St. Claire had been watching them, of course, and approached them in slow deliberate steps that made Carly certain they were about to be thrown out. In her late fifties, she was married to Myron St. Claire, the president and CEO of one of New Orleans's oldest and biggest banking chains. The ball had become a bit of a chore for her. It took a tremendous amount of effort and work to ready the third-floor ballroom of her large home to host the event every year, but Myron loved it so she always capitulated.

Carly held her breath for a few seconds as Emily stopped a few paces away and took in Poppy Valente. Myron gravitated to his wife as she readied herself to pass judgment. No one expected her calm, almost playful greeting.

"Carly, sugar, I hope this stunner doesn't kill you one night from pure pleasure. You promised to introduce us, I believe."

Carly immediately performed the introductions, and Poppy shook hands with Emily and Myron.

"Carly, would you do an old woman and friend a favor?" asked Emily. "Lend me your spouse for the next dance. I promise to return her in the same condition in which I found her." Addressing Poppy she continued, "Only, would you consider a waltz? I don't think I could contort my body like Carly does. And since I haven't had the opportunity, let me give you our congratulations now. Myron and I are thrilled for you both."

She said the final words softly, so that only they could hear. When the music started again, Poppy then danced with Emily and Carly with Myron, and everyone present joined in the merriment and hit the dance floor. When the witching hour arrived and the lights were dimmed, Poppy's mask fell away at a quick tug from Carly. She returned the favor and they barely had time to kiss, when Carly's ex-husband barged up and grabbed her by the arm, loudly telling her what an embarrassment she was. He attempted to drag her out of the room, but a large hand closed around his throat with a vise grip and lifted him from the floor.

The crowd parted as Poppy walked past them with Thomas attached to the end of her arm, walking on his toes and pawing futilely at her hands. Carly later told Matlin and Sabrina that she had worried for Thomas briefly, as she followed them out to one of the balconies.

Poppy tended to become more controlled in her actions, the more out of control her emotions got, and her calm, low voice warned just how mad she was. "Listen to me, asshole. You see that woman there?" She swung Thomas around to face Carly. "Never lay a hand on her again unless she invites you to do so. Understand?"

"She let him go," Sabrina said. "And he never messed with them much after that, not to their faces anyway. The St. Claire butler never darkened his doorstep again, and he was dropped from a number of other social events as well."

"But he was downright spiteful after that," said Matlin. "During the divorce it was just horrible, so you can see why Poppy's reluctant to go through that again. It's a knee-jerk reaction, that's all."

Sabrina nodded. "We both saw how she looked at you."

"I didn't mean for anything to happen between us, but for once in my life, I felt connected to someone after just a couple of days—it's hard to explain. The time we've had together hasn't been strained like the beginning of some relationships. It's been perfect, but I haven't been totally honest with her, so I think I don't have a chance here. I just want…" Julia couldn't continue because of the lump in her throat.

"Oh, honey, we know what you want. Trust us, it's what that hardhead wants as well."

"I'm not Carly and no matter how hard I try, I won't ever be able to replace her."

Matlin took hold of Julia's hands. "Aside from Poppy and Elizabeth you won't find two people who loved Carly more than Sabrina and me, and you're right, you'll never replace her. But Carly had her time, and what Poppy needs now is a woman to love who'll love her in return. She doesn't want a substitute for Carly. If you try to be that for her, she'll turn away from you. So just be what you've been up to now—yourself. I promise it'll be enough."

"Do you think she'll forgive me for lying to her? I had a million opportunities to tell her the truth, and I didn't." Julia twisted her napkin around a finger as she thought of something else. "Poppy wouldn't fire Ray, would she?"

"Let's deal with one thing at a time, okay? But if it makes you feel better, I think by tomorrow night we'll all be laughing about all this, and you and Poppy will be fine."

Matlin sounded convincing enough to get Julia to nod her head and relax a little.

CHAPTER SEVENTEEN

The next morning Julia fed and changed Tallulah and left her in Rayford's care, then set out toward Poppy's bungalow. It seemed deserted, so she made her way to the back, hoping to find Poppy in the rocker having her first cup of coffee. Julia was confronted by an empty chair. Figuring Poppy must be inside, she knocked on the screen door. "Can I help you, señorita?" A maid walked out of the bathroom with an armload of towels.

Startled, Julia said, "I'm looking for Ms. Valente."

"She no here, and it no look like she stay here last night. She might be gone, I don't know."

Julia's stomach churned, and she took the stairs as fast as she could. They would never have the chance to resolve any of this if Poppy hadn't even stayed to face her. Frantically she ran back to her bungalow and called the front desk, asking where Poppy was. No one seemed to have a clue, but they said a porter had collected luggage from her bungalow.

Disbelieving, Julia sank down on her sofa and stared out the window. Rayford was about twenty yards away, pushing Tallulah in her stroller. He'd said he would probably take her out on a few errands. Julia tried to think, but her brain felt foggy. This whole situation was too much. It had to end, and she could think of only one place she wanted to be.

Making an effort to sound calm, she called Miguel and requested a flight out. "It'll just be me and the baby." Julia didn't turn around when she heard the door open and close.

"Does Poppy plan to—"

"No," Julia snapped, clutching the phone in one hand and dragging her suitcase out from the storage closet. "I'm sure Poppy is not interested in my plans at all. Good-bye."

"Where are you going?" Rayford watched her throwing clothes into the case, his expression a mixture of awkwardness and concern.

"I'm going home, Ray. Even if it is going to be hell, I'm going back. I can't stay here any longer." Julia fell against his chest, crying. It hurt so much that Poppy had just left without saying good-bye.

The more Julia thought about it, the more she understood that kiss they'd shared the night before should have been the beginning of a new phase in their relationship, not the end of what they had. She could see from the look on Poppy's face, when their lips parted, that she wanted the same thing. But perhaps Carly would always loom too large between them.

"What happened? I thought you were going to stick it out with me for a while until you decided what you wanted to do?" Rayford ran his hands carefully up and down Julia's back as if that would make her calm down.

She moved away from him. "There's some stuff I didn't plan on, so I've got to get out of here. Will you help me pack up and get the baby ready?"

"Sure. If that's what you want."

"It is."

"When are you coming back?"

"I'm not."

Rayford fell silent, then ordered up a golf cart and plunked himself down on the sofa. Less than fifteen minutes later he found himself standing next to the helipad waving Julia and his niece good-bye. He had gotten part of the story out of Julia while he helped her pack, and now that she was airborne, he was planning a trip of his own to knock some teeth out. He was going to find the asshole who had hurt Julia and tell her exactly what he thought of her.

He waited until the helicopter disappeared beyond the horizon on its way to Aruba, then headed for the pool area. After the time they had spent on the island, he knew Poppy always had breakfast there when she wasn't lifting anchor to take Julia and Tallulah sailing. Rayford's self-control vanished when he saw her sitting at one of the tables looking relaxed and content, not a trace of remorse for the way she'd just blown Julia off.

He balled his fist and did what would make him feel better. "*You*!

What'd you do to Julia, you big ape?" He didn't care that guests were milling around; he wanted answers.

Poppy stood, intent on getting her red-faced manager away from the now-attentive guests filling the tables around them. Not that they were her main concern, but she didn't enjoy airing her private life in a public setting. Even the wait staff had stopped their actions, anxious to see what was going to happen next.

"I didn't do anything to your—" Poppy didn't finish due to the fist connecting under her left eye. It happened so fast she didn't have time to defend herself. The force of Rayford's blow threw her back and into the pool, and when she resurfaced, she could see the water around her was stained with blood.

Rayford looked suddenly unsure of his actions, taking several steps back and mumbling something vaguely apologetic. No sooner than her hands had hit the pool deck, Poppy was on him like fury. She grabbed his collar and cocked her fist back to retaliate, but hesitated. There was something about his eyes she'd never taken note of; they were exactly the same shade of green as Julia's.

Lowering her fist a little, she said, "First off, didn't your parents teach you not to go around hitting women, even if they're bigger than you are?"

Those familiar green eyes widened, still riveted on her fist.

"And for the record, I didn't do anything to Julia. If you were home more often instead of flirting with the front-desk workers, maybe your wife wouldn't have flown out today."

She was still toying with the idea of hitting him, when she heard loud laughter and turned to see Matlin and Sabrina cracking up.

"What's so damn funny?" she demanded.

"You. Dripping wet and in the throes of a jealous rage," said Sabrina.

"Jealous rage? I'm the one with a black eye."

"She's not his wife, you idiot. She's his twin sister," said Matlin.

"She's what?" Poppy lowered her arm and loosened her choke hold. "But she wears a wedding ring and your application said…" She broke off, realizing the application said…nothing.

Feeling like someone had let the air out of her sails, she let Rayford go and dropped back into her chair. When she wiped her face to rid it of water, she blinked with shock at the sight of blood across her hand. But the pain of her face couldn't compete with the pain in her heart. Julia had left without saying good-bye, which only meant Poppy had blown her chance.

"I don't know about where you come from, but in our world girls like Julia don't get pregnant without a big fancy wedding first." Rayford finally summoned a response. The ring belongs to our grandmother. She didn't want people looking down on Julia because she had a baby and wasn't married."

"You're saying this is some kind of family cover-up for the sake of appearances?"

"What's it to you? Who the hell are you to make my sister feel like shit? Because that's what you did. If I had cause, I'd fire you."

Poppy found a napkin and pressed it to the cut under her eye. She lifted her gaze to Matlin. "You helped with this?"

Matlin said, "Oh, boy."

"So let me get this straight. They came here, posing as married, with your full knowledge, but they're really siblings. Have I got that part right?"

Rayford answered on Matlin's behalf. "Yes, but since the owner's never going to find out, what's the harm?"

His answer made Matlin and Sabrina put their heads down.

"We'll get to that eventually, Mr. Johnson," Poppy said. "What I want to know right now is why Julia's on a helicopter out of here? Why is she running away?"

"What did you expect? If you didn't want a future with her, you shouldn't have led her on." Rayford's voice rose sharply. "You blew it, lady. You should be thrilled with yourself—she looked like shit when she left." Before anyone could stop him, he threw another punch.

This time Poppy didn't care who was around; she was going to kill him. One of the staff ran over and dragged Rayford away before she could do serious damage. Poppy was intent on following them, but Sabrina seized her arm and told her she had to stop and wipe the blood off her face.

Poppy pressed another napkin to the new cut above her eye. "Not a word out of either of you, and find the Texas slugger and get him the hell off my island."

"Let's not be hasty here," said Matlin. "Anyway, I think you need stitches."

"Stitches can wait."

"Are you sure you're all right?" asked Sabrina.

"I'm fine." She might have screwed up a little, but she had never lied to Julia about anything. Julia wasn't getting away that easily. She had some explaining to do. "And blondie's not going anywhere until I talk to her." Poppy figured if she sounded irrational, she could blame it on the blows to the head.

She pulled out her phone and called Miguel, demanding, "How's she getting off Aruba? I know you know, and I know you're going to tell me."

"I can't tell you that. She made me promise. She very upset when she left."

"Miguel, I have two black eyes, and I'm bleeding because of that Neanderthal brother of hers. Do you for one minute think I'm in a good mood? Because let me tell you, my Mexican friend, I'm dying to hit someone just to make myself feel better, and I'd hate for it to be you."

Poppy was so caught up in talking to Miguel, she barely noticed Matlin and Sabrina were steering her toward the infirmary.

"I'm no afraid of you, Poppy, so stop threatening me," Miguel said as the nurse on duty greeted Poppy and showed her into a curtained cubicle. "I'm no going to tell you where she gone."

"Mickey, I just want to talk to her, so tell me what flight you booked her on." Poppy was on the verge of begging, but when it came to her friends, she was all bluster and no action. Miguel would know the threat of a beating was hollow. After a long pause, he said, "It leaves this afternoon. American Airlines flight 1210."

Poppy thanked him curtly and ended the call. She attempted to get to her feet, but the nurse examining her cuts said, "It's going to need surgery so it won't leave a scar, Ms. Valente. I can put butterfly bandages on both cuts, but I don't want to attempt anything else. I suggest you don't wait too long before you see a surgeon."

"Okay. Fine." She sat still and unflinching while the nurse treated her.

Sitting in the small room, letting the woman take care of her injuries, gave her time to think, and the jumble of emotions that had ripped through her died away, leaving a feeling she was all too familiar with. Defeat. In that instant, it was like she woke up from a stupor and figured out Julia was really gone.

"You *will* go after her, won't you?" asked Matlin from the chair in the corner of the room.

Poppy repeated the question in her mind. After the nurse had left the cubicle, she said, "I don't think so. I may have misinterpreted her situation, but mine was crystal clear. So if she really was interested, she'd be here now and not at the airport trying to put a thousand miles between us." The bleakness that had set in when she lost Carly was taking hold, and she wanted nothing more than to go back to her bungalow and lock the door. "Matlin, I know you're only trying to help, but I just want to be left alone for awhile."

Poppy jumped off the table intending to go back to her bungalow, but wobbled as her feet hit the ground. Just before the blackness set in and she fell forward, she heard Matlin yell, "Nurse, get back in here!"

❖

Fingers running through her hair woke Poppy up. Focusing on her surroundings she could see that she was back in her room in the bungalow and any chance of catching up to Julia was gone. Both Matlin and Sabrina were asleep on the sofa across from the bed, snoring softly against each other. Carly was the only one keeping vigil over Poppy, and the sight of her sitting on the bed made Poppy smile.

"Look at you, my love. You're quite the sight," Carly said softly. The bruise around the cuts had darkened, leaving Poppy with two perfect black eyes, and the fall had contributed a huge purple lump on her right brow and yet another butterfly bandage.

"Tell me I don't have about thirty stitches on my face?"

"No, but you have enough of those butterfly things to start a collection." Carly squeezed Poppy's cheeks together for emphasis and laughed at the result. "Since we have so little time, let's plan your next step, honey. 'Cause let me tell you, you haven't done so well working this out on your own. That girl loves you, and you let her get away. You know, you're supposed to get better with age, not the other way around."

"Please, baby, I'd rather not discuss my love life with my dead wife, if it's all the same to you. I just don't understand why she left," Poppy mused out loud.

"She left, rock head, because she thinks your past still dictates your present and your future." Carly pushed Poppy back onto the bed. "You can't blame her or get angry because she's worried that you'll be stuck on me forever. Julia's important to your future, honey, so don't screw this up."

The verbal kick in the pants got Poppy moving, and after a momentary bout of dizziness she headed toward the office. She'd been planning a gift for Julia, and the timing could not be better. "Bob, this is your commander speaking." Poppy waited for the question he was going to ask and hoped her foggy mind could remember the code word.

"This is Eagle One, sir. What's the mission code word and what's your position?" asked the pilot.

"The code word's Gypsy Lady, and my position is Carly's Sound. Now listen up, I have a mission for you." Poppy gave him a list of things to do, picturing him taking diligent notes. "Got all that, soldier?"

"Aye, aye, sir, I won't let you down. Should I arm myself?"

"No! I'll be there before the plane leaves so don't shoot anyone. Do you copy?"

"Yes, sir," yelled Bob before hanging up.

"Crazy son of a bitch," Poppy muttered, and she ran toward the marina.

The fastest shuttle in the fleet, as luck would have it, was moored, and the keys were still in the ignition. Poppy just hoped there was enough gas left in the big boat's tanks to get her to Aruba.

From their lounge chairs behind the bungalow they were sharing, Lizzie and Susanna watched the boat cruise by at top speed and wondered who was going to get into trouble with Poppy for making so much noise close to shore.

Susanna's hands stopped midmotion, but didn't lift away from Lizzie's back. "Ooh, someone's going to get fired for gunning that bad boy along here," she said, applying sunscreen as she strained to see if she could make out the driver.

"Like you wouldn't relish the chance to take that thing out for a spin." Lizzie looked behind her with a smile firmly in place.

"Would you protect me from the wrath of Valente?"

"Get those hands moving again and I'll consider it." Lizzie caught a blush coloring Susanna's face just as she turned toward the water again. Before she could say anything else, her phone rang, and Poppy didn't even say hello before she started issuing commands.

"Lizzie, get your hands on a passenger manifest for me, and before you ask why, don't. I'm in a hurry, and I need you to just do it."

"Okay, but is it all right if I ask why you sound like you're stuck in a wind tunnel?"

"I'm in one of the shuttles headed toward Aruba because the *Piper* would take too long."

The explanation sounded like it was missing the main entrée so it would take a little longer on Lizzie's part to get the rest. "Didn't we hire people to drive those around for us?"

"I'm not going to pick up guests, sweetheart."

"Since you're not going to be doing anything for the next, say, forty minutes, how about you humor me?"

"Julia and I had a little misunderstanding, and she left for the airport. Thinking I was fully to blame for what happened, Rayford punched me in the face twice. So now I'm on my way to Aruba to have a talk with Ms. Johnson and set things right."

"Why, that little..." Lizzie rolled over and sat up, but shot her hand out to keep Susanna from moving. "Wait till I get a hold of Matlin for hiring the little creep. You fired him, didn't you? Wait a minute, shouldn't he be shaking your hand for not sleeping with his wife? They must have some kind of understanding relationship."

"The little shit ran before I could retaliate so I'll have to hunt him down to fire him, but I'll worry about that later, Scarlett. For now I just need that manifest. And by the way, I'm actually looking for his sister, not his wife."

"His sister? What does his sister have to do with you tracking down Rayford's information?"

"It's his sister I'm looking for, Lizzie. You met her, on numerous occasions. Cute blonde with an equally cute baby."

Lizzie pulled the phone away from her ear and looked at it in confusion. "Did the blows to your face impair your judgment? You're not making a whole lot of sense here, boss."

"Considering what's happened to me in just a day, I could write a tell-all book, kid. Just get me that list, and I promise to entertain you at lunch tomorrow."

CHAPTER EIGHTEEN

M a'am, I need you to come with me." Bob marched up to a stiff-backed older woman, took her elbow, and tried to drag her from a line of people waiting for their luggage.

"Is there a problem?"

"I have my orders, ma'am. That's all I can tell you for the moment." Bob was so busy maneuvering around the crowd, he never saw the large purse headed toward his head. When it struck, it left him momentarily stunned.

"You're one of them people they warn you about when you travel out of the country, ain't you? You have picked on the wrong old lady. I can tell you that, asshole."

Fending off another blow, Bob said, "Ma'am, I'm not trying to rob you. I can assure you of that. I just wanted to escort you to your granddaughter." Torn between trying to find his glasses and letting go of the feisty Texan, he spotted Julia across the small terminal and waved at her.

"Granny?" Julia hurried over, startled to see her grandmother poised to strike Poppy's pilot. "What are you doing here?"

"Julia, honey, I wanted to surprise you." Tallulah Johnson kept one hand on the back of Bob's collar as she smiled at Julia and the baby. "Not that I'm not thrilled to see you, but could you be a dear and find an officer to arrest this thief?"

"Granny, that's not a thief. Bob, what are you doing here?"

"The commander asked me to come by and make sure you saw your grandmother before you left."

"Is Poppy on her way here?" Julia moved Tallulah's stroller away from the throng of travelers hurrying by.

"That's confidential information, ma'am."

"Uh-huh." Julia concluded she would need to escape quickly if she didn't want to run into Poppy. "Granny, you can let him go. We have to get out of here, though. Can you see your luggage?"

Leaving a chagrined Bob talking to himself, Julia loaded the bags her grandmother indicated and hustled her out to a cab. She ordered the driver to take them to the Esmeralda Verde, certain the Valente resort was the last place Poppy would think to look for her.

Less than half an hour later, she and Granny Tallulah sat in her room, looking out at what had seemed like paradise up until now. Julia had rebooked her flight out of Aruba and arranged for her luggage to be delivered to the resort, and she'd just put Tallulah down for a nap. Her grandmother had ordered up a sandwich and a glass of milk— amazingly, the resort actually had peanut butter and jelly. She was trying to get Julia to join her in eating the snack.

"Julia, honey, you can't go without food. It's not good for the baby, or for you."

"I'm just not hungry, Granny." Julia fought back tears. All she wanted right at this moment was to be off the island and back on her grandmother's ranch in Texas.

Granny had taken care of Julia and her brother almost from the time they were born. Julia's parents traveled abroad for such extended periods they always seemed distant to her, as a child. Granny often said Julia and Rayford had brought her so much pleasure over the years, she thought of them as her own. No one was better qualified to know when Julia was upset by something minor, like a spat with a friend, or something more serious, like having to tell her parents she had gotten pregnant. That hadn't been pretty.

She gazed at Julia with eyes that saw everything. "Take a few bites, and when your mouth's not full you can tell me what's got your britches in a twist to leave this beautiful place. Not that I mind having you and my great-granddaughter back home with me, but I just got here and was looking forward to getting some sun on these old legs."

Julia slowly ate half the sandwich as a delay tactic before confessing. "I met someone, Granny."

"Oh, Julia, that's wonderful. I want you to have the same love in your life your grandfather and I had. You never got to know him, but he was such a romantic fella. There were always flowers or some little thing he'd get me so I wouldn't forget who his favorite girl was," Granny Tallulah reminisced.

"Trust me, Granny, I've been wined and dined plenty in the past two months. Not to mention sailed, and serenaded as well."

Julia thought back to the bug song Poppy was always singing to Tallulah, and a smile broke out across her face. Just as quickly, she reminded herself that Poppy had let her go, and she knew the pain in her heart must be obvious.

"What's his name and where do I find this Romeo?"

Julia smiled at the tone of outrage. No doubt Granny Tallulah imagined some playboy had played fast and loose with her beloved granddaughter. "Poppy."

"Sounds like some kind of cartoon character. If this guy's so wonderful and you love him, sweetheart, then why aren't you with him? What did he do?"

"She *is* wonderful, Granny, and I'm not with her because she doesn't want me." Julia waited for the outburst. Her grandmother had never been a judgmental person, but Julia had never mentioned she was gay.

"I *see*. Well, this Poppy individual can't be very intelligent if she doesn't want you. What makes you so certain about that?"

"It's a long story."

"I'm not going anywhere."

Julia smiled and took her grandmother's hand. For the next hour she told the story of herself and Poppy, from their first meeting in the coffee shop in New Orleans to the kiss they'd shared the night before. When she was done, Julia fell into the arms that had soothed away her childhood fears and cried.

"You haven't even talked to her about this, sweetheart," Granny Tallulah said. "You're jumping to some big conclusions here, and she does after all think you're married to your ornery brother. God help the woman who finally gets *that* job."

At the thought of her brother's romantic history, Julia laughed along with her. "I'm not sure how much difference it would make if she knew I wasn't married. She acts like it's a big deal, but I think there's much more to it than that. Her partner, Carly, was married with children, and Poppy had no trouble starting that relationship."

"Then what do you think the problem is?"

"Carly died, and Poppy is never going to let her go. Everything in her life is about Carly, and I can't compete with a dead woman."

"Have you asked Poppy if you need to?"

"No, I left so that I didn't have to…I'm not sure I could cope with the answer. "

Granny frowned, a faraway look on her creased face. "Are you quite sure you didn't have your own reasons for running away?"

"What do you mean?"

"I'm not a shrink, but I know you very well. You never got over your parents leaving you all the time. I think it's made you rather untrusting."

Julia's first impulse was to respond with a flat denial, but then she allowed the idea some room. Granny was right; she was very slow to trust anyone, and time and again she had puzzled over Poppy's kindness to her and Tallulah, wondering about her motivations. She had been reluctant all along to believe Poppy genuinely cared for them both. Julia had discovered a long time ago that it was easier not to hope for anything; if she believed her parents' promises about coming back soon or ending their continuous travels, she was only disappointed when they didn't follow through.

"I think you have a point," she conceded. "I guess I don't trust her."

"Has she done anything to deserve that?" Granny asked quietly.

"No."

"Then maybe together we can come up with a solution to your Poppy problem. It sounds to me like she hasn't passed up the opportunity to get you two beauties tied up in one neat package. You never gave her the chance."

Julia groaned. "Why are you right about everything all of the time?"

"Because I've had about seventy years to figure this stuff out." Granny Tallulah took Julia's hand. "Promise me you'll think everything through very carefully before you write this girl off."

Julia leaned across the table and kissed her grandmother on the cheek. "Thanks for listening, Granny. I promise I won't make any rash decisions."

❖

Poppy turned a few heads when she ran into the Aruba airport looking like a victim of some horrible accident. Her eyes were now a serious shade of black, and the front of her shirt was covered in blood. She was ready to throw up when she saw Bob was alone.

"I'm sorry, sir. That old woman hit me in the head with her purse and tried to have me arrested."

"Am I too late? But I thought there was plenty of time before Mrs. Johnson's flight left."

"There is, but she's gone."

"Gone? Where did she go?"

"She left in a taxi with her baby and that violent old lady." Bob rubbed a reddish mark on his head for added effect.

Poppy couldn't resist teasing him gently. "You let her get away with beating up on you?"

"I'd never hit a woman, sir."

"Maybe I should lock you in a room with a man named Rayford and let you teach him some manners." Poppy led Bob outside. "Which way did they go?"

She already had her suspicions. Julia had probably assumed Poppy would start at the port and slowly work her way down, trying to find out which of the many hotels she'd checked into. "She told me she doesn't want to be found," Bob said, helpfully.

"Aruba's not that big." Poppy thanked him and told him to take the rest of the day off. With any luck she wouldn't be needing him until the next morning. She drove one of the Valente jeeps to the resort and went straight to Jorge's office.

"What room is she in?" Her manager looked intentionally blank, so Poppy offered some encouragement. "Before you say you don't know who I'm talking about, think about how much you love your job. I'm not threatening you, but I need to speak with Mrs. Johnson urgently."

Jorge took a deep breath and put his hands on the counter to keep them steady. "You know I can't tell you, Poppy. She asked me not to, and she's a Valente guest."

Wondering what it was about Julia that forged such loyalty in so little time, she said, "I'll tell her I tortured it out of you."

The manager took in Poppy's appearance with a quizzical expression. "Have you been in an accident?"

"Don't even ask." In her most rational manner, Poppy said, "You know I can find out anything I want by talking to the housekeeper,

Jorge, so let's save me time and you a career change. What's her room number?"

Jorge considered the request for no more than a second or two and said, "She's in the same suite you stayed in last time."

❖

Poppy didn't go to Julia's room right away. Instead she took a shower and changed into the clothing she'd quickly packed. It felt good to be rid, finally, of the evidence of her one-sided battle with Rayford. As she took the elevator down two floors, she thought about what she was going to say to Julia.

This time, they had to be completely honest with one another. She didn't care why Julia had pretended to be married; it hurt that she had not owned up to the deception much sooner, but Poppy could understand how it was to put off a difficult discussion. She'd done so herself. She took a calming breath as the elevator doors opened and strolled along the hallway to Julia's room. An older woman with warm green eyes greeted her at the door and, without a trace of surprise, said, "You must be Poppy. Come on in here and have a seat."

When Poppy followed with a bit of a lag, the woman was already pouring two cups of coffee like she had been expecting her.

"How'd you know my name?" Poppy asked.

"My granddaughter did a fairly good job at describing you. I bet if you took off those fancy sunglasses, there would be some pretty blue eyes waiting there for me. Now come talk to an old woman and tell me what's going on. I've heard my granddaughter's version."

Reluctantly, Poppy removed the glasses, exposing the bruising she'd intended to cover. "I've been looking forward to meeting you, Mrs. Johnson. Julia's told me so much about you. As for what's going on between me and Julia, with all due respect, that's something I need to talk with her about. Is she here?" "

"No."

Poppy felt her shoulders slump before she had a chance to hide her dismay, but a familiar cry made her look sharply around.

"I didn't say they'd left," Tallulah Johnson said. "Julia just went out to run an errand."

"May I?" Poppy got up and went into the next room, emerging

with the baby a moment later. She sat on the comfortable chair and started singing to the little girl in Spanish. Tallulah listened intently, then reached up and put her little hand on Poppy's cheek, as she often did.

"She's taken a real shine to you, I see," said the other Tallulah as she watched. "Her mama was a lot like her at that age. Maybe she still is, since she's taken a shine to you too."

Poppy held Tallulah close to her and inhaled the sweet, innocent smell that always clung to the baby. When she looked up, she found the elder Tallulah staring at her. "I feel the very same way, and I just want the chance to talk to her."

Tallulah leaned forward and patted Poppy's knee. "Julia's important to me, and I love her more than life itself. I don't want her hurt."

"I understand," Poppy said. "Let me tell you something. Julia's important to me too, ma'am. I've spent the past two months of my life with her and Tallulah, and they've brought me more joy than the last two years. I want the opportunity to build on that." She took the hand on her knee and squeezed it. "I'm not out to hurt her. Can I see her?"

"You'd better get downstairs. I think she's making reservations at the restaurant. This is just a hunch on my part, but I'll bet she'll be happy to see you."

When Poppy smiled, Tallulah Johnson could see what her granddaughter had fallen for. Poppy reminded her of her late husband Fred. Not a man of many words, he had a look about him that made her want to follow him into hell if necessary.

"My granddaughter's a stubborn one, but once she sets her mind to something you better be in it for the long haul. I hope you know that going in."

"Yes, ma'am, I do. If you'd be so kind as to excuse me, I have some apologizing to do." Poppy stood up and handed Tallulah her sleeping namesake.

❖

"What happened to your face?" Julia lifted her hand to Poppy's face, softly touching the swelling on one cheekbone. The bruises looked angry and painful, but strangely enough, they somehow brought out the blue of Poppy's eyes.

Poppy had led them away from the restaurant to the first empty conference room she could find and closed the door. They'd walked the entire way in silence, waiting for more privacy before starting their much-delayed talk. When the solid wood door closed behind them, Julia had to lean against the oak surface to fight off the urge to fall into her arms like she had the day before. *Has it been only a day since that happened?*

Julia had never thought she could miss someone so much. Her heart had almost jerked from her chest when she saw Poppy approaching. She looked a little out of place with a light-colored linen suit and her trademark white cotton shirt, but all the same, heads popped up like fishing corks, and women lowered their sunglasses discreetly as she passed by. Julia noticed the same inviting looks everywhere she went with Poppy. The two black eyes peeking out from the sunglasses and the white bandages on her forehead didn't take away from her striking appeal.

"Don't we have more important things to talk about than my face?" Poppy asked, noticing that the wedding rings were gone from Julia's finger.

"What happened? Please tell me."

"Your brother punched me for hurting your feelings." Poppy took a step closer, then stopped to gauge Julia's reaction. Her intention was not to push Julia, but she didn't want to hold back anymore.

"Tell me poor Rayford isn't hospitalized somewhere in the Caribbean?" Julia could feel the body heat emanating off Poppy as she moved even closer.

"No, poor Rayford's just where you left him, looking just the same. I don't even think anyone's told him exactly who he knocked into the pool in his frenzy to protect you."

"Oh, he's going to love finding *that* out." Julia had to laugh. "He had you down for some lazy cousin of the owner, trying to take full advantage."

"Yes, he made that fairly clear."

"Thank you for not killing him."

"For you, anything."

Julia caught herself staring at Poppy's mouth and looked away while she could still resist the urge to kiss her. "Why are you here?" She crossed her fingers behind her back and prayed for the answer she wanted out of Poppy.

"I could say I have a list of reasons, but words aren't what the moment calls for, I think." Poppy closed the gap between them even more, encouraged that Julia wasn't taking a step back for every one she took forward.

"No?"

Poppy shook her head. They stared at each other without saying another word. Going with her gut like she had so many years before, Poppy took the plunge and bent down to reach the lips she had been thinking about since her first taste of them.

Julia needed no further encouragement and molded herself to the body she had visited in her dreams since they had met. The kiss was slow and soft, the kind of kiss you tell your grandchildren about when you describe how you fell in love with the person sitting next to you fifty years down the line. Julia was certain she would remember it that way. The big hands with the interesting calluses from strumming too many guitar strings were holding her close, and the fingers in her hair belonged to the person she wanted that future with. Poppy had slowly swept her off her feet, with her gentle manner and sweet soul.

"Don't ever leave me again without talking to me first," Poppy said, when they paused to breathe. "That's all I ask of you."

"I'm sorry. I thought I wasn't what you wanted or needed."

"Never be afraid to ask me what I want or need. I can promise I'll always answer you honestly. Last night I was scared. That's not really a good excuse, but I was. I'm sorry I hurt you."

"Could we start the day again?" Julia ran her hands under the lapels of Poppy's jacket, almost unable to believe the solid body holding her was real.

"I'd like that. This morning I was afraid I would lose you before you understood what you've come to mean to me."

The answer made Julia want to grab Poppy and Tallulah and run back to Carly's Sound. Just seeing that beautiful smile, though, she knew the location would never matter as long as Poppy was with her, looking at her the way she was now. This kind of happiness seemed impossible. "Not that I'm complaining, but how'd you find me?"

"Tallulah told me." Poppy kissed Julia again just because she was so close.

"Smart girl, that daughter of mine. Now tell me why you're really here?"

"I thought I answered that, but if you need more, I wanted to see you and that daughter of yours, first off. Secondly, I want to take you out on a date. That's if you want to go out with me."

"You went through all this trouble to take me out on a date?"

"It seemed so much more civilized than clubbing you and dragging you back to the bungalow."

Julia wished they were already back on the *Pied Piper*. With Poppy kissing her neck with such distracting sensuality, she was starting to eye up the conference table as the nearest flat surface.

"I thought you'd left," she said. "That's what the woman cleaning your room told me this morning. I thought my heart would break at not ever seeing you again."

"Why would I have left?" Poppy looked genuinely surprised. "The first rule of business is you never walk away until you get what you came for."

"Is that what I am to you? Business?" Julia stepped out of Poppy's embrace.

"Business? No, you're much more than that. Don't you realize how special you are to me?"

"Perhaps you should show me," Julia invited, and Poppy closed the gap between them until they were barely touching, then held out her hand.

Without hesitation Julia took it and was once again pulled into a heated kiss, one she hoped with all her heart would be the first of many in her lifetime.

CHAPTER NINETEEN

"Where was this taken?" Tallulah stood in the open-air lobby of Carly's Sound looking at the picture hanging on one of the posts. She had never seen such a commotion among a hotel staff as that when their boat had docked in the small marina. They were treated like they owned the place.

"It was taken from the porch of the last bungalow on the east side of the island, Granny." The long legs and the rocker in the picture were so engrained into her brain, Julia could slap herself for not recognizing them the first time she had seen the photo.

"Actually, it's the last one on the southeast side of the island," Poppy corrected. "Don't tell anyone, but in a rare fit of selfishness, I took the stretch of beach with the best view of the sunrise." She turned slightly to introduce Lizzie to Julia and her grandmother.

The women spoke for several minutes as the Johnsons' luggage arrived, then Poppy led them out to a waiting cart and they drove to the house reserved for Julia and her grandmother.

Lizzie had been surprised by the choice of accommodations, but recognized the statement Poppy was making. Julia was not just a casual acquaintance to be cast aside when Poppy was ready to return to everyday life in New Orleans. She was happy for them both as she waved a good-bye and went back into the lobby, but there was also a hollow feeling in her gut. What would it mean if Poppy had a new family?

Poppy thought about Lizzie as the cart stopped in front of a beach house set back from the path and well hidden from the other buildings close by. Unlike the bungalows around it, this one had a wide porch that encircled the whole structure, making it resemble a Louisiana Acadian home. The house had been the last built, not as an afterthought, but as a gift from Lizzie to Poppy. She thought if the bungalow Poppy had shared with her mother was too full of memories, she could start fresh on the exact opposite end of the island.

But the architectural differences were not its most striking feature. Thousands of orchid plants filled the gardens that surrounded it. Their colors cascaded smoothly from one to the next, forming a rainbow effect that was breathtaking. It was as if the landscape designers had taken the delicate, whimsical flowers and painted them in almost formal lines.

Julia had never seen anything like it before. Orchids were by nature beautiful but temperamental. To get them to cooperate on such a grand scale was a major feat. "Poppy, this is one of the most beautiful things I've ever seen." She couldn't take her eyes off the floral masterpiece. "I can't believe you haven't shown me this place before now."

"It was just finished a couple of days ago, so don't think I'm holding out on you. The grounds crew wasn't too thrilled with me when I told them what I had in mind, but I think they did a great job."

"That's a major understatement," said Tallulah.

Poppy took the baby indoors so Julia could enjoy the walk to the wide porch.

Tallulah whistled loudly once they crossed the threshold. "Hot damn, now this is living." She walked to one of the large chairs next to the fireplace and dropped into it.

"There are three bedrooms. The staff set one up for the baby," Poppy explained as Julia followed them in.

"How'd you rate scoring such a great setup?" Tallulah asked Poppy.

"Granny, you never did ask what Poppy does for a living." Julia took in the hardwood floors and the complete wall of windows along the back of the house looking out on water so perfect it resembled a painting.

"You said Ray worked for her, so I thought she was a manager."

"I really don't know if it's important. What I do for a living won't change your grandmother's opinion of me, will it?" Poppy said, laying a blanket out on the floor. "It didn't change your opinion of me."

"If you tell her, though, maybe we can talk her into coming here regularly. Granny works way too much, and you have enough places to keep her busy for a while, if you invite her, that is."

"Wait a doggone minute. You own this place?" Tallulah crinkled her brow and plowed ahead with more questions. "How old are you?"

"I just turned thirty-three." Poppy didn't take her eyes off Julia's face.

"I'd have to say you made a wise decision when you chanced coming out here with Ray, sweetheart. If Poppy has the ability to grow some extra appendages, your mother would be thrilled." Tallulah had a twinkle in her green eyes, and Poppy could see the feisty nature of the woman shining through.

"Trust me, Granny. I wouldn't be too interested if she did."

"Do the three of you think you could do without me for awhile?" Poppy asked, wanting to escape before she started blushing.

"We'll have to muddle on alone if we don't have any other choice. I mean the accommodations are so shabby and all." Julia tried to sound serious. "Do you really have to go?"

"I need to check on a few things. Besides, it'll give you time to catch up with your grandmother, and she can issue any warnings about me she doesn't want me to hear."

They both laughed at Tallulah's snort. Poppy had the feeling if Tallulah wanted to say something, she wouldn't much care who was in the room. She kissed Julia, then kissed Tallulah senior on the cheek. Her last stop was to get down on the floor and kiss the baby good-bye.

"I think that one's pretty gone on you, darlin'," Tallulah said as the front door softly closed.

Julia smiled. She still had doubts, but the more she thought about it, the more she realized that her own insecurities played a bigger role in her worries than they should. She had no idea how long it would take for Poppy to profess any kind of love for her or talk about their future, but she was willing to wait.

"I don't expect her to fall on one knee and pop the question, but I'd like it if she did," Julia said. "I want to tell her I've found the person I'll be with for the rest of my life and not have her run off on me. Do you understand?"

Her grandmother responded with a tranquil smile. "I suspect Poppy doesn't give her heart away easily, and that's a good thing. When someone takes their time, it means they plan to commit forever."

❖

The sun had set before a freshly showered Poppy showed up with flowers for both Julia and her grandmother. The two bouquets couldn't have been more different. Julia wondered how Poppy could have found out yellow roses were her favorite flower, let alone getting it right for her granny as well.

Tallulah accepted her yellow daisies with a shy smile and placed them on the mantle. As Julia made way for her to go ahead, Granny Tallulah took her arm and smiled at Poppy.

"If you don't mind, I'm really tired from traveling, and I'd rather dine in. Is that possible?"

Poppy hesitated briefly, then said, "We can all dine here."

"No, no." Tallulah waved a hand impatiently. "You girls go and have a nice evening. Can I order room service?"

"I'll have the chefs send over a selection of dishes," Poppy said.

Julia felt as if her grandmother was virtually pushing them out the door. "Are you sure?"

"Absolutely."

"I think that's a hint." After wishing Tallulah good night, Poppy took Julia's arm and said, "I see where you get some of your determination from."

She drove them to her bungalow and pulled into the back, where a tent had been set up near the shore with a tarp close by to stop some of the breeze. Under the canopy was a formally set table complete with candles and crystal.

Julia's eyebrows climbed almost into her hairline as she stepped down from the cart and took it all in. "You certainly know how to impress a girl, Ms. Valente, I give you that. This is beautiful. Are you doing the cooking tonight?"

"Not that I don't love cooking for you, but I'll let you in on another little secret of mine."

Julia loved this more playful side of Poppy as the smile played around her lips. "What?"

"Why have such a great staff working for me, if I can't take them out for a spin on occasion? I haven't had many first dates, so I like to make them memorable."

A familiar voice greeted them from the beach. "Look at you, all dressed up with a beautiful woman on your arm, dining at the most romantic table in the Caribbean tonight," said Marta, as Julia took her place by Poppy's side.

"Julia Johnson, may I present Marta Rojas, the most extraordinary chef you'll have the pleasure of dining with. Marta, this is Julia."

"Your beautiful girl and I already met, mija." The chef took one of Julia's hands between both of hers and smiled. "You see now why wishing is a good thing?"

"Yes, ma'am, I'm learning it has its advantages." Julia almost laughed. She had an odd sense that some kind of conspiracy had been afoot on Carly's Sound that neither she nor Poppy was aware of.

"Bueno, you sit and we gonna feed you. I've been slaving all afternoon on the meal for you both, so please relax and enjoy." When Marta stepped toward the bungalow, four waiters appeared out of nowhere and started their dining experience with a bottle of chilled white wine.

"Aren't you just full of surprises." Julia watched as Poppy swirled the almost clear liquid in her glass before taking a small sip and nodding her approval to the waiter.

"What?" Poppy's smile was not quite hidden behind her wineglass as Julia teased her.

"This." Julia waved a hand. "Why go to all this trouble?"

"I wouldn't dream of treating you any other way, so I suggest you get used to it."

"Thanks. I've never had anyone take that kind of trouble before." Julia reached across the table and placed her hand over Poppy's, feeling the familiar comfort she always did when she touched her. She tried to ignore the fact that the platinum wedding band was still on Poppy's finger.

"You're a special woman who deserves no less." Soft music drifted across the gardens, completing the romantic setting. "Dance with me?"

Poppy stood up and extended her hand in invitation, openly admiring Julia's body as she rose. The white thin-strapped dress she had chosen to wear looked good with the sun she'd gotten in the past two months. Poppy lifted the small hand covering hers and kissed it. "You look beautiful tonight," she said.

"Thank you," whispered Julia. When she placed the side of her face against the pale pink shirt Poppy wore, she realized Poppy smelled like the ocean. It was a fresh, salty scent that made her want to bury her face into Poppy's neck. As she was led around the sand, she felt like they would start floating at any moment. "This is perfect," she said, and was not sure if Poppy even heard.

They were both lost in the moment, it seemed, and Julia was content to stay that way. The rest of the evening was just as special. They sat down to a wonderful meal served by Marta and the resort staff. During dessert, Marta joined them and told Julia some stories of Poppy's adolescent years that made Julia want to kiss away the pout on Poppy's face. On the drive back to the beach house, Julia was surprised when Poppy gently shook her awake.

"I'm sorry I fell asleep on you. God, that would have been embarrassing if I'd fallen out of the cart."

"Not to worry. It wasn't the company, I hope."

Poppy got out to help Julia down, but instead of walking her to the front door, she carried her. The sprinklers had just soaked the ground, and Poppy said she didn't want Julia to ruin her heels. When they reached the porch she put her down gently, but didn't release her.

Julia's arms were still lightly draped around Poppy's neck. Standing two steps higher, she could see into the blue eyes that looked darker than usual. With one of her hands, she played idly with the short ponytail at the back of Poppy's head.

"Thank you for a wonderful evening," she said. "When can I see you again?"

"Anytime you want to. With Julia so close, Poppy had to kiss her. She willed her hands to stay still on Julia's hips, but she felt the tie slip from her ponytail and gentle fingers run through her hair. "Maybe I can find a good reason to lift anchor on the *Piper*, and we can see where we want to go from there?"

"What would it take?" Julia asked.

"Your saying yes."

"I can't think of too many questions you could ask me that my answer wouldn't be yes. Nights like this are the stuff of fairy tales. I never imagined I would actually live one, but all it takes to make me happy is just being with you."

Julia's lips were so close, Poppy could feel the soft brush of them against her own. She wanted to accept their invitation, but the timing didn't feel exactly right. She wasn't quite sure why, or what she was waiting for.

"What do you want, Poppy?" Julia framed the question for her. "Is there something I can do to make you feel the same way?"

"I haven't wanted anything in so long, it's hard to find an answer," Poppy said truthfully. "I feel alive again, and happy, and I also want more. Can I ask you to be patient with me?"

Julia slumped on the other side of the door until she couldn't hear the whirl of the electric motor on the cart Poppy was driving. Was Poppy ready to move forward? Julia didn't know, but she wanted it so much she was willing to give her as much time as she needed. And, for a change, she believed they had all the time in the world.

❖

On her ride back to the bungalow, Poppy took a detour to the untamed side of the island and let her mind wander back to the past. She knew she had to let it go before she could fully embrace the future and give Julia and her daughter the certainty they deserved. She also realized that part of her saw this as a betrayal, and another part feared forgetting Carly.

She conjured a memory of gentle fingers drawing circles on her back. It was early on a Monday morning, and the light was just coming through the windows in their New Orleans home. She could feel Carly's nipples pressing into her back and the tangle of sheets around her legs. They had spent a lazy Sunday at home, knowing their week was going to get hectic with business.

The construction crews were set to begin to clear the areas where the guests' bungalows were going to be built on Carly's Sound. Poppy and Carly were scheduled to join them within the next two days.

"Good morning, sexy," Carly said. "What are you thinking about?"

"How happy I am, and how tied into that you are." Poppy flipped over so she could kiss Carly good morning. The kiss was slow and knowing. After ten years it was hard to surprise each other during sex, but she knew no amount of years would kill the passion between them.

What she didn't know was that Carly had found a lump in her breast. Later, they would share their amazement that Poppy hadn't found it sooner, considering how attached she was to that part of Carly's body.

Carly said she was going to the doctor that afternoon, and Poppy asked, "Want me to come with you?"

"No, I want you to make me come first, then we'll see about you," said Carly as she pushed Poppy's head down her body. Sometimes she teased that Poppy's sensual mouth wasn't only good for singing love songs.

It was the last time they'd made love without a sense of urgency. A few hours later, they had walked from Dr. Susan Jackson's office to the hospital for Carly's biopsy, and three days after that, life stopped being normal.

Poppy slowed down and pulled over. She always felt like throwing up when she relived that terrible moment.

Susan had looked so calm. Gently, she'd said, "Carly, you have breast cancer, and we have to remove your right breast."

Sitting on the hospital bed, Poppy felt like someone had driven a stake through her hope.

Sweating as memories of those months crowded her mind, she got out of the cart and walked. Carly had always referred to this area as the wild side of their paradise. No vegetation grew here among the solid black rocks that stuck out of the water for hundreds of yards offshore. Some looked like square pillars that had broken off of a castle giving the area an abandoned air. Others were sharp and jagged like they had just cooled from the volcanic eruption that had formed the land where they now sat. With the ever-present trade winds, the waves reached about fifteen feet at their crest before slamming into the unyielding shoreline sending up an impressive spray. Once every wall of seawater lost its battle with the rock, another took its place.

Poppy stared out to sea and yearned for another day, standing here with Carly alive and healthy next to her. During the painful treatments, Poppy never cried or talked about anything but hope and optimism in front of Carly. In private, she cursed God for what Carly was going through.

At the end of a beautiful day in early June, eighteen months after it all began, Carly had asked Poppy to carry her out to the beach. It was another gorgeous sunset in a string they had witnessed since they'd moved to Carly's Sound.

"Promise me something?" Carly asked.

"Anything."

Poppy held Carly in her lap on one of the chaise lounges out by the water. Carly was weak, and her breathing had been difficult all day. The disease that had started in her breasts was now in her lungs and bones. Her constant pain made death seem like a welcome friend.

"Promise me you'll find someone who makes you happy. You've given me so much, that I want you to be happy again. You deserve nothing less. There's someone out there waiting for you, my love. Promise me you won't turn away when she finds you."

Poppy could feel Carly's strength ebbing and tightened her arms, sensing Carly was hanging on for the words that would sustain her one more time.

"I love you, Carly, with all my heart. Safe journey, my love."

Once the words left Poppy's mouth, Carly took her last breath.

For a good while after the sun went down, Poppy just sat there holding her, knowing it would be her last opportunity to do so. She choked out eighteen months' worth of tears she had stored up over Carly's illness until she had no emotion left. She'd been carrying the pain that remained ever since.

But could she let it go? In doing so, would it mean letting Carly herself go? Why was she stuck on this now, after the wonderful evening she'd spent with Julia? She had lived with the pain and loneliness from the moment Carly had died on that beach. She wasn't even sure how she would feel without it.

"You're thinking about it because it's time." Carly stood next to Poppy on the beach, bathed in a brilliant light. "You don't have to let me go. You just have to learn to put me where I belong. We've come as far as we can, and I can't go the rest of the way with you."

"I'm not sure if I want to go without you," Poppy said on a sob. Her head hurt and the cuts around her eyes were killing her, but the pain didn't compare to the despair in her heart.Carly gave her some time to collect herself, then asked, "Do you have doubts about your girl?"

Poppy had to repeat the question to herself a couple of times to move her thoughts to the here and now. "Why do you ask?"

"Because I'm dead and it fills my days to ask annoying questions of the living." Carly's tone made Poppy laugh, dispelling the gloom that had dragged her down.

"The situation I find myself in is very unique," Poppy reflected aloud. "For most of my adult life I loved you more than I thought I was capable of loving anyone. So much so that when you left me here alone, that's what I predicted for the future—I'd be alone."

"But then…"

"But then I found my way back to being happy. It's kinda stupid, but a small part of me feels guilty."

Poppy gazed at the inky vastness of the water and the bleakness of the land. She and Carly had picnicked along these rocks often. Despite its uselessness as a tourist attraction, this area had been one of Carly's favorite places on Carly's Sound. They had come up with the name for the resort and island standing where they were now. Carly had always made the comment it was where you could hear the land the best.

"This was the one place we never needed words," said Poppy loud enough to be heard over the pounding.

"I love this place so much because it's always reminded me of you," Carly said.

"Flowers and pretty beaches I could understand, but our relationship compares with this place?"

"Yes. This place is constant, just like you were for me. Those waves are you, Poppy. They'll never stop pounding into these rocks and I always equated that to how you loved me. Your love hit me with such force that it filled every space in me you could reach, and just when I thought it couldn't get better, you did it over and over again to the point where I expected it.

"Don't get me wrong, I never took you for granted, but I had spent my life expecting the people I was with to choose the distractions over me. I never got their all because there was always someone prettier or more exciting who would come along to usurp my place. But not with you, never once did that happen with you. You, my darling, where there every day. I got all of you, but like those rocks, I was never overwhelmed." Carly stopped for a moment and ran a hand over the rough surface of a rock. The explanation she was giving was slowly curving the corner of Poppy's lips upward.

"The other side of the island has all the flowers and sand you mentioned, but here it's just as beautiful to me. The way you loved me was so perfect and so raw in its intensity, you didn't need all the trappings," explained Carly.

"Thank you for telling me all that."

"I told you because I want you to release the guilt of having to let me go. Look around you, Poppy. Use this place as an example of what your heart should look like when you think about Julia. No distractions. She's a wonderful choice, my love. You don't need to hear this from me, but congratulations."

"Thank you. Maybe I'll find a way to plant one little shrub out here. I promise Julia will get all of me, but there'll always be that one little sliver that'll belong to only you."

"Good thing you're hooking up with a landscaper."

Poppy smiled shakily. "So you aren't upset with me?"

"Poppy, you need the other half of your soul, sweetheart, and she's waiting for you in the opposite direction than you were just headed. I'll always love you, and I know you'll always love me, but it's time for you to follow your heart, honey. You need to live in the here and now. It's the only way to your future."

The admonishment in her tone was so familiar, Poppy smiled and carefully brushed her tears away. Carly had always been a clear talker, no matter what the subject. It was nice to hear things hadn't changed.

"You were the other half of my soul, Carly."

"There's room in your heart for someone else. Trust me." Carly was getting dimmer as she finished talking, but Poppy still felt surrounded by her love. She reached, wanting to cling to the vision before her.

"Don't leave me again," she pleaded.

"I'm not leaving yet, honey, but our time is growing short. Start thinking with the part of your heart that's trying to burst free, the part that wants to love and live again."

With that she was gone, drawn back into the heavens leaving a shooting star as proof she was there, leaving Poppy rooted in place, wondering what to do next. She looked up and followed Carly's path, then gazed inward and gave a voice to her wishes. There was only one answer she could come up with.

"Julia."

❖

The elder Tallulah was pulled out of a pleasant dream when she heard someone cursing in the yard, followed by footsteps on the porch.

Whoever it was paused at the door before knocking, as if hesitant of doing so because of the late hour.

She opened the door and was rewarded with a disarming smile. "I'm sorry to disturb you, but I have to see—"

Tallulah held up her hand and gave the flirt at her door a smile of her own. She surmised that the cursing she'd heard was in response to the mud caking Poppy's shoes.

"Come on in. You don't need to explain, but take your shoes off first. If you mess up the nice carpets in here, I don't think the owner would appreciate it. Be real quiet, though. The baby's in with her. She doesn't like to let the little one out of her sight if she doesn't have to."

"Thanks, Mrs. Johnson, I owe you one." Poppy stepped into the house and gave Julia's grandmother a kiss on the cheek.

"A nice vacation at some other exotic location might be an even trade," Tallulah said. "I hear tell Mexico's nice this time of year."

"I'll keep that in mind."

CHAPTER TWENTY

The next morning Poppy woke up to feel someone running a finger slowly across her eyebrows. There was a weight on her chest, as well as along the rest of her body, and after the cobwebs cleared she realized who it was. Poppy kissed Julia hello and caressed her cheek, loving the feel of the soft skin under her fingertips.

"Good morning," she whispered.

The burr of her voice made Julia look up at her and smile. "I'll have to wish on shooting stars more often."

"Huh?"

"After you left last night, I was feeding Tallulah and saw a shooting star from the bedroom window. I wished it would bring you back to me, and it did." Julia kissed Poppy again. "Now as much as I'd like to give the star all the credit, how did you get here?"

"I saw the same star. It told me to look into my heart and make my wishes come true."

Julia put her head back on Poppy's chest and just soaked up the warmth of the body beneath her. "I asked you last night what you wanted. Does your being here this morning mean you've started to figure it out?"

"Yes, I have. With a little help, I sure have."

"What do you want?"

The question was so like the one Carly had asked at the beginning of their relationship, and she had given an honest answer then. Now would be no different. Poppy just spoke from the heart.

"I want you. I want a life with you and Tallulah, and I want to make music in the sun. I want to take care of you and have you two take care of me. And when we're done, I want you to feel like you've lived a good life because of it."

"I want that too." Julia stroked the inside of Poppy's left hand before moving to her fingers. She stopped when she came across the ring finger and almost cried. The wide banded ring was gone, and in its place was a prominent tan line as the only sign it had ever graced Poppy's finger.

Poppy knew why Julia had stopped, and she just curled her fingers around the smaller ones in her palm. They would have to wait for another time to savor the significance of the gesture as the soft sounds coming from the bassinet interrupted their morning.

Julia rolled onto her side so she could watch Poppy get up to retrieve Tallulah. Poppy had kept on her shirt from the night before, but had taken off her pants and shoes. The sight of the rumpled-looking woman wearing only the shirt and boxer shorts made her laugh.

"I see that your mother's not a boxer woman," Poppy told Tallulah. The cooing infant turned her green eyes to her and reached out for her face again like she had the previous afternoon. Walking back to the bed with her, Poppy asked Julia, "Got milk?"

Julia took Tallulah and got comfortable to feed her, settling against Poppy when she sat a little behind her for support.

With her arm around Julia, Poppy used one of her fingers to rub the wispy fuzz on the baby's head. "Her hair's starting to lighten up, don't you think?"

"Yeah, Ray and I both had almost white hair until we were like five. Then it became more like the color we have today."

There was one other question Poppy hadn't asked in the whole time they had known each other, the story of Tallulah's conception. She wondered if it was really important who'd fathered the baby she had come to love, then decided she had a right to ask. If she was going to spend the next twenty years helping rear Tallulah, she wanted to be sure she wouldn't be treading on anyone else's toes.

"Julia, is there someone…" She started the question but didn't know how to finish.

"I got drunk at a party one night, and one of Ray's friends decided he liked me. It was the most irresponsible and stupid thing I've ever done." Julia sounded so disparaging of herself, Poppy wished she hadn't asked. "I've gone over and over that night, trying to find a way to excuse my behavior, but there isn't one. I woke up the next morning next to this guy who didn't want another thing to do with me. It did wonders for my self-esteem when he told me I was like a piece of wood in bed."

"Sweetheart, you don't have to do this. I just wanted to know if there's someone we have to share her with. How she got here doesn't matter to me." Poppy whispered into Julia's ear and held her as best she could without disrupting the baby's meal.

"I want you to know," Julia insisted. It was best, her granny had always told her, to start on something important with no secrets. She wished she'd remembered that a bit sooner. "There's too much I've kept from you." Taking Poppy's hand for reassurance, she continued her story.

"For a week I went from total guilt, to joy, to denial. I thought about the alternatives and tried to drown out the objections of my parents once I found the courage to tell them, but in the end she was growing inside of me and I wanted her. I figured I'd find someone who'd love her as much as I do, and want to help raise her, so the decision was easy."

"Doesn't he want to be involved in her life?"

"No, he said he'd fight paternity so I didn't push it, since I don't want anything from him. When the time comes, I'll have to explain that to her and hope she understands."

"When that day comes, we'll both explain it to her." Poppy kissed Julia's temple and pressed closer into her.

"Thank you. I couldn't have conjured up someone more perfect to share her with." Julia turned a little and looked up to eyes that held a little hint of anger. Not directed at her, but on her behalf.

"The guy's a fool to give up the chance at getting to know her. She's a great kid."

"He's a fool who had to drink his meals through a straw for weeks after Ray got done with him. I love Ray, but sometimes he does his thinking with his fists." Julia kissed the lips so close to hers.

Poppy blinked slowly once they were done and tried to forget about the pain in her face. "Really? I would've never guessed that about him." Ignoring Julia's snort, she lifted Tallulah up to burp her.

Julia held the sheet up to her chest and watched her daughter give Poppy a milky smile. The night before when Poppy had crawled into bed with her, Julia had felt right at home next to the big body. If Poppy was expecting an argument, she must have been surprised when Julia just rolled over and nestled into her.

"What's the game plan?" Julia asked.

"That's easy. After we finish opening this place, you and I will find a place to live. Or I'll find you two a place to live, and I'll move in next door, if you'd prefer that. We have plenty of time to figure it all out. Where would you like to live?"

"Anywhere where you are," was Julia's answer.

Poppy grinned. "I think I'd like to explore your reasons for saying that. Want to come to my place for breakfast?"

"I'll go put Tallulah to bed and see if Granny's awake."

❖

A short while later, now at Poppy's bungalow, Julia got out of the shower and stepped out onto the patio, wrapped in one of the big fluffy robes she had found in the bathroom. She felt tears well up as Poppy stood and stretched out her arms for her.

"What's the matter, baby?" Poppy could feel Julia's hot breath against her chest and felt a small flutter of worry at the uneven rise and fall of her shoulders. Were they going too fast? "We don't have to—"

"I want to," Julia said, tears welling again. "I just can't believe this is really happening. And I was just thinking, in the shower, I haven't even asked you if you want to be a parent or just be a part of Tallulah's life."

"Honey, could you do me a favor and shut up for a minute." Poppy put her palm on Julia's cheek and with her thumb dried some of the tears away. "I've been as clear as the Mississippi River when it comes to my feelings, haven't I? I'm sorry about that."

Julia shook her head to protest, but the finger pressed to her lips stopped her from doing so.

"I woke up this morning with you by my side, and for the first time in forever I didn't want to cry as soon as the sun came up. You make me feel alive, Julia. After everything, I feel like there's someone I can count on again. There's someone I want to be with and sing to. I know that sounds crazy, but it's a big part of who I am."

Even as she spoke, Poppy felt flooded with certainty. She had lived well up to now; her success was there for everyone to see in the bricks and mortar she had laid over the years. She'd experienced joy and overwhelming pain, and now it was time to live and take chances again. All that her life had taught her up to now had brought her to this place, with this woman.

"I know that being with you means being committed to two people, not one. But the thought of helping you raise Tallulah doesn't scare me. I love her." As Poppy gazed into Julia's darkening green eyes, she felt ready to step into the future with her. To live life again. Taking Julia's hand in her own, she said, "I love you, Julia."

At the words, Julia's tears started again. "I love you too."

"Do you want to take a chance with me? I promise to give you my best for as long as you'll let me stay with you. Would you be willing to share Tallulah with me? If you say yes, I'll spend my life making you two happy and working hard to make us a family." Poppy kissed Julia's palm softly.

The feel of her lips shot a sensation of heat to Julia's core, and she leaned forward to accept a kiss that made her moan. "I want you in my life, and Tallulah will thank me one day because you are."

They both stopped talking then, and Julia ran her fingers into Poppy's hair, drawing her forward. She slipped her tongue into Poppy's open mouth and savored her taste. This was their beginning, here on the shores of Poppy's beautiful island. Hand in hand they walked into the bedroom to experience that beginning in all its possibilities.

A little nervous, Julia opened Poppy's robe and allowed her eyes to travel slowly over the tall, muscular body unencumbered by clothes. It looked as good as it had the night she'd watched Poppy walk into her bungalow after getting out of the outdoor shower. Interpreting Julia's hesitance for cold feet, Poppy tried to reassure her. "We can take it slow. We have all the time in the world."

"I've waited all my life for you. Make love to me."

Poppy pulled off Julia's robe and let it drop to the floor. With a slow touch, she ran her hands along the smooth, creamy skin, loving the goose bumps she raised as she went. When Poppy stepped back to look at her, Julia stood nervously under the scrutiny of her soon-to-be lover's gaze.

For Poppy, the sight of the full and heavy breasts and the small patch of blond hair flooded her passions. With a quick flick of her wrist, she turned down the bed and pulled Julia to her. She wanted to feel that beautiful body against her own, with no barriers between them.

Julia moaned as her skin came into contact with Poppy's. Only for a split second did she wonder if Poppy would be turned off by the aftereffects of her pregnancy. The reassuring hands running down her back and the heat in Poppy's eyes melted her doubts. As Poppy touched lower, Julia moaned again and felt herself grow wetter.

"I love the feel of you," said Poppy. Julia offered up no resistance when she rolled them over so she could look down on her body. "You're so perfect."

Julia could feel the hot blush in her cheeks extend all the way down her throat to her chest. "I'm still recovering from what my little bundle of joy did to my body, so I don't think so."

"Baby, I mean it. You're beautiful."

Poppy used just her fingertips and started at Julia's forehead. Slowly she dragged them down the slope of her pink cheek to her breastbone, where she stopped to place a kiss on her neck. Not wanting to miss out on the visual tour, she watched the progress of her fingers down to Julia's right breast. The touch narrowed to one finger as it slowly circled just the areola. With each lazy circle the skin puckered more and more until the nipple looked painfully hard.

"Honey, please," said Julia, hoping to break the spell Poppy seemed to be in.

"Please what?" Blue eyes met green, and Poppy smiled at the way Julia's nostrils flared. "Are you trying to tell me you have two of these beauties?"

Any response to the funny question died on Julia's lips as Poppy sucked the nipple into her mouth. Julia arched her back to increase the contact and gasped when Poppy switched from sucking to biting down gently. They could have done just that for the rest of the night and it would have been better than all of Julia's prior experiences. The only other time she had felt this raw energy coursing through her was the night she'd seen Poppy naked for the first time.

Julia was so turned on she could feel the sheet getting wet under her. She tugged on Poppy's ponytail, wanting to feel those lips on hers again. She closed her eyes when Poppy's tongue slid into her mouth. The kiss was unlike any of the ones they'd shared since admitting their feelings. She now knew Poppy loved her, but the hand squeezing her breast and the kiss meant she also desired her.

The sensations in Julia were building, and she pressed so hard into Poppy, she got her to roll over onto her back. "Honey, I need you to touch me." Julia felt so wet and ready, she was rubbing against Poppy's abdomen trying to find relief.

Poppy groaned as she ran her fingers down between them and encountered the wetness that painted Julia's skin with slick moisture every time she moved. Poppy took her time, wanting to savor the first touch of her lover's center. When her fingers finally dragged across Julia's core, Julia pulled her lips away from Poppy's and took a deep breath.

Poppy stopped at Julia's entrance and waited. With what looked like physical difficulty, Julia opened her eyes to meet those of the woman waiting to claim her. "Yes, honey, I want you."

Still not rushing her movements, Poppy barely slipped in one finger to the knuckle before pulling out again. Julia was about to protest its departure when another joined it, and they went in all the way. She felt so full and Poppy looked so loving, it undid Julia and her eyes filled with tears.

Poppy's first instinct was to want to pull out, thinking she'd done something wrong. "Did I hurt you?"

"No." Julia wiped away a tear that had escaped. "Don't move your hand yet, baby. You feel so good I just want to enjoy having you inside me."

"I love you." Poppy waited until she felt a slight twitch in Julia's hips before pressing her thumb against her clitoris. The move pushed Julia up higher as she gripped Poppy's shoulders for the ride. Poppy could only smile when two pink nipples appeared inches from her face.

The first swipe of Poppy's tongue against her chest made Julia push her center harder against the fingers, taking her toward the best climax of her life. It was a delicious feeling to let go like this with the person you loved. She wanted the moment to last, but she could feel the tightness beginning. "Oh, my God, honey, don't stop."

"Come for me, baby," said Poppy before suckling Julia's breast again. The words and the move sent Julia over the edge.

Julia stopped moving altogether, and Poppy thought something had gone wrong.

After an intense moment, Julia slumped against her, knocking them both to the mattress. Her inner walls flexed, not wanting to lose Poppy as she began to ease out.

"I have a confession to make," Julia said after she'd caught her breath. "When we first met and you took us out for the first time on the boat, I went to your house that night to make sure you'd made it back all right. When I got there you were getting out of the outdoor shower and walking naked into the house. Marta caught me staring, but even then I couldn't look away from you. You woke something up in me without even laying a hand on me, and I've been dreaming of nothing else but touching you ever since."

Poppy pulled Julia down so that she was lying on top of her.

"I guess this can only mean one thing." Poppy kissed the top her head.

"What?"

"We need more bushes around that damned shower."

Julia struck quickly, giving Poppy no chance to defend herself from the hard pinch to her bottom. With equal quickness Poppy rolled them over so she was pinning Julia to the mattress, and with one hand she captured the two smaller ones of her tormentor.

"You've got me, you big brute. What are you going to do with me?" Julia raised her head and bit down on Poppy's neck before sucking the flesh into her mouth.

"I think I'll keep you." Poppy let go of her hands and kissed her.

"Oh, honey, you ain't getting rid of us now."

Free, Julia let her hands wander over Poppy's broad back and down to the place she had only seen from a hundred feet, Poppy's butt. She had to sit up a little to reach it, but the hard, perfect cheeks were worth the uncomfortable position. She felt Poppy's breathing start to quicken at the caresses, so she moved her hands, running her fingernails slowly up her back, applying enough pressure that it left some light red marks.

The muscles in Poppy's arms and chest were standing out in vivid relief from the exertion of holding most of her weight off Julia, but it was getting more difficult as Julia kept changing the direction of her hands. To revel in the feeling, Poppy bent and joined their lips in a kiss.

Her arousal climbing, Julia parted her mouth and opened her legs wider to accommodate the big body. She squeezed her hand between them and opened herself up, feeling the new flood between her legs. With the same hand, she spread Poppy apart so they could slide against one another. The evidence of Julia's excitement mingled with Poppy's equally drenched folds. With the first deep moan from Poppy, Julia spread her legs wider, looking forward to the ride.

"That's it, baby, let go for me," she said, reveling in the power in Poppy's body as she pumped harder and faster.

"Oh, Julia, I'm coming." Poppy could feel Julia's nails dragging up her back, and it was driving her crazy.

"Come on, love, we'll do it together." When her hands moved down to Poppy's butt again and squeezed, it was the final catalyst. Poppy pumped faster, but Julia was there to meet her thrust for thrust until there was no turning back. With one final push, Poppy brought them both over the edge.

Poppy didn't know how long she lay in Julia's embrace or why tears were streaming down her face. The hands that only moments ago were all over her now rubbed her back slowly, and Julia's legs were wrapped around her waist, making Poppy feel like she was using her whole body to reassure her.

"I'm sorry, baby, I must be crushing you," she said with a small crack in her voice. She tried to roll off but only met with resistance when Julia tightened her hold.

"I like you just where you are, love. Don't move. Are you okay?" She had felt the hot tears on her shoulder when Poppy came crashing down on her after they had made love. Julia just knew her heart wouldn't be able to take it if Poppy regretted they had moved their relationship forward like this.

"I'm great, as a matter of fact. Just got a little intense there for a minute. It's embarrassing, really, but it's been a long time. I don't usually cry after sex, but I just felt so happy I went with it."

"Well, I think it's great you trust me enough already to do that. You don't ever have to be embarrassed for showing your emotions, especially if it's because I've made you feel good. I want us to always be honest with each other, even when you think I might not like what you have to say." The tie of Poppy's ponytail had come undone, and Julia ran her fingers through the thick curly hair.

The pensive look on her face made Poppy ask, "How are you doing, baby?"

"Wonderful. I was just wondering how your hair would look if you cut it."

"A lot curlier than it does now. The length tends to pull the curls down a bit, but when it's short it's downright springy. Why do you ask?" Poppy wanted to soak up the afterglow with Julia, but she was starting to get distracted by the smooth flesh stretched out beneath her own.

"I was just thinking how it'd feel curled around my fingers if it was short. Have I told you how much I love curly hair?" The mouth sucking on her neck made Julia lose her own interest in the conversation, and her mind focused instead on the hand burning a path up her body.

"I have my own confession to make to you, beautiful." Poppy could almost feel Julia's moans, they were so deep.

"What…What is it?" Poppy's hand was doing interesting things to her body, impairing her ability to form coherent sentences.

"Ever since I got in this bed with you, I've been wondering what you might taste like. Is that part as sweet as the rest of you?" Poppy asked.

Because of the cuts on her partner's face and the bruises around her eyes, Julia opted for the only safe alternative to what Poppy had in mind. Taking two fingers, she sat up and ran them through her sex, thoroughly coating them, and then she pressed them to Poppy's mouth. Those blue eyes made her feel beautiful, releasing Julia of all her inhibitions, and when Poppy's warm tongue welcomed her fingers, Julia pushed Poppy's hand down between her legs.

She wanted to be free to move and let Poppy enjoy watching her, so she positioned Poppy's fingers so she would be doing all the work.

Poppy gasped. "God, baby, that's so sexy."

When the walls around Poppy's fingers clamped down, Julia stopped moving. Once she had reached the pinnacle of her excitement, it was her turn to drop bonelessly onto Poppy's chest.

❖

Several hours later, Julia opened her robe and let it drop to the floor, then pulled the drawstring on the cotton pajama pants she'd put on, enjoying the way Poppy followed their path to the floor. "Why are you dressed?" she asked.

Poppy would have signed over the deed to one of the properties to watch Julia walk naked across the room again. "I need to do some work today."

The sunlight filtering in through the closed blinds gave Poppy a perfect view of Julia's breasts as she bent to spread Poppy's legs apart. Poppy took advantage and kissed her as Julia dropped down to her knees at the side of the bed. The kiss lasted long enough for both of them to run out of air; then Julia encouraged Poppy to lean back on her hands.

Poppy's new position made it easy for Julia to unbuckle the alligator skin belt so she could reach the buttons of the fly of the linen pants. "Lift, please."

Poppy did, getting turned on by the way Julia dragged her pants and boxers down slowly until they puddled at her ankles.

The buttons of her shirt came next, and Julia kissed each newly exposed patch of skin as she uncovered it. When Poppy went to remove the garment, Julia stopped her. "I'll do it, honey. Just not yet. Lean back on your hands again."

Curious as to what her partner had in mind, Poppy did as she was asked.

Julia thought she'd never seen a more enticing sight. With care she lifted Poppy's feet to get rid of the clothing they wouldn't need, tossing the pants and underwear over her shoulder. She used her thumbs to open Poppy to her gaze.

"But, baby, your surprise is up here."

"And your thank you is down here." Julia bit down gently before she started sucking. Poppy's hips shot forward.

"Oh, yeah." It wasn't poetic, but it was all Poppy was capable of.

Before long they were naked again and in need of a nap. Poppy had her hands on Julia's backside, and Julia draped over the top of her.

"In case I haven't told you, honey, your hair looks great." Gone was the ponytail, and in its place the kind of hairstyle that Julia could imagine running her fingers through all day. The fact that Poppy must have cut it herself, just for her, made her slightly breathless.

"If I'm going to get this kind of reaction, then, hell, is there something else about me you'd like changed?"

"Nope, you're perfect now. Is there something about me you'd like for me to change?" Julia was having trouble concentrating on their conversation; Poppy's fingers were wreaking havoc with her senses yet again.

"Well, there is something." The fingers stopped and Julia looked up. "But it's more like a favor than something I want you to change. Would you have dinner with my parents tonight so that they can meet you?"

The inevitable would have to happen sooner or later, and Poppy could only hope Isabelle was in a good mood when she met the new woman in her daughter's life.

"Of course. What should I wear?" The question was a stall tactic on Julia's part. "I didn't realize they were here."

"They're actually arriving later today, so you can meet them tonight, and you can wear whatever you feel comfortable in."

"Of course they're coming. It's your opening," rambled Julia, until something Poppy had said broke through. "Wait, you're not coming?" She pushed herself up a little higher so she could get a better look at Poppy's face.

"No, I thought I'd give you the opportunity to get to know them without me." Poppy almost laughed at the look on Julia's face. Not having the heart to keep up her joke, she kissed the tip of Julia's nose and tried to wink up at her.

"That was mean, Valente. Just be prepared for my revenge."

CHAPTER TWENTY-ONE

"Where are you?" Julia asked wordlessly through clenched teeth.

Poppy had gone to her office after they had gotten up to get some work out of the way, and Julia hadn't seen her for the rest of the afternoon. Her busy lover had called around three to say she was running late and would meet Julia in the restaurant before her parents arrived.

Julia had been sitting by the pool entertaining Poppy's parents for almost an hour, now, and there was no sign of their only offspring.

Every time Julia looked across the table, she felt certain Isabelle Valente was working out an inventory list in her head, ticking off Julia's various shortcomings.

"You know, my Poppy, what she need is a good person to settle her down and give me grandbabies to spoil. You like babies, no?"

"I love babies, yes." Julia smiled. She wanted the same things with Poppy.

The early chill between her and Isabelle had thawed a little, and Julia thought at this rate they might be friends by the time Tallulah was in college. She met Raphael's amused eyes as he signaled the waitress for another drink. She was intrigued at how similar Poppy was to him; the trademark looks that set her apart did the same for him.

"Papi, look what I found under a bush on the way over here." Poppy walked to the table with Tallulah in her arms, bending to drop a kiss on her father's cheek before moving around the table and giving her mother a big hug.

Raphael immediately got up and took the cooing baby out of Poppy's arms, bouncing her in delight. Julia stole a quick glance at Isabelle and saw tears in her eyes as she watched her husband play with the baby.

Before she made official introductions, Poppy gave Julia a soft kiss on the lips and handed her a beautifully wrapped gift. "I believe my mother's been waiting for this moment from the day I was born, so why don't you do the honors, love."

Unable to resist, Julia ran her fingers through Poppy's freshly washed curls before turning her attention to the gift. She had an idea of what was in the box from their early conversation about Poppy's parents. She had waited until Poppy was there to tell the couple about Tallulah. Wanting grandchildren was one thing; accepting one who was no blood relation was something else.

"Mami, a little something for the next cocktail party you host," said Poppy as Julia handed her mother the box.

Inside was a framed picture of Poppy and Julia with Tallulah, coming into Aruba's port aboard the *Piper*. The harbormaster's wife had taken the picture, in an unguarded moment, and had captured the beginnings of a family. Poppy's head was thrown back in laughter as Julia leaned against her, holding the baby.

"May I hold her?" Isabelle asked Julia.

"Of course you can, Mrs. Valente. This is my daughter, Tallulah."

Julia was touched when Isabelle took Tallulah from her husband and just held her against her chest. The baby quickly fell into the role of spoiled grandchild and started cooing as if for a woman who would fulfill her every whim.

"Oh, Julia, she's beautiful." Isabelle held Tallulah away from her shoulder to study the small face. "She look like my Poppy when she was a baby. Soft blond hair, but the eyes they were blue. Then the Valente took over. A big moose I get, like Raphael."

"And you wonder why I never want to go out to dinner with you?" Poppy teased, making Julia laugh. As her parents continued to dote over the baby, she leaned over and kissed Julia again, murmuring, "Did you survive the Spanish Inquisition?"

"It wasn't too bad. Though various federal law enforcement agencies could learn something from her techniques. I missed you."

"I missed you as well, but I'm glad we don't have to fly down to south Florida."

Isabelle looked up from the baby, apparently ready to finish the questions she had about the new women in Poppy's life. "Que paso?"

What happened? She ran her fingers over the wicked-looking bruises surrounding her daughter's blue eyes.

Picking up a cue from Poppy, Raphael said, "Not now, Isabelle. Poppy had an accident, and in time it will heal. Let's be grateful for that and enjoy our night with Tallulah and Julia."

Poppy gave him a tiny nod of thanks. He knew his wife well enough not to have shared the contents of Poppy's phone call about Julia's brother and what had happened between them. For the rest of the evening she and Julia talked with her father, while her mother fussed with Tallulah.

They returned to the beach house early so Julia could feed the baby with her soon-to-be mother-in-law looking on. Sitting in the rocker in Tallulah's room, breast-feeding and talking with the woman who had once nurtured Poppy the same way, Julia felt overwhelmed. To know Tallulah would have at least one set of doting grandparents filled her heart.

"Are you mad I didn't tell you about her right away?" she asked.

"No, that was sneaky, Julia, but I forgive you if you let me spoil this little girl. I never thought Poppy would have a family that would include a baby. Carly, well, let us say I didn't agree with that choice, but who am I? Just the mother. We grew to be friends, she and I, but it was a long road. I promised myself when she die, and I saw the suffering in my child's heart, I accept Poppy's choices for her life no matter what. But now look at what she has found."

Julia tried to find the words to express what this acceptance meant to her, but she could see Isabelle understood. Poppy's mother just smiled, opening her arms as if to embrace Julia and her daughter.

"Raphael and I welcome you to our family. You and your daughter will never want for anything."

"We just want Poppy, Mrs. Valente, and we promise to always take good care of her." Julia reached out and took the woman's hand in her own, squeezing firmly.

"You've lost your baby, now, sweetheart," teased Poppy from the door. "Once my mother gets her hooks into her, Tallulah will have more stuff than we do."

If she expected a snappy comeback from her mother, Isabelle surprised her by walking up to her and hugging her, then leaving the room to sit with her husband.

In a now familiar routine, Poppy took Tallulah and hummed softly to her while Julia adjusted her clothing back into place. By the middle of the second song, Tallulah was sleeping and Julia was dressed. They both stood by the baby bed and watched Tallulah sleep for a minute.

"I never thought this kind of happiness could exist for me," Julia said. "When I was pregnant with her, I was always sad because my parents gave me such a hard time. I thought they should have been happy because they'd be grandparents. I don't know why I was surprised that they weren't—they didn't like being parents, either."

At the catch in her lover's voice, Poppy slid an arm over her shoulder. Julia's granny had told her how little parental love the Johnson twins had received from their parents, and Poppy thought this explained a lot. She was even willing to cut Rayford some slack over his immaturity. The kid obviously hadn't had a male role model worth a dime in his life, and his protectiveness of his twin scored points with Poppy, albeit misguided.

She said, "I think you made my mother's day."

Pensively, Julia said, "How ironic that I had to travel to what seems like another world to find the people who'll give my daughter the kind of home and family she deserves. I love you, Poppy, and I want to thank you for introducing me to your parents." She felt the strong arms encircle her completely, and her old sorrows just disappeared.

"You're welcome, my love. Try to remember, Tallulah's our daughter now. Think you can share?"

"I'll share anything and everything with you." Julia's face was sweetly solemn. "I love you."

They kissed, long and deeply, and Julia felt at home in a way she never had. This was where she belonged; a deeply buried part of her had recognized that from the moment she first saw Poppy. This was meant to be, and she was going to do everything within her power to cherish every moment they were given.

❖

"Oh, my God! I punched the owner of Valente Resorts and my sister's girlfriend, not once, but twice? Miguel told me who she was that day, and I thought he was just messing with me." Rayford grabbed the folder they had given him in training and started leafing through it. His face was as pale as Julia had ever seen it.

"What are you doing?" she asked.

"I'm looking to see where she owns all her properties because, believe me, if there's one near hell, that's where she's going to transfer me. That's if I don't get fired."

"Calm down. Poppy's in the vacation business, so I'm sure all her properties are in decent locations. Besides, I thought you wanted to be transferred?"

Rayford hesitated. "I like it here, Jules. Miguel's great, and I really love my job. I know it sounds corny coming from me, but it's true. Once the guests started to arrive, all the training made sense. All that's down the drain now."

His shoulders slumped, and Julia knew exactly what that was about. Their father would have one more opportunity to be disappointed in him. "Nothing's going to happen to you, so chill," she said, smiling at him.

"Yeah, how do you know?"

"Let's just say I'm in the position to protect you from the fury of Poppy Valente."

"Isn't this all a little rushed? You were trying to get away from her a couple of days ago." He squinted at her as if thinking of something else. "She didn't do anything to you, did she? I can kick her ass."

Julia ignored the threat. "I'm happy, Ray. She makes me happy."

"So you love her, huh?"

"Very much."

"What about Tallulah?"

"Poppy loves her. She loves both of us, and I trust her enough to know time won't change that. This isn't a fling."

"I'm happy for you, sis. And just remember, I can take her down. So if she ever…"

"Let's not go there," Julia said dryly.

"Sounds like I need to do the manly thing and have a talk with Poppy, make sure she's clear on her responsibility to the two of you." Rayford bit his lower lip, his anxiety transparent. He'd been avoiding Poppy like she was the first human case of bird flu since she and Julia got back from Aruba. "I'll head over there when I feel better and do just that."

Hoping he would have the good sense to conduct himself like an adult, Julia said, "Good idea. Just don't talk too much."

❖

"Maybe a shot of the tequila you're so fond of?"

Poppy could just make out Lizzie's suggestion over the crying going on next to her ear. Jokingly, she said, "I don't think her mother would appreciate me liquoring up the kid."

Lizzie laughed. They had spent the afternoon babysitting and working on the contracts she'd put together, and she no longer felt concerned that Poppy might push her aside now that there was a new woman in her life. At the same time, she wasn't all that sure she was ready to see Poppy with someone who wasn't Carly.

On the credenza behind Poppy sat a slew of pictures, which, like all the ones scattered throughout the bungalow, depicted happier times. Lizzie decided to do some redecorating, as a goodwill gesture, as soon as she could get her hands on pictures of Julia and Tallulah.

"What's the matter, pumpkin. You don't recognize my face? You can blame your Uncle Rayford for messing up my features."

"I'm sure he feels just terrible about that." Hearing her mother's voice made Tallulah cry harder. "Hi, Elizabeth."

"Hey, I know at least one person who's missed you besides Randy Raccoon over there," Lizzie teased. "I'm going to go take a walk before dinner. Page me if you two need anything."

"Remember, eight o'clock tonight over at the beach house," Poppy said as Julia took the baby from her and moved to the sofa to feed her. For the first time in twenty minutes she didn't have to raise her voice. As soon as Lizzie had left she said, "I think this is the first time some girl has come in here and exposed a breast without kissing me hello first."

"Does that mean it usually happens *after* they kiss you hello?"

"So many times, it's hard to keep track." Poppy leaned over and pressed her lips to Julia's.

"We're going to have to do something about this." Julia ran a finger lightly over the cut on Poppy's forehead. "You were my secret weapon before you became damaged goods. Now my princess doesn't recognize you."

"The truth comes out. You love me only for my babysitting abilities." Poppy kissed the tip of Julia's finger and laughed. "We could always ask your brother to take her off our hands when she gets too cranky."

"Not funny, Valente. I was thinking more along the lines of you seeing a medical professional."

The sight of Julia feeding the baby softened the teasing look on Poppy's face. Watching the beautiful act made her understand what Isabelle had tried to explain about children and the passage of time.

"I made an appointment today to have them stitched. If they scar too badly I can always have something done about it when we get back to the States."

"Anything else running around in here?" Julia tapped her finger on Poppy's temple, sensing she had a lot on her mind.

"I was just thinking about my mother. For years she's been telling me what a blessing children are, and I was just agreeing with her. Watching you do this makes me feel so lucky." Poppy put her hand on the back of Tallulah's head as she took a break to blow a milk bubble. "I love you two very much."

When the baby was finished, Julia sat in Poppy's lap for a while, content to enjoy the beginning of desire, but willing to wait until they were alone. The quiet of the room put the baby to sleep, so she left Poppy in the end to take Tallulah back to the house. Poppy joined Lizzie, and for the first time since the opening of the resort, they inspected the property together.

Law school and experience had taught Lizzie her profession, but everything she knew about the hospitality business had come from the person next to her.

"Congratulations. She seems to be a wonderful woman," Lizzie said.

It sounded sincere enough, but Poppy was aware of a strain between them. "Thanks. You want to tell me what's bothering you? And don't say it's nothing."

Lizzie's jaw clicked shut, and she smiled at the reprimand. "It's nothing."

"Nothing a trip to the woodshed won't cure." Poppy gave Lizzie a mock glare.

"I said it was nothing," Lizzie reiterated, which made Poppy's eyes close to slits.

"And I called you a liar, so spit it out." Poppy took Lizzie's hand. "I know you, well enough to know something's bothering you. Don't shut me out."

Lizzie looked down at the hand holding hers and tried to formulate the right words. She wanted Poppy to be happy. She knew that was the mature way to feel, but she couldn't help but think everyone had to have a character flaw. Jealousy was hers. "She seems like a nice person."

"I'm guessing you mean Julia?"

"Yeah, and you look like you've taken to parenthood as well." The soft, thoughtful tone Lizzie was using hit Poppy between the eyes like a club. "I'm glad it's something you won't miss out on."

"Honey, you're my family too. Don't think so little of me that I'd forget that."

"I know. It's just Mom…" Lizzie didn't know how to finish. She let out a long sigh. "I shouldn't have said anything."

"You have every right to say whatever you want to me, whenever you want. I think we've both earned that privilege in each other's life. It's time for me to exercise it now." Poppy steered them toward her bungalow. "I want you to understand what Julia means to me, and why I chose not to fight it anymore. Your mother meant everything to me."

"I know, and she's gone, so I'm happy you're moving on."

"You make it sound like I'm moving out of an apartment and leaving an old sofa behind."

Lizzie laughed at the analogy. "I'm just a little jealous." Poppy saw her duck her head at the admission. The time had come for the talk they'd ignored even when Carly was alive.

"You'll find someone. Just give yourself time."

"I know that, but the waiting…it's hard." Lizzie tried to stay in control of her emotions.

"But the rewards are worth every minute. Have I ever told you about the night two blondes and a brunette walked into a bar?"

"Yeah, the Stevens clan are quite the punch line," said Lizzie with a laugh.

"Last time around I fell for the brunette and got you as part of the deal. This time it's the blonde, and I'm getting Rayford. For every silver lining…a dark cloud." They both laughed, and Poppy asked, "Are we okay, now?"

"We're fine. Go make sure there's no emergency for the night, and I'll go on ahead and tell them you're right behind me."

❖

A few evenings later, Poppy and Julia walked to the large common area by the main pool, holding hands. They smiled at one another when they saw Poppy's mother fussing with Tallulah. The newly minted grandmother had come by and taken the baby to get her ready.

"I think you were right. We may've lost her," said Julia, looking at their daughter. Tiny palm trees covered the new dress Tallulah had on, and from the smile on her face, she was content to be in Isabelle's arms. "But I don't mind, after seeing the kind of final product she puts out."

Carly's two oldest friends smiled when Poppy and Julia reached their table and exchanged a hug. Poppy knew their adoring looks would've normally had Matlin and Sabrina gagging by now, but the two were teary when Poppy pulled Julia to her and they started to dance.

From her seat, Lizzie focused her camera and took some candid shots of the oblivious couple. She had been dreading this day from the moment her mother had gone, the opening of the place Poppy identified most with her memories of Carly. For a long while, Lizzie had been afraid to mention Carly's Sound, knowing it sent Poppy somewhere dark within herself.

"But look at you now," whispered Lizzie.

Her closest friends and family stood and held their champagne glasses up in salute.

"I found this place what seems like a million years ago, but even then I could envision what it could be one day," Poppy said. "For everything we build in life, we must begin with the foundation. Mami and Papi, thank you for being mine." She lifted her glass toward her parents before taking a sip. "And thanks for those guitar and piano lessons. They sure have come in handy."

Everyone laughed before lifting their glasses and drinking to the Valente couple.

"Susanna, thank you for all the late hours, last-minute trips you made down here, and for keeping focused on the outcome. It's nice to never have to question if you'll be there for me, no matter what." Poppy's glass went up in her assistant's direction, and she drank again.

"Mickey, there are no words that'll make you understand how grateful I am to you. You finished what we started." Poppy stopped when her throat closed with emotion from seeing the unshed tears filling his eyes.

"You two." She tilted her glass in the direction of Sabrina and Matlin, eliciting a protest from both of them.

"Be nice, or we start telling stories about you when you're done," threatened Sabrina.

"Be quiet so I can be nice to you," Poppy shot back. "Don't ever think a day's gone by for the past two years I haven't realized how much you miss her. Just like Lizzie and I, you lost something precious." Poppy took a deep breath as Sabrina and Matlin nodded their heads.

She could almost hear them talking about her speech-making later: *She's worse than a greeting card commercial.*

"This place," Poppy cocked her head back in the direction of the guests' bungalows, "is your finest hour, my little trio of terror," said Poppy, making reference to Carly, Matlin, and Sabrina. "Here's to everything you've done for me, taught me, and shared with me." Poppy toasted the two and took another sip.

The last person Poppy looked toward was Lizzie, which made her start crying. Poppy opened her mouth a couple of times, but all that came out was, "To Lizzie."

Everyone repeated the toast, and Julia took Poppy's glass and pushed her in Lizzie's direction. The second Poppy opened her arms, Lizzie didn't hesitate accepting the offer. Poppy didn't let her go until she had calmed down.

"We need to raise our glasses one more time," said Poppy when Julia handed her glass back to her. "To Carly. You held me up so I could dream big and accomplish more than I could imagine. You loved me, and it made me feel invincible. And your belief in all of us made this place possible."

Draining her glass, Poppy smiled when she saw Carly standing between Lizzie and Matlin.

"Thank you, Poppy. Now it's time to get on with the business of living and doing it well," Carly said.

Poppy nodded and took Julia's hand, leading her to the dance floor again. "It's a party, people. Shake off the gloom and enjoy it," ordered Poppy of the misty-eyed ensemble.

The band Miguel had hired out of Aruba kept the guests happy until after three in the morning, and when they weren't dancing, everyone enjoyed the buffet and open bar.

"I had a good time," said Julia as they walked back toward the house via the beach. It was about an hour before sunrise, and she was amazed Poppy didn't look tired. "The next time, though, I want to see a real Valente opening."

Poppy laughed as she looked down at the water swirling around her feet. "I'll see what I can do."

"Should I go and try to get Tallulah from your parents?" Julia's breasts were starting to get tender.

"If I had a gun, maybe. Unarmed, I'm not so sure we'd be successful, baby." With a small grunt Poppy dropped into the rocker on their porch. There was just one piece of her past she had to let go, and the time had come to set it free.

CHAPTER TWENTY-TWO

A re you sure you don't want me to come with you?" Julia asked for the fourth time that afternoon. She gazed down at an old tin container in the shape of the cartoon character Betty Boop. Poppy had taken it from the cedar box on her mantle and put it in a waterproof bag.

"Baby, come and sit with me for a minute." Poppy walked Julia to the porch and pulled her onto her lap, setting the bag on the floor next to them.

In her lap sat her future, which she kissed and held until Julia relaxed against her. On the floor sat her past, which was waiting to be set free of its confines. What seemed like an impossible task only a few months before was something Poppy knew she could do now.

Lizzie was waiting on the *Piper* so she wouldn't have to do it alone, but Poppy wanted to take the time to reassure Julia before she left.

"Baby, there's one more thing I have to do for Carly, and it's something she asked me to do before she died. She found this charming container at some flea market, and while I'm sure she's loved occupying it, the time has come to let her go."

Julia smiled at the funny tin bombshell, evidence of Carly's sense of humor. She could only imagine how hard it must be for Poppy to be severing this final tangible link to her.

"I put off doing this," Poppy said. "I didn't want to let go, but it turns out she's in here." She pointed to her heart.

Julia leaned in and kissed her. She loved the fact Poppy was always honest with her feelings, and that she was not going to forget the woman who had shared most of her adult life. As much as Julia wanted to go with her, not out of jealousy, but out of concern for her well-being, she knew this small journey was one Poppy and Elizabeth needed to take alone.

"Our future has just begun, and I don't want any old baggage getting in the way. I love you."

"I love you, too. Promise you'll be careful?" Julia asked when their lips parted.

"I promise, baby."

❖

When Poppy lifted anchor, the sun was low in the sky, Carly's favorite time of day. They had often sat out on the porch or on the beach and watched the big orange ball make its final descent into the water. As she pointed the sailboat away from the island, Poppy remembered all the dreams they had voiced during those sunsets.

For once, the thoughts and memories didn't make her want to cry out of pain, but out of the happiness that she'd had the opportunity to share them with the woman she'd loved. There had been so many firsts with Carly, but Poppy was starting to get comfortable with the idea that there would be more in her lifetime, with Julia.

Carly's appearance at her side was exactly what she'd expected. She didn't care whether the ghost she'd been seeing over the past months was a figment of her imagination. Saying good-bye this way was better than anything she'd hoped for.

"You once told me, you get only one chance at the big game," Carly said in a thoughtful tone. "To do it justice you must live every day to its fullest, because the one thing that pisses God off more than anything is for any of us to die without having enjoyed her life. Do you remember that?"

"Yes, I do. And you did an admirable job of living yours, even if you did get off to a late start. I like to think you made up for lost time once you cut loose. My life was always fun and never dull with you around."

"You made a good choice in Julia."

"I appreciate that, Carly. She's really special to me. I love her, and I promise to be good to Tallulah. Though it'd be nice if the kid had a nickname." Poppy laughed.

"Ask her mother what her middle name is. I'm surprised she hasn't told you already. Remember I love you, and I'll always be looking out for you, my love. Take care of my baby. Like her mother, she'll always need you."

"Will you be all right?"

Carly looked to the horizon. "There's a great adventure out there waiting on me, love. Don't worry about me anymore." She moved closer. "You kept your vows to me, and you did so with such devotion I know what paradise is, so I know what to look for now."

Poppy closed her eyes to keep the tears from slipping out, but it was no use. "I'm going to miss you so much. I still have a hard time believing I lost you."

Carly grew solid one last time and moved to embrace the person who had most helped pave the way to her happiness. "I love you, and I'll miss you too, but don't think of this as our ending. Because we loved each other, Julia will know how close to perfect life can be with you. She'll give you things I never could."

"I promise never to forget you."

Carly kissed her one last time and stepped away. "I know that, sweetheart. That's why I'm ready to go. The one thing that makes that possible is you're ready to let me go as well."

As Carly started to fade, Lizzie moved to Poppy's side, and for a while they let the yacht take its own course. Then they popped the top of the container off and watched Carly's ashes take to the wind, scattering, it seemed, in all directions at once.

"Good-bye, my love, safe journey," said Poppy.

She slipped the rings Carly had worn from the time of their ceremony till the day she died into Lizzie's hand, and then held the crying woman in her arms. They had come full circle, ending the life they had started in these waters years before. Like Carly's ashes, the pain Poppy carried for so long was swept away by the wind. She felt at peace with her memories and with the hand fate had dealt.

It was time to get back to the life that awaited her.

❖

That night as Poppy held Julia close to her, she remembered something Carly had said. "Baby, can I ask you something?"

"Sure you can, sweetheart. What is it?" asked Julia, kissing Poppy's bottom lip.

"What's Tallulah's middle name?"

Julia's lips stopped their teasing. She remembered the first time she had held her daughter and wondered what to name her. It was as if someone whispered the name into her ear, and it seemed to fit. "You wouldn't believe me if I told you."

"Try me." Poppy felt a shiver pass through the body draped over hers, and she ran her hand along Julia's back for comfort.

"Her full name's Tallulah Carly Johnson. I just liked the name Carly, but I wanted to honor the woman who'd raised me, so Tallulah came first. I didn't know how you'd react, so I thought about changing it, if it makes you uncomfortable."

To her surprise, Poppy laughed loudly and freely.

"*You always were dense when it came to how women felt about you, so I thought I'd point you in the right direction just this one time,*" said Carly. Poppy couldn't see her, but she heard the distinctive voice in her ear.

"No, baby," she assured Julia. "It doesn't make me uncomfortable. She'll probably grow up to think we named the island after her, and that's okay with me. I love you, and I look forward to whatever comes next."

About the Author

Originally from Cuba, **Ali Vali** now lives in New Orleans with her partner. As a writer she couldn't ask for a better more beautiful place so full of real life characters to fuel the imagination. When she isn't writing or working in the yard, Ali makes a living in the non-profit sector.

Her next book will continue the Casey Family Sagas. Read *The Devil Unleashed*, coming in 2006.

Books Available From Bold Strokes Books

The Traitor and the Chalice by Jane Fletcher. Without allies to help them, Tevi and Jemeryl will have to risk all in the race to uncover the traitor and retrieve the chalice. The Lyremouth Chronicles Book Two. (1-933110-43-0)

Promising Hearts by Radclyffe. Dr. Vance Phelps lost everything in the War Between the States and arrives in New Hope, Montana with no hope of happiness and no desire for anything except forgetting—until she meets Mae, a frontier madam. (1-933110-44-9)

Carly's Sound by Ali Vali. Poppy Valente and Julia Johnson form a bond of friendship that lays the foundation for something more, until Poppy's past comes back to haunt her—literally. A poignant romance about love and renewal. (1-933110-45-7)

Unexpected Sparks by Gina L. Dartt. Falling in love is complicated enough without adding murder to the mix. Kate Shannon's growing feelings for much younger Nikki Harris are challenging enough without the mystery of a fatal fire that Kate can't ignore. (1-933110-46-5)

Whitewater Rendezvous by Kim Baldwin. Two women on a wilderness kayak adventure—Chaz Herrick, a laid-back outdoorswoman, and Megan Maxwell, a workaholic news executive—discover that true love may be nothing at all like they imagined. (1-933110-38-4)

Erotic Interludes 3: Lessons in Love ed. by Radclyffe and Stacia Seaman. Sign on for a class in love…the best lesbian erotica writers take us to "school." (1-933110-39-2)

Punk Like Me by JD Glass. Twenty-one year old Nina writes lyrics and plays guitar in the rock band, Adam's Rib, and she doesn't always play by the rules. And, oh yeah—she has a way with the girls. (1-933110-40-6)

Coffee Sonata by Gun Brooke. Four women whose lives unexpectedly intersect in a small town by the sea share one thing in common—they all have secrets. (1-933110-41-4)

The Clinic: Tristaine Book One by Cate Culpepper. Brenna, a prison medic, finds herself deeply conflicted by her growing feelings for her patient, Jesstin, a wild and rebellious warrior reputed to be descended from ancient Amazons. (1-933110-42-2)

Forever Found by JLee Meyer. Can time, tragedy, and shattered trust destroy a love that seemed destined? When chance reunites two childhood friends separated by tragedy, the past resurfaces to determine the shape of their future. (1-933110-37-6)

Sword of the Guardian by Merry Shannon. Princess Shasta's bold new bodyguard has a secret that could change both of their lives. He is actually a *she*. A passionate romance filled with courtly intrigue, chivalry, and devotion. (1-933110-36-8)

Wild Abandon by Ronica Black. From their first tumultuous meeting, Dr. Chandler Brogan and Officer Sarah Monroe are drawn together by their common obsessions—sex, speed, and danger. (1-933110-35-X)

Turn Back Time by Radclyffe. Pearce Rifkin and Wynter Thompson have nothing in common but a shared passion for surgery. They clash at every opportunity, especially when matters of the heart are suddenly at stake. (1-933110-34-1)

Chance by Grace Lennox. At twenty-six, Chance Delaney decides her life isn't working so she swaps it for a different one. What follows is the sexy, funny, touching story of two women who, in finding themselves, also find one another. (1-933110-31-7)

The Exile and the Sorcerer by Jane Fletcher. First in the Lyremouth Chronicles. Tevi, wounded and adrift, arrives in the courtyard of a shy young sorcerer. Together they face monsters, magic, and the challenge of loving despite their differences. (1-933110-32-5)

A Matter of Trust by Radclyffe. JT Sloan is a cybersleuth who doesn't like attachments. Michael Lassiter is leaving her husband, and she needs Sloan's expertise to safeguard her company. It should just be business—but it turns into much more. (1-933110-33-3)

Sweet Creek by Lee Lynch. A celebration of the enduring nature of love, friendship, and community in the quirky, heart-warming lesbian community of Waterfall Falls. (1-933110-29-5)

The Devil Inside by Ali Vali. Derby Cain Casey, head of a New Orleans crime organization, runs the family business with guts and grit, and no one crosses her. No one, that is, until Emma Verde claims her heart and turns her world upside down. (1-933110-30-9)

Grave Silence by Rose Beecham. Detective Jude Devine's investigation of a series of ritual murders is complicated by her torrid affair with the golden girl of Southwestern forensic pathology, Dr. Mercy Westmoreland. (1-933110-25-2)

Honor Reclaimed by Radclyffe. In the aftermath of 9/11, Secret Service Agent Cameron Roberts and Blair Powell close ranks with a trusted few to find the would-be assassins who nearly claimed Blair's life. (1-933110-18-X)

Honor Bound by Radclyffe. Secret Service Agent Cameron Roberts and Blair Powell face political intrigue, a clandestine threat to Blair's safety, and the seemingly irreconcilable personal differences that force them ever farther apart. (1-933110-20-1)

Protector of the Realm: Supreme Constellations Book One by Gun Brooke. A space adventure filled with suspense and a daring intergalactic romance featuring Commodore Rae Jacelon and a stunning, but decidedly lethal, Kellen O'Dal. (1-933110-26-0)

Innocent Hearts by Radclyffe. In a wild and unforgiving land, two women learn about love, passion, and the wonders of the heart. (1-933110-21-X)

The Temple at Landfall by Jane Fletcher. An imprinter, one of Celaeno's most revered servants of the Goddess, is also a prisoner to the faith—until a Ranger frees her by claiming her heart. The Celaeno series. (1-933110-27-9)

Force of Nature by Kim Baldwin. From tornados to forest fires, the forces of nature conspire to bring Gable McCoy and Erin Richards close to danger, and closer to each other. (1-933110-23-6)

In Too Deep by Ronica Black. Undercover homicide cop Erin McKenzie tracks a femme fatale who just might be a real killer…with love and danger hot on her heels. (1-933110-17-1)

Course of Action by Gun Brooke. Actress Carolyn Black desperately wants the starring role in an upcoming film produced by Annelie Peterson. Just how far will she go for the dream part of a lifetime? (1-933110-22-8)

Rangers at Roadsend by Jane Fletcher. Sergeant Chip Coppelli has learned to spot trouble coming, and that is exactly what she sees in her new recruit, Katryn Nagata. The Celaeno series. (1-933110-28-7)

Justice Served by Radclyffe. Lieutenant Rebecca Frye and her lover, Dr. Catherine Rawlings, embark on a deadly game of hide-and-seek with an underworld kingpin who traffics in human souls. (1-933110-15-5)

Distant Shores, Silent Thunder by Radclyffe. Doctor Tory King—and the women who love her—is forced to examine the boundaries of love, friendship, and the ties that transcend time. (1-933110-08-2)

Hunter's Pursuit by Kim Baldwin. A raging blizzard, a mountain hideaway, and a killer-for-hire set a scene for disaster—or desire—when Katarzyna Demetrious rescues a beautiful stranger. (1-933110-09-0)

The Walls of Westernfort by Jane Fletcher. All Temple Guard Natasha Ionadis wants is to serve the Goddess—until she falls in love with one of the rebels she is sworn to destroy. The Celaeno series. (1-933110-24-4)

Change Of Pace: *Erotic Interludes* by Radclyffe. Twenty-five hot-wired encounters guaranteed to spark more than just your imagination. Erotica as you've always dreamed of it. (1-933110-07-4)

Honor Guards by Radclyffe. In a wild flight for their lives, the president's daughter and those who are sworn to protect her wage a desperate struggle for survival. (1-933110-01-5)

Fated Love by Radclyffe. Amidst the chaos and drama of a busy emergency room, two women must contend not only with the fragile nature of life, but also with the irresistible forces of fate. (1-933110-05-8)

Justice in the Shadows by Radclyffe. In a shadow world of secrets and lies, Detective Sergeant Rebecca Frye and her lover, Dr. Catherine Rawlings, join forces in the elusive search for justice.(1-933110-03-1)

shadowland by Radclyffe. In a world on the far edge of desire, two women are drawn together by power, passion, and dark pleasures. An erotic romance. (1-933110-11-2)

Love's Masquerade by Radclyffe. Plunged into the indistinguishable realms of fiction, fantasy, and hidden desires, Auden Frost is forced to question all she believes about the nature of love. (1-933110-14-7)

Love & Honor by Radclyffe. The president's daughter and her lover are faced with difficult choices as they battle a tangled web of Washington intrigue for...love and honor. (1-933110-10-4)

Beyond the Breakwater by Radclyffe. One Provincetown summer three women learn the true meaning of love, friendship, and family. (1-933110-06-6)

Tomorrow's Promise by Radclyffe. One timeless summer, two very different women discover the power of passion to heal and the promise of hope that only love can bestow. (1-933110-12-0)

Love's Tender Warriors by Radclyffe. Two women who have accepted loneliness as a way of life learn that love is worth fighting for and a battle they cannot afford to lose. (1-933110-02-3)

Love's Melody Lost by Radclyffe. A secretive artist with a haunted past and a young woman escaping a life that has proved to be a lie find their destinies entwined. (1-933110-00-7)

Safe Harbor by Radclyffe. A mysterious newcomer, a reclusive doctor, and a troubled gay teenager learn about love, friendship, and trust during one tumultuous summer in Provincetown. (1-933110-13-9)

Above All, Honor by Radclyffe. Secret Service Agent Cameron Roberts fights her desire for the one woman she can't have—Blair Powell, the daughter of the president of the United States. (1-933110-04-X)